SWEEP OF THE BLADE

ILONA ANDREWS

SWEEP OF THE BLADE

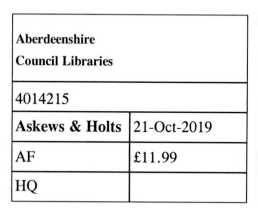
Sweep of the Blade
Copyright © 2019 by Ilona Andrews
Ebook ISBN: 9781641971041
CS Print ISBN: 9781080143986
IS Print ISBN: 9781641971072

NYLA Publishing
121 W. 27th St, Suite 1201, NY 10001, New York.
http://www.nyliterary.com

[1]

THEN...

The hot wind flung brown dust into Maud's face. It scoured her skin, clogged her nose, and piled in her hair. She tasted grit on her tongue, dirt tinged with bitter metal, and pulled the hood of the tattered cloak tighter around her face.

Around her the endless plain rolled to the horizon, interrupted in the distance by low hills. Here and there stunted thorny plants jutted out of the dirt, desiccated and twisted by the winds. Far to the north, bur, the shaggy herbivores that made Earth elephants look small, stomped their way across the plain, grazing on the scrawny vegetation. There was no beauty on Karhari; no golden fields of grain, no forests, no oasis. Just dry dirt, rock, and poisonous salt deposits.

Ahead, by the crossroads barely marked by solar lights, the blocky metal box of the Road Lodge jutted against the wastes, tall walls and narrow recessed windows pitted from the frequent onslaught of wind and dust. A reinforced double door punctured the wall in front of her. Maud shouldered her needle rifle and

1

headed to it, carrying the canvas sack in her left hand high enough it didn't bump her legs. The canvas was liquid-proof, but she didn't want it touching her all the same.

The door clanged, split in half, and slid into the wall. Maud walked inside, and the doors shut behind her back. The stench of unwashed bodies and klava caffeine washed over her. The delicate perfume of drunk vampires.

She grimaced, pulled the needle rifle off her shoulder, and dropped it through the slot in the electrified wire cage by the entrance. She kept her blood sword. The owner only cared about projectile weapons. If the patrons decided to bash each other's skulls in, she didn't give a damn as long as their tab was paid.

The inside of the Lodge consisted of a long rectangle, with a bar counter on the right and a collection of grimy booths and tables on the left. Toward the end of the room, a spiral staircase led upstairs, to seven shabby rooms, each little more than a box with a bed and a bathroom hidden behind a partition.

The Lodge catered to travelers, doubling as an inn and a bar. It sat on the crossroads like a trap, catching the dregs that washed up from the wastes of Karhari—mercenaries, convoy guards, raiders—lost souls who had no place to go and wandered the planet of exiles until they found their place, or someone relieved them of the heavy burdens of their life and possessions.

It was barely past noon and most of the Lodge's patrons had either left, trying to make it to the next rest stop before dark, or hadn't arrived. Only a few vampires milled at the tables, nursing the dark klava swill. They paid Maud no mind as she walked over to the bar.

The bartender, a large vampire woman with greasy greying hair and pitted armor, eyed her from behind the counter. Maud held the sack out to her. The woman pulled it open and fished out a blood-smeared counter defilade launcher with a hand still

2

attached to it. Barely the size of an Earth submachine gun, the launcher fired high-energy pellets at 1,200 rounds per minute. Two pellets would make a hole in the armored side of the Lodge. The launcher's magazine carried 2,000. Firearms of that caliber were outlawed on Karhari. The owner of the weapon had paid a fortune to smuggle it, destroyed a lodge, then spent his time riding around holding random lodges and inns for ransom.

The vampire woman sniffed the bloody gun. "Did he put up a fight?"

Maud shook her head. "Left my bike in plain view on the eastern road. He stopped to check it. Never saw me."

The bartender scowled at her. "How did you know where he'd be coming from?"

"The west is House Jerdan's territory; they patrol with infrared and they would've stripped the launcher off him. The closest place to rest to the south is four days; to the north, five, and that road gets frequent convoy traffic. Too risky. Someone might have noticed him and if he took too long driving back and forth it would give you enough time to get a defense together. No, he went east and camped for a day. No sane vampire will camp longer than one night during the storm season."

The bartender nodded. "You do good work, human, I'll give you that." She reached behind the counter, put the gun away, and pulled a heavy bag out. "Water or cash?"

"Neither. I need the room till the end of the month."

"It's yours." The barkeep put a large cup of mint tea on the counter. "The drink is on the house."

"Thanks."

Maud pulled the hood deeper over her face, took her tea, and made her way to the familiar ratty booth at the far wall, near the staircase. She slid into the metal seat and tapped the ancient remote terminal unit on her wrist. The piece of junk blinked and buzzed softly. Maud slapped it. The terminal blinked again and came to life. Maud pulled up the keyboard and sent a single glyph to the only other terminal connected to hers.

Safe.

Two glyphs appeared in response. *Safe, Mommy.*

Maud exhaled and sipped her tea. It was lukewarm, but free. She tapped the terminal again, running an integrity check on the armor. She could still remember the time when controlling her armor was intuitive and easy, almost as mindless as breathing. But to do that, she would have to have a crest of a vampire House. She had lost hers when her husband's political machinations had gotten the three of them exiled to this anus of the Galaxy. No, not lost, Maud corrected herself. It was taken away from her when father-in-law had personally ripped it off her armor.

The memory of that day stabbed her, and Maud closed her eyes for a moment. She'd begged her mother-in-law for her daughter's life. It was too late for Melizard and her, but Helen had been only two at the time and Karhari was an ugly, vicious place, the junkyard of vampire souls, where the Houses of the Holy Anocracy sent the garbage they didn't bother killing. She'd pleaded on her knees and none of it mattered. House Ervan expelled them. Their names had been struck from the House scrolls. Their possessions were confiscated. Nobody had argued in their defense.

Helen was five now. The memories of their life before Karhari were so distant, sometimes Maud wondered if she had dreamed them.

She surveyed the dozen vampires getting drunk on caffeine. A predatory strain of the same genetic seed that had sprouted into humans, vampires were bigger, stronger, and more powerful than an average *Homo sapiens.* They occupied seven main planets and had colonies on a dozen other worlds, all of which together made up the Holy Cosmic Anocracy, governed by three powers: the military might of the Warlord, the religious guidance of the Hierophant, and the judicial wisdom of the Judge. Within the Anocracy, power lay with the Houses—clans, some with only a few dozen members, others numbering in hundreds of thousands.

The vampires had obtained the secret of interstellar flight when they were still in a feudal period, and their society had changed little since they launched their first ship into space. They still built castles, they wore armor, and they held on to the ideals of knighthood: honor, duty, and loyalty to the family and House. To the ragtag lot in the Lodge now, all those things were distant memories, vague and abandoned. One only had to look at their armor.

To a vampire knight, the syn-armor was almost holy. Deep black and glossy in mint condition, the high-tech nanothread mesh was custom made for each knight and paired with a sophisticated AI unit within their House crest. A vampire knight spent the majority of their time in armor, taking it off only in the privacy of their quarters. Repairing it was an art and keeping the armor in battle condition was a point of pride.

The vampires in Lodge still wore armor—they had been knights once, after all—but instead of sleek lines and glossy black, their suits were a dented mess of charcoal and grey, with sections from other suits tacked on to patch the holes where the nanothreads had been damaged beyond repair. They looked like they'd painted themselves with glue and rolled in a metal junkyard.

Her own armor was no longer black either, but at least she had managed to keep her nanothreads alive.

The door of the Lodge slid open, and a large vampire strode inside, swaddled in a black cloak. At 5'9" Maud was tall for a human woman, but he had almost a foot on her. The vampire pulled back his hood, releasing a black mane of hair that fell to his shoulders. The kind of hair that said that he was wealthy or could leave the planet to a place where water was plentiful enough to wash it. The only water on Karhari came from deep within the planet. During the short rainy season, the water filtered through the porous rock, forming underground lakes, and the vampires pumped it like oil. It tasted foul and cost an arm and a leg.

Maud had pampered her hair with conditioners and masks since she was a teenager. Their first night on Karhari, she had slashed it all off, almost two feet of black locks. It was her sacrifice to the planet. She sat on the floor of a grimy bathroom in an arrival hostel, with her husband and child sleeping just a thin wall away, her hair all around her, and cried silently, mourning Helen's future and the life they lost.

The newcomer turned, saw her, and made a beeline for her booth. If he were human, she would have put him somewhere between thirty and forty. He had a masculine face, heavy jaw, bold features, but with just enough aristocratic refinement to keep it from being brutish. A jagged scar chewed up the left side of his face, cutting through his cheek to the bionic targeting module glowing weakly in the orbit where his left eye used to be.

Renouard. *Ugh.*

Maud put her hand on the hilt of her blood sword under the table.

Renouard marched down the aisle between the tables. A taller younger vampire got in his way. Renouard looked at him for a long moment and the younger mercenary decided to take a seat. Renouard's reputation preceded him.

He slid into her booth, taking up the entire bench, and pondered her. "I thought you left, Sariv."

She really hated that nickname. "Why haven't you?"

"I had a small bit of business to take care of."

Renouard bared his teeth at her, displaying his fangs. Vampires showed their teeth for many reasons: to intimidate, to express joy, to snarl in frustration. But this one was a leer. *Look at my teeth, baby. Aren't I amazing?*

She drank the last swallow of her tea and studied her empty cup.

"Since your pretty boy husband got himself killed, you've never stayed in the same place longer than a day or two."

Melizard was owed a blood debt. A debt she collected over the last six months, as she went after every vampire complicit in his murder and their relatives and friends dumb enough to track her down to get revenge. She'd stabbed the last murderer a month ago and watched his heart pump his blood onto the dirt.

She gave him a cold flat stare. "My memory is quite good. I do not recall you being there. Don't presume to comment on my habits, my lord."

Renouard grinned. "Ahh, and there is the wife of the Marshal's brat. I keep waiting for this place to smother you, but you do endure, Sariv. Why are you here?"

She raised her eyebrows. She wasn't going to even dignify it with an answer.

"You've been threading your way through the wastes, towing your crazy child with you for months, then the week before last you parked yourself at this Lodge. You're waiting for something. What is it?"

She yawned.

"Tell me." His tone gained a menacing quality.

A hiss came from the stairs. Maud leaned back to bring the stairway into her peripheral vision. Helen crouched on the stairs, wrapped in a tattered brown cloak. Her hood was up, but she was looking straight at them, the long blonde hair sliding out of the hood and two green eyes, glowing slightly, fixed on Renouard.

"There is the demon spawn," Renouard said.

Helen opened her mouth, showing two thin sickle fangs, and hissed again. Crouched like that, she looked like a vicious little animal backed into a corner, a feral cat who didn't want to fight, but if you tried to touch it, it would slice your hand into ribbons.

She couldn't have heard them all the way from upstairs. Or at least Maud hoped she hadn't. With a child that was half-vampire, half-human, Maud had given up on all her preconceived notions long ago.

"Are you waiting for someone to take you off this rock?" Renouard's upper lip trembled, betraying the beginning of a snarl. "If so, you're waiting in vain, my lady. Karhari is under a restricted access seal. Only the handful of Houses who are charged with guarding Karhari or those designated as vital trading partners are granted a permit. There are less than ten traders, all vampires, and I know every one of them."

"It's truly rare to find a man who enjoys the sound of his own voice as much as you do."

"The Houses guarding the planet are paid by the Anocracy to keep you exactly where you are, and you have no way to pay for the passage from a trader. The cost to smuggle you out is too high. You barely earn enough to keep you and your demon from dying of thirst. If you're waiting for an outsider to come to your rescue, their craft will be shot down the moment it enters the atmosphere."

She stroked the hilt of her sword under the table.

Renouard leaned forward, taking up his side of the table and some of hers. "I'm your only chance. Take my offer."

"You want me to sell my own daughter to the slave market."

"A vampire-human hybrid is a rarity. She's worth some money. I promise you, in a month, she and the planet will be a bad dream."

If she threw the cup at his face, he'd jump to his feet and she could drive the knife on her left hip under his chin and into his mouth. Hard to talk with your tongue impaled.

"If you don't want to sell her, leave her here. She grew up here. This hellhole is the only place she knows. She doesn't remember House Ervan. Void, she's probably forgotten her own father by this point. Leave her here. It will be a kindness."

She felt the sudden need to take a shower to wash off the few molecules belonging to him that happened to land on her skin.

"Come with me. We'll burn our way through the galaxy. I'll keep you too busy to brood. I'm quite good at making women forget their problems."

He reached for her.

She thrust the sword between them under the table. The point grazed his thigh.

"It seems you've forgotten what happened the last time you failed to keep your hands to yourself."

His affable expression was completely gone now. An ugly snarl twisted his features.

"Last chance, Maud. Very last chance."

"You have a shuttle to catch."

"Fine. Rot here." He rose. "I'll be back in six months. We can revisit it then, if there is anything left of you to bargain with."

Maud watched him walk away.

Helen slid into the booth next to her. "I don't like him."

"Neither, do I, my flower. Neither do I. Don't worry. He won't bother us again."

"Mommy?"

"Yes?"

Helen looked up at her from the depths of her hood. "Will somebody really come for us?"

The fragile hope in her daughter's voice nearly undid Maud. She wished so badly she could say yes.

Two weeks ago, when they stopped at the Lodge for the night, she had run into an Arbitrator. The galaxy, with all of its planets, dimensions, and thousands of species, was too large for any unified government, but the Office of Arbitration, an ancient neutral body, served as its court. To meet an Arbitrator was rare. To meet a human one... Up until two weeks ago Maud would've said it was impossible.

Humans didn't get out much. Through a twist of cosmic fate, Earth sat on the crossroads of the galaxy. It was the only twelve-point warp in existence, which made it a convenient hub. Instead of squabbling over the planet, the interstellar powers, in a rare moment of wisdom, formed an ancient agreement with represen-tatives of humanity. Earth would serve as the way station for the galactic travelers passing through on their way to somewhere else. They arrived in secret and stayed at specialized inns equipped to handle a wide variety of beings. In return, the planet was desig-nated as neutral ground. None of the galactic powers could lay claim to it, and the existence of other intelligent life remained a secret to all human population except for the select few families who minded the inns.

The few rare humans who made it off-planet were like her, children of innkeepers, all marked with a particular magic that allowed them to defy the rules of physics within their inns. The Arbitrator felt different, suffused with power, unlike any human she had met before. She had stood by the bar, trying to figure out if he was Earth-born, when he turned to her and smiled. For a second, she stumbled. He was shockingly beautiful.

He asked her if she was from Earth, she told him she was, and he casually offered to deliver a message to her family.

She'd frozen then while her mind feverishly tried to find someone to whom she could send the message. When she was pregnant with Helen, her brother Klaus and her younger sister,

Dina, had come to House Ervan to tell her their parents' inn had disappeared. One moment the charming colonial was there, hiding a microcosm inside, the next it vanished, taking everyone inside with it. When Klaus had come home from running errands, he had found an empty lot. Nobody, not even the Innkeeper Assembly, knew where or how the inn had vanished.

Her siblings were going to search the galaxy for answers. She wanted to join them, but she was pregnant and Melizard begged her to stay by his side. He was in the middle of another scheme, and he had needed her.

Two years later, just as her husband had started on the path that would land them on Karhari, Dina and Klaus had come again. They found nothing. Klaus wanted to keep looking, but Dina had enough. She was going back to earth. Of the three of them, Dina longed for normal life the most, always wanting things the innkeeper families couldn't have, like friends outside the inn or attending high school. Maud still recalled the bad feeling that had washed over her as she watched the two of them walk toward the spaceport. Something told her to grab Helen and follow them. But she loved Melizard and she had stayed...

By now Dina probably had a normal job. Maybe she was married, with children of her own. Klaus was universe alone knew where. She told the Arbitrator as much and he smiled at her again and said, "I wouldn't worry too much about it. Messages have a way of getting where they need to go."

Maud took off her necklace, scribbled a few words with the coordinates of the Lodge on a piece of paper, and handed them both to him. It felt right somehow, as if this was a test and she had given the correct answer. Now they waited.

She had no idea how long it would take. Her mercenary job had earned them two and a half weeks of stay, the rest of her money would buy another two weeks or so, then she would have to search for jobs.

Helen was still looking at her, waiting for an answer.

Will somebody really come for us?

"Yes," she said. "If your aunt or uncle get our message, they will come for us and they will take us away from here."

"To a different place?" Helen asked.

"Yes."

"With flowers and water?"

Maud swallow the hot clump that wedged itself in her throat. "Yes, my flower. With all the beautiful flowers and water you can imagine.

———

MAUD DRANK HER MINT TEA. NEXT TO HER HELEN NIBBLED ON A dry cookie and flipped the digital pages of a book. The book, *Weird and Amazing Planets*, a paper-thin single use tablet, showed photographs of landscapes from different planets. It had cost Maud a month's worth of water, but Helen had found it at a trader's stall and hugged it to her, and Maud couldn't say no. There were almost a thousand photographs and by now Helen knew every one by heart.

The Lodge was full tonight. First, two convoy guard teams, each consisting of a dozen vampires, came in one after another; then, to make things interesting, a group of fourteen raiders. The two convoy guards, the traders, and the lone travelers had taken the tables along the perimeter of the Lodge, near the walls, and the raiders were left with a chunk in the middle, exposed and surrounded. The convoy guards and the raiders were eyeing each other, but so far nobody had gotten drunk enough to start any trouble. If a brawl broke out, she'd grab Helen and head upstairs.

The door of the Lodge slid open, and three travelers made their way inside. The first was tall and broad, his cloak stretched over his wide shoulders in the familiar way it did when the fabric rested on vampire armor. The man right behind him wore dark pants and a windbreaker, his movements graceful and liquid. He didn't move, he glided. Or rather, he stalked in, ready to fend off an attack.

The windbreaker looked Earth-made.

Human.

Her heart sped up. The man pulled back the hood of his windbreaker. Maud scrutinized his features: scarred face, russet-brown hair, clean shaven...

The human inhaled, scanned the room with his gaze. His irises caught the light, reflecting it with an amber glow for a split second.

Disappointment slammed into her. Not a human. A werewolf, a refugee from a dead planet.

The towering cloaked figure headed for the bar. The werewolf followed. A third person trailed them, wearing a tattered gray robe. The cut of the robe was achingly familiar. It looked like an innkeeper robe.

You're imagining things, Maud told herself. *It's a gray robe.* There were millions of them in the galaxy. It was the simplest and most common garment, second only to a cloak. In the end, all colors faded to gray.

The robed traveler took a seat at the bar. The bartender took the order and came back with two cups. The larger man half-turned to watch the room, blocking Maud's view of the robed traveler.

Move, you oaf.

He leaned his elbow on the bar. The armor on his arms was jet-black. A new victim added to the never-ending trickle of exiles? No, he didn't hold himself like an exile. She'd seen enough of the new arrivals over the years. They broke into two categories: the first thought they would own the planet in two weeks and the second were desperate and broken. Both held themselves tight, ready for an attack to come at any moment. If this vampire got any more relaxed, he'd start stripping his armor off.

A few moments passed. The raiders sized up the newcomers. Much easier prey than either of the convoy guard teams. If the raiders got into it with the guards, the other team would likely jump in, but nobody cared about three strangers. The guards would sit back and watch.

Anticipation hummed through the room like a low-voltage current.

The raider leader rose and casually moved back, giving himself room for a charge, resting his hand on the big blood hammer at his waist. Almost simultaneously, the largest raider, his face ruined by a deep scar, got to his feet and lumbered toward the bar.

"Stay close to me," Maud whispered, and squeezed Helen's hand.

Helen squeezed back.

The huge raider made it to his destination and stopped in front of the cloaked figure. The raider had a bit of height on the newcomer, but not much. His armor, an ugly mess of gray and black, looked like it had gone through a car crusher and was then somehow muscled back into some semblance of the right shape.

"You're not from around here," the raider declared.

The Lodge went quiet in anticipation of a good show.

"Such keen powers of observation," the cloaked man answered, his voice deep.

An old House. Crap.

The accent was unmistakable, cultured and still carrying traces of the original home world, the planet that gave life to the vampire species. Everybody in the room recognized this. Her husband's family did their best to imitate it, going so far as to hire voice coaches for the children. Maud pulled her dagger and her sword out under the table. Things were about to get ugly.

A grimace twisted the raider's face. "Your armor is clean. Pretty. Do you know what we do to pretty boys like you here?"

The tall vampire sighed. "Is there a script? Do you give this speech to all who enter here, because if so, I suggest we skip the talking."

The raider roared. His mistake.

The cloaked man waited until the sound died. "A challenge. I love challenges."

The raider grabbed his sword. The cloaked man punched him in the jaw. The blow swept the larger vampire off his feet. He went airborne and landed into a booth.

Okay then.

The raider scrambled up and swung his blade. The cloaked man ducked under the strike and smashed his fist against the raider's ribs. The shoddy armor split with a dry burst. The edge of the breastplate popped free. The cloaked vampire grasped the broken breastplate and yanked it upward. The entire armor collapsed with a deafening crunch, locking the vampire into a rigid straitjacket.

Every vampire in the Lodge winced. Maud did too.

"Nice," the werewolf said.

"If one is going to wear armor, one must properly maintain it."

The raider tried to rise. The armor on his left arm fell off completely, the one on the right twisted his limb so far back, his shoulder had to be dislocated. He managed to stagger halfway up. The cloaked vampire kneed him in the face. The raider collapsed, his face bloody. The other vampire kicked him. The raider went still, drool and blood dripping from his open mouth onto the floor.

He wasn't just a random knight. This one had a lot of martial training. If he headed for the doors now, he and his friends could walk out. Vampires respected strength. Even this lot would acknowledge his victory. If he stayed...

The cloaked man surveyed the room. "Anyone else?"

He did *not* just say that.

Seven raiders stood up.

The werewolf muttered something under his breath and pulled a large knife from a sheath on his waist. The blade shone with emerald green.

"Might as well get it over with." The vampire tore off his cloak and hurled it aside.

State-of-the-art armor. House Krahr crest, as old of a blood-line as you could get. The sigil on the shoulder was blurred, some-thing higher-ranking vampires did when they weren't acting in official capacity. Stunning face and a mane of blond hair.

Oh dear universe. What the hell was a high-ranking knight of Krahr doing brawling on Karhari? She knew almost nothing about House Krahr except that it was large, aggressive, and one of the original Houses. Had one of Krahr's knights visited House Ervan, her husband's family would've treated him as an honored guest. Back before the exile, they probably would've paraded her in front of the visitors and had her recite one of the ancient sagas in a dialect nobody had used for three hundred years. *Look at our pet human doing cute tricks.* The thought brought bile to her throat. Why did she let it go on for so long?

The Krahr knight stepped forward, and she finally got a look at the person behind him. The figure in the gray robe slid off the stool. The hood had fallen back, revealing a familiar face framed by blond hair.

The hair on the back of Maud's arms rose. She looked again, terrified she was mistaken.

"Mommy," Helen whispered, "who is that lady?"

Somehow Maud's lips moved. "That's your aunt."

Half of the room was now standing. The vampires roared in unison, bellowing a challenge.

Too many. Because of that idiot's hubris, the werewolf and her sister would have to cut their way to her through at least thirty pissed-off vampires. She had to act, or they would never make it.

"Helen, get down low and head for the door."

Helen slid her book into her little backpack, shouldered it, and slipped under the table.

Dina's gaze connected with Maud's. Her sister grinned.

Maud jumped onto the table and sprinted to the raider leader. He was focused on the Krahr knight. He never saw her coming. She primed her blood sword a moment before she reached him. The weapon whined as the bloodred high-tech liquid surged through it, rendering it nearly indestructible. The raider leader turned, reacting to the telltale noise, and she beheaded him in a single smooth stroke.

Blood splashed on the tables. Vampires roared and attacked.

She sliced someone's arm in half, the blood sword cleaving through the subpar armor like it was baking foil, spun away from a female vampire's outstretched hand trying to grab her, and kicked another female raider in the face.

Around her the Lodge was chaos, vampires shouting, tables flying, and blood weapons screeching as they were primed. She registered it all with adrenaline-saturated detachment. Nothing mattered except killing until they reached the door or there was nobody left to kill.

Someone grabbed her cloak and jerked at it. It came loose as it was designed to do, buying Maud an extra second. She dropped to her knees, buried her dagger in the nearest vampire throat, rolled off the table to avoid an incoming mace, and slashed across a raider's face with her sword. He bellowed in rage, and she sank her blade into his side, in the gap between ill-fitting armor sections.

Maud twisted, checking on Helen. Her daughter had dropped to all fours and was crawling under the tables to the exit. *Good girl.*

Dina was screaming something. Maud spun, trying to parry and keep her in view, but the raiders closed in on her, locking her into a ring of bodies. *Too many...*

A deafening roar tore from behind the raiders. Bodies went flying like they were made of straw. The huge female vampire in front of her collapsed, blood spray flying from her ruined skull, and the Krahr knight burst into the ring, his fangs bared. He brained the raider to her right with a vicious swing and hammered a savage uppercut into the stomach of the one on her left. The faulty armor cracked with a sound of crushed nut shells. The raider doubled over, and the Krahr drove his left elbow into the back of his neck. The blow swept the raider off his feet, sending him to the side. One moment there were two bellowing vampires. The next there was only the Krahr knight, brandishing his mace.

The raiders stared, awestruck for a moment, and Maud used every fraction of it to stab and slice as much as she could. The ring around them widened and suddenly she found herself back to back with the Krahr.

"My lady," he said in that deep cultured voice. "I apologize for not arriving sooner in your time of dire need."

Hell would freeze over before she would owe another vampire. "Not that dire, my lord. Please don't bestir yourself on my behalf."

She dropped, spinning, kicked a vampire's legs from under her and stabbed her in the throat on her way down.

He smashed his mace into the shoulder of a raider with a bone-snapping crunch. "I insist."

She parried a swing that nearly made her drop her blade and drove her dagger into the raider's groin, punching through the damaged armor by pure luck. "No need."

He struck at the vampire on his left, took a hit to the shoulder from another, grunted, reversed his swing, and hammered a devastating blow to the new opponent. The vampire bent forward from the impact and the Krahr drove his fist into the back of his head.

"Please, allow me this small diversion. I'm but a guest on your planet. It was a long trip and I have sat for far too much of it."

Argh. He out-mannered her. As absurd as his claim was, he backed her into the role of the host and the laws of vampire hospitality dictated that the guests were to be indulged.

Wait, I'm not a vampire. Why does it even matter?

A male vampire kicked. She stumbled back, bounced off the Krahr's broad back and threw herself into the fray.

Out of the corner of her eye she saw Dina fighting her way to the exit, the orange energy whip hanging loose and sparking on the floor. Helen was in her arms. What was she doing? Helen's best advantage was in her size and speed. Now neither of them could move.

She doesn't know, Maud realized. Her sister had no idea what kind of a child her daughter was.

The werewolf thrust himself in front of them and began carving a path to the door.

"My lord!" Maud called. "We're leaving."

He grunted. "I'll be there shortly."

"My lord!"

"I'll cover your retreat."

Dina and Helen were only a few yards from the door. Maud charged at the remaining vampires. In two swings she was through the gauntlet.

"Arland!" the werewolf screamed, his voice cutting through the noise of the Lodge.

So that was his name. Maud looked over her shoulder and saw him, drenched in blood, mowing down bodies.

"Arland!" the werewolf snarled.

The Krahr turned, saw them, and began backing up toward the door.

The heavy metal doors swung open. Dina ran out, clutching Helen to her, and the werewolf followed. As Maud sprinted through the doorway, she saw the barkeep waving at her with a small surreal smile.

A narrow black shuttle waited on the landing strip and they ran toward it. The doors slid open. Maud leapt into a seat and plucked Helen from Dina's arms. The werewolf landed in the pilot's seat and started the pre-flight check, his fingers flying over the controls.

Where was the Krahr? If he didn't emerge in the next ten

seconds, she would go back in and get him. He fought for her and her daughter. She owed him that much.

A ball of bodies rolled out the door and collapsed into eight individual fighters. Arland appeared, fangs bared, face splattered with blood. It was like something out of one of the Anocracy's pseudo-historical dramas—a lone hero on a strange planet, standing against impossible odds, roaring his rage to the heavens.

Arland swung his blood mace. It smashed a female fighter's skull in a gory explosion of blood and brains. Before the swing was finished, the Krahr knight turned, grabbed the one to his left by his throat, shook him once like a rag doll, and tossed the dead body aside. The perfect blend of sheer brutality and efficient precision was beautiful to watch.

The Krahr knight kicked a huge raider to his left, driving the full power of his armored leg into the vampire's knee cap. The man dropped, and Arland backhanded his jaw with his mace, almost as an afterthought, turned and sank the head of the mace into the ribs of the raider on his right. A hammer landed on his back. Arland shrugged it off as if he'd been smacked with a flyswatter, spun, too fast on his feet for a man of his size, and slammed the mace against his attacker's right arm. The arm went limp. The vampire turned and ran. Arland hurled his mace. It soared through the air and bounced off the vampire's smaller back. The armor, already dented and hanging together on a prayer, cracked, and the raider flew into the side of the building, bounced off and fell to the ground.

Wow.

Vampires took pride in ground combat; her husband was one of the best, but this, this was on another level. Where did House Krahr even find him? What did he do for them?

She turned to Dina and pointed at Arland. "Who the hell is that?"

"The Lord Marshal of House Krahr," Dina said.

Oh sweet galaxy, he was the military head of his House. How in the world did Dina manage to rope him into this rescue?

The two remaining raiders charged in concert. The Marshal braced himself for the attack, roaring a challenge. When one of the raiders got close, he stepped to the left, crouched, and dove low into the charging vampire. The attacker had no time to react to the sudden shift in the center of gravity. The momentum carried him forward while the Marshal drove him up and over his shoulder in one smooth movement. The raider fell on his head. His neck snapped with a dry crunch. The Marshal scooped up the dead vampire's hammer and brained the last remaining raider with it.

Maud remembered to breathe.

The Marshal sprinted to the shuttle.

Sparring with him would be amazing. She could go all out without holding back.

In a couple of breaths, he jumped into the cabin and landed in the seat next to the werewolf.

The door of the Road Lodge slid open and a mob of vampires tore out, snarling and roaring.

"Do you even know how to fly, werewolf?" the Marshal growled.

"Buckle up." The werewolf pulled a lever and the slick craft sped into the sky.

Gravity sat on Maud's chest. It was real. They were leaving. She hugged Helen to her.

"What happened?" Dina asked. "Where is Melizard? Where is your husband?"

"Melizard is dead. He led a revolt against his House. They stripped him of all titles and possessions and sent us to Karhari.

Eight months ago he crossed the wrong local and the raiders killed him."

"We killed them back," Helen said.

"Yes, we did, my flower." Maud smiled at her and petted her hair. "Yes, we did."

It was over. It was finally over.

The Marshal turned around and looked at her. He seemed shell-shocked, as if her existence somehow upset the structure of his universe and he couldn't quite reconcile the two. She'd seen that look before. None of the vampires expected a human to know which end of the sword to point at the enemy, let alone wear their armor. Dina must've told him something, so he'd expected a human, but he hadn't expected *her*, and she clearly blew his mind.

Maud met his gaze. Shockingly handsome. His features were strong and masculine, carved without any weakness, yet neither crude nor cruel. His thoughtful eyes, a deep intense blue, took her measure, noting her armor and lingering on her bloody sword. He looked back at her face, and Maud saw surprise and respect in his eyes, an admiration of a fighter appreciating a peer's skill.

Something forgotten and repressed stirred inside her.

"Well fought, my lady," he said quietly.

"Well fought, my lord," she answered on autopilot.

"Are you or your daughter hurt?"

"No, my lord."

"All is well then."

He smiled at her. He was handsome before, but he was impossible now.

No, she told herself. *No. You tried before, you tried your best for years, and they threw you and your child away like garbage.* She wouldn't become involved with another vampire again. She wouldn't even entertain that idea, no matter how hard he fought or how much admiration reflected in his eyes when he looked at her.

She was done with all things vampire.

———

Three weeks later

ARLAND LAY NAKED ON THE METAL EXAMINATION TABLE. BLOODY blisters sheathed his body. Some had ruptured, leaking polluted, foul blood that smelled of acid and decomposition.

Panic flailed and clawed at Maud's insides. She took his hands. His fingers were like ice. He looked at her, his blue eyes brimming with pain. It cut Maud like a knife.

You fool. You stupid fool.

They were besieged in Dina's inn. An alien had asked her sister for shelter and she took him in, knowing that his entire species was a target of a planet of religious zealots. A clan of assassins had targeted the alien. She and Arland had been helping to hold them off, fighting side by side, sparring, eating in the same kitchen, repairing their armor at night at the dining room table in a comfortable silence. He provoked her, she responded, then she provoked him, and he parried. She watched him play with Helen, treating her like a treasured vampire child. She noticed when he smiled. She trained with him and she told herself that none of it mattered. They were just friends fighting for the same cause.

Today the assassins managed to introduce a seed of the World Killer into the inn. A flower with the power to wipe out the entire planets, the World Killer was impervious to fire and acid. Made of energy, it passed through every barrier they could throw in its way and only became flesh when it was about to attack. It would kill and grow and kill again until nothing alive remained on the planet and the five of them, Dina, Sean, Helen, Arland, and she would become its first victims.

They stood frozen in the kitchen, afraid to make the slightest movement. Then Arland declared that his blood was toxic to the flower. She saw him look at Helen, look at her, and she knew deep in the very core of her soul that he would sacrifice himself for them. The enormity of that realization smashed into her, throwing her so off balance, she couldn't even think.

She remembered his voice, so calm it chilled her. "Lady Maud, if I die, say the Liturgy of the Fallen for me."

Saying the Liturgy of the Fallen fell to the one you treasured most. Your spouse. Your lover. Your one who was everything. She couldn't dishonor that confession and she answered him in the language of vampires. *"Go with the Goddess, my Lord. You won't be forgotten."*

He had thrown himself at the flower. It stung and seared him, wrapping around him like a constrictor snake. It pierced him again and again, poisoning him until it brought him to his knees. He'd screamed, his voice raw with pain, tears streaming down his face, and still he fought it until he finally grasped its root, tore it open and spat his own blood into it. It died.

And now Arland would die too.

They made him release his armor while Helen cried and begged him not to die, then they brought him here into the medward. He had grown so weak. There was barely any strength in his fingers. Her sister kept washing him, rinsing the polluted blood off his body, but his wounds bled and bled. There was no antidote.

She couldn't lose him. She couldn't. Thinking of getting up in the morning, knowing she would never see him, shredded her soul. She wanted to scream and rage, but he was looking at her face, their stares forging a fragile connection. She held his hand

and looked back at him, terrified this tether would snap and he would be gone forever.

She saw death in his eyes, coming closer and closer. Vampires died surrounded by family or on the battlefield. She had to help him. She had to...

Maud made her voice neutral and calm. "Dina, do you have a vigil room?"

"No."

"Then I'm going to make one. Off the kitchen."

She closed her eyes, reaching for the magic of Gertrude Hunt. Dina's inn responded, moving first slowly then faster, pulling apart floors and walls, forming a new space, shaping a massive tub, growing the proper plants... It would give him the peace of mind. If he was reassured that proper rites would be said and prayer offered on his behalf, he might hold on.

Hold on, she willed. Please, hold on. Please don't leave us.

She opened her eyes, took the showerhead from Dina, and kept washing him.

His chest barely rose.

"Don't go," she begged. "Hold on to me."

He smiled at her, so weak it almost broke what little resolve she had left.

"Fight it," she said. She grasped his hand, trying to pour some of her vitality into him.

"Everything is slowing down." His voice was quiet. He raised his hand, his fingers trembling. She leaned into his palm, and he stroked her cheek. "No time."

"Fight it. Live."

His eyes dimmed.

A knock sounded. A door opened and Caldenia ka ret Magren strode into the room. Once a galactic tyrant, now Gertrude Hunt's only permanent guest, with a bounty on her head that would let you buy a paradise planet. She carried a small box.

A cure. Maud had no idea how she knew it, but she believed it with every heartbeat.

Her fear had paralyzed her, and Maud turned numb.

Even as the needle pierced Arland's skin and his wounds stopped bleeding, she still couldn't bring herself to hope. She directed the inn to transport him, she watched him slide into the mint bath in the vigil room, and then she sat by him and whispered prayers, one after another.

Around them the inn was quiet. Dina had left somewhere. Sean and others were in the kitchen, but they might as well have gone to the moon.

Live, Arland. Live. Don't leave me. Don't leave Helen.

A warm wet hand touched her. Maud opened her eyes. He was looking at her, his blond hair wet, his skin still too pale, but his blue eyes were brighter and deep within his irises, she glimpsed the same iron will that drove him into battle.

"My lady," he said quietly.

"Never do that again," she whispered.

"Stay with me," he asked.

"Where would I go?"

He smiled then. She rolled her eyes and went back to the rites.

———

THE PRACTICE MACE WHISTLED OVER MAUD'S HEAD. SHE DROPPED into a crouch and kicked out, aiming to sweep Arland's legs. The Marshal of House Krahr leaped up and back, avoiding the kick. Maud lunged to the left, rolled to her feet, and came up in time to dodge another blow.

He forced her across the white marble floor. Sweat drenched her face.

Around them the grand ballroom of Gertrude Hunt glowed in all of its glory. The enormous light fixtures on the ceiling were off, and glittering nebulae shone on the dark walls and the tall ceiling far above, clusters of stars sparkling like constellations of precious gems. The only illumination came from the delicate glass flowers blooming on golden vines that twisted around the towering turquoise columns.

She used to spar with Melizard like this, but their practice matches always had spectators. Like everything, her late husband put on a show meant to impress and further his ambitions. Maud once told him she was uncomfortable with the attention, and he told her that he wanted everyone to witness his human wife's skills. He spun it as a way to improve her position with House Ervan. Now, years later, she understood that it was always about him, never about her.

Arland never paraded her or himself in front of an audience. If someone had come to practice beside them, he wouldn't object. He was a knight of an old House and politeness was ingrained in his bones. But he never invited attention. However, their practice sessions were theirs alone, private, quiet, just for the two of them. And she never held back.

He told her he loved her. She remembered every word. It was etched in her memory. He stood before the tub where her catatonic sister sat, watching them with unseeing eyes, knowing that they were about to go into battle that might end them both and told her the truth.

When I first saw you, it was like being thrown from a shuttle before it touched the ground. I fell and when I landed, I felt it in every cell of my body. You disturbed me. You took away my inner peace...

Arland charged her. She danced away, spun around him,

tapped his back, and was away before he could chase after her again.

...You taught me the meaning of loneliness, because when I don't see you, I feel alone...

Arland lunged, thrusting. An unexpected move, one particular to a sword, not a mace. It caught her by surprise. She took the blow in the chest and staggered back. He advanced and got a slice of the practice sword across his neck for his trouble.

...You may reject me, you may deny yourself and if you choose to not accept me, I will abide by your decision...

Arland dropped the mace and rushed her. She should have avoided him, but the last battle for the survival of Dina's inn had taken a lot out of her. Her emotions were a mess, her brain felt like it was overheating trying to wrestle her thoughts under control, and Maud was still too damn tired. His fingers caught her right wrist, and he pulled her to him, turning her so her back pressed against his chest. His hands clamped her upper arms in a steel vise. He'd caught her like that before, and she knew from experience that getting out of this hold was impossible. Even if she pulled up her legs, hitting him with her dead weight, he would simply hold her above the floor.

They stood in a kind of embrace.

...But know that there will never be another one like you for me and one like me for you. We both waited years so we could meet.

He let her go. She picked up her sword and walked back to the practice weapon rack.

Arland loved her. And she loved him too. She had known it the moment he asked her for the Liturgy of the Fallen, because it felt like the fear that he would die would wrench her heart out of her chest. But then he ruined it all and asked her to marry him.

Maud dropped her sword and her buckler onto the practice weapon rack and pulled on the inn's magic. The inn obeyed, parting the floor under the rack and letting it sink down into storage, but it responded sluggishly, almost as if it was confused by her directions. The response at her parents' inn had been instant. Here, it was like giving commands to a sibling's dog. It obeyed her because she was family and a human, but it knew she was not *its* human.

It would get better with time, if she stayed. And staying at the inn made all the sense in the world. She and Helen would be safe here. Dina could use the help, and Helen loved it. The inn responded to her much better than it did to Maud. All inns instantly took to children.

But what would happen when her daughter realized she couldn't have friends?

What would happen when he left?

That last thought gave her the shove she needed. Maud turned to Arland.

"I love you," she told him. "But I can't marry you."

His handsome face stayed perfectly neutral, but she caught the splash of happiness in his eyes. It dimmed instantly, but she caught it.

"May I ask why?"

"Because love is simple, but marriage is complicated."

"Explain."

She crossed her arms on her chest, using them as a shield. "When you look at Helen, what do you see?"

"Potential."

She could've kissed him for that, but that wouldn't help. "If you didn't know her background, would you say she's a human or a vampire?"

"A vampire," he said without hesitation.

"Because of the fangs?"

"Because of her predatory drive. Fangs make her *look* like a

31

vampire. They can be obtained by surgical means, but the instinct to identify and strike at the opponent's weaknesses can't be fabricated or learned. One either has it or doesn't. She has it."

That was her assessment as well. "If I stay here, in my sister's inn, Helen would have to confine herself to the grounds. She can't attend a human school. Other children wouldn't be safe around her. They wouldn't know what she was but they would know she was different. They would ignore her or torment her, and she would retaliate."

Arland's expression hardened. "I have no right to offer my opinion, but would imprisoning her in the inn be the best thing for Helen?"

Imprisoned. That's how he saw it. That's how she saw it too.

Within the inn, the innkeepers possessed almost god-like power. They built rooms for a hundred different species in minutes. They bent the laws of physics and opened passages to planets thousands of light years away. They saw the oddities and wonders of the galaxy pass through their doors.

But the human world of the innkeepers was small, the friends few, and even though the galaxy lay at their door, most of them rarely stepped over the threshold. Outside of the inn, they were vulnerable. The children of the innkeepers grew up at home, apart from human society, and when they grew up, they became innkeepers or the ad-hal, the enforcers of the innkeepers. Sometimes they left Earth the way she and her brother had. Almost none of them entered human society. Once they learned to use their magic, there was no putting it back into a box.

"What would happen to Helen if we took her to House Krahr?"

Arland frowned. "She would run wild around the keep with other children like her. I'd like to see the Sentinels try to wrangle her into a classroom. In fact, I would pay good money..." He caught the expression on her face. "That is, she

32

would receive a fine education in line with the other scions of House Krahr."

"You once told me that she should be a *rassa* in the grass, not a *goren* on the porch."

Rassa were fierce ambush predators, while gorens, smaller and tamer, served vampires like dogs served humans.

Arland cleared his throat. "I may have been too blunt."

"No, you were right. Helen is a *rassa* and at House Krahr she would be among other *rassa*. It would be more dangerous, but she could find her place there the way she could never find it here. Then there is me. I've worn the armor of a vampire for six years. I'm not the same human woman who left her parents' inn. I'm not even the same woman who had been exiled to Karhari almost three years ago. I don't know where my place is. I haven't figured out where I belong."

"With me," he said. "You belong with me. Maud, all of these are arguments in favor of our marriage."

She nodded, "I know. And that's a problem. I'm a widow of a dishonored knight. My husband tried to murder his own brother to become the marshal of his House. I am a human. I know how vampires treat outsiders. I've lived that life. Your House will see me as a human woman who has nothing, no status, no honor, no purpose. No use to anyone. A woman who has a half-vampire child and would do anything for the sake of that child, including seducing the pride of their House and then manipulating him to get what she wants."

Arland raised his eyebrows. "I've survived countless attempts at manipulation before. I appear to be too dense for it. However, I am open to being seduced."

"Will you take this seriously?"

"I don't care what my House thinks."

"But I do. For years I was an exemplary wife to the son of a vampire Marshal. Nobody could find fault with my behavior or with my daughter. I worked for the benefit of House Ervan. I organized their banquets, I taught them to deal with their alien neighbors, I memorized their rituals, rites, poetry...I know more Ancestor Vampiric dialects than most vampire scholars. Yet, when my husband committed treason, his House threw us away like garbage. None of my accomplishments mattered. I didn't exist outside of my husband."

His face turned hard. "I'm not Melizard and House Krahr is not House Ervan."

Maud nodded. "I know that. But the imbalance between us is much greater than between Melizard and me. I don't want to be the pet human, Arland. I won't let myself be treated that way again. My trust in your society has been shattered. I swore to myself that I would never return to the Holy Anocracy. I wanted to save myself and Helen from rejection. I can probably take it. It would crush me, but I would survive it. I'm an adult. Helen is a child. The first time it happened, she was too young to fully understand it, but now she is old enough. I can't put her through it. To have found a home and a father and then to have it ripped away from her for the second time would be too unfair. I can't let anyone throw us away again. I won't. But I can't keep my promise to stay away from the Anocracy either, because the thought of you leaving terrifies me and because my child is half-vampire. She deserves to know where she came from."

"I am the reflection of my House," Arland said. "I love you. I see you as you are, a woman who would be an asset to any House. If you come with me, those close to me will see you as you are as well, and they will come to love you. There is not a person alive who wouldn't care about Helen."

"Tell it to her grandmother."

34

Arland bared his fangs. "I will when opportunity arises. Marry me."

"I can't. But I can't let you go either. I want to come with you, and I don't know if I am doing it for Helen, for myself, or because I am too weak to do the right thing and thinking about not being with you makes me desperate. I won't lie to you, Arland. I used to finesse my husband, because he left me no choice, and I will never do that again. I can't promise I will marry you. I can't even promise I will stay with you. I can promise that I will try to prove to your House that I am worth it. This is so much less than you deserve. I have only two conditions. One, you do not pressure me into marriage. Two, if I want to leave, you will provide me with a passage back to Earth. Take us with you or don't. The decision is yours."

She stared straight ahead, looking in his direction but not seeing him.

"Maud."

She met his gaze.

"How quickly can you pack?" he asked.

[2]

NOW...

The stars died, replaced by total darkness.

Maud hugged her shoulders. The cold, slightly rough texture of the armor felt familiar under her fingertips. Reassuring. The plan was to never wear armor again, but lately life had taken a baseball bat to her plans.

The floor-to-ceiling display only simulated a window, with the cabin itself hidden deep within the bowels of the destroyer, but the darkness yawned at her all the same, cold and timeless. The Void, the vampires called it. That which exists between the stars. It always made her uneasy.

"Are we dead, Mama?"

Maud turned. Helen stood a few feet away, hugging a soft teddy bear her aunt bought her for Christmas. Her long blond hair stuck out on the right side, crinkled from her sleep. From here she could almost pass for a human.

"No. We're not dead. We're traveling in hyperspace. It would take too much time to get where we need to go under normal propulsion, so we thread through a wrinkle in the fabric of space like a needle. Come, I want to show you something."

Helen padded over. Maud swept her up—she was getting so big so fast—and held her to the display.

"This is the Void. You remember what Daddy told you about the Void?"

"It's where the souls go."

"That's right. When a vampire dies, his soul must pass through the Void before it is decided if it goes to Paradise or to the empty plains of Nothing."

"I don't like it," Helen whispered and stuck her head into Maud's shoulder.

Maud almost purred. These moments, when Helen still acted like a baby, were more and more rare now. Soon she would grow up and walk away, but for now Maud could still hold her and smell her scent. Helen was hers for a little while longer.

"Don't be afraid. You have to look, or you will miss the best part."

Helen turned. They stood together, looking at the darkness.

A tiny spark flared in the center of the display. The brilliant point of light rushed toward the spaceship, unfurling like a glittering flower, spinning, its petals opening wide and wider, painted with all the majesty of the galaxy.

Helen stared, her eyes opened wide, the starglow of the display playing on her face.

The dazzling universe engulfed them. The ship tore through the last shreds of darkness and emerged into normal space. A beautiful planet hung in front of them, orbiting a warm yellow star, a green and blue jewel wrapped in a turquoise veil of gently glowing atmosphere. Daesyn. It wasn't Earth, but it could've been her prettier sister. Two moons orbited the planet, one large and purple, closer to the surface, the other tinted with orange, smaller and distant. The sunsets had to be spectacular.

"Is this the planet where Lord Arland lives?"

"Yes, my flower." Maud set Helen on the floor. "You should get dressed."

Helen scampered off, like a bunny released from its hutch.

The turquoise planet looked at Maud through the screen. The home world of House Krahr.

This was crazy. Certifiable.

If she went on logic only, she should've never come here. She should've never brought Helen here.

The planet grew on her screen.

Maud hugged her shoulders. It would've been so much more prudent to walk away and stay in her sister's inn. To relearn being a human after trying for so many years to become the perfect vampire.

Being in love in the inn was simple. They were fighting for their lives every day. It left little room for small things, but in ordinary life those little things often became important enough to shatter relationships. Jumping headfirst into vampire politics was unwise, especially House Krahr politics. Melizard would've cut off his arm to own this ship, and Arland drove it back and forth like it cost him nothing. The threshold was that much higher.

When she had married Melizard, she had hoped for acceptance, second family, and trust. She found none of it. Now...Now she just wanted to find out if House Krahr was worth it. She was no longer willing to settle. They would take them in as their own, or they wouldn't need to bother.

A sphere slipped from behind the curve of the planet. It didn't have the usual pitted look of a satellite. She squinted at it.

What the hell...

Maud pinched her arm. The sphere was still there. Three rings wrapped around it, twisting one over the other, each consisting of a metal core bristling with a latticework of spikes. From here the rings appeared delicate, almost ethereal. She touched the display, zooming in on the rings.

Not spikes. Cannons.

House Krahr had built a mobile battle station. Her mind refused to accept the existence of so much firepower concentrated in one place.

Dear universe, how much did that thing cost? Arland had mentioned that because of her sister's help, their House was doing well, but this, this was off the scale.

Maud's fingers went to the blank crest on her armor. The crest controlled the armor's functions and granted her entry to the Holy Anocracy and permission to operate within its borders as a free agent, a mercenary. She wouldn't be trapped on Daesyn. If things went sour, she could always grab Helen and go back to Dina's inn, she told herself. She made Arland promise to provide a passage, but Dina had insisted on sharing the proceeds of the sale of weapons they collected during the attack at the inn. She could easily buy a passage back.

"Mama?" Helen asked. "Are we there yet?"

"Almost, my flower."

She turned. Helen had put on the outfit they bought at Baha-char, the galactic bazaar. Black leggings, black tunic over a crimson shirt. She looked like a full-blooded vampire. But she was only half. The other vampires would not let her forget it. At least not until she beat every last one of them into submission.

"Come here." Maud crouched and adjusted Helen's belt, cinching her daughter's tiny waist. She reached for the small box waiting on the shelf next to the bed and opened it. A strip of black metal lay inside, ten inches long and one inch wide. Maud took it out and placed it on Helen's left wrist. Tiny red lights sparked inside the metal. The strip curved around Helen's wrist, joined into a bracelet, and shrank, adhering to her skin. Thin rectangles formed on its surface.

"Do you remember how to use it?" Maud asked.

Helen nodded.

"Show me."

Helen tapped the center rectangle with her finger. A translucent screen showing the layout of the ship flared into life one inch above her wrist.

"Call Mommy."

Maud's own unit came to life, tossing her own screen out with Helen's image on it.

"Good."

The harbinger unit served as the Holy Anocracy's version of a smartphone. Equipped with a powerful processor, it made calls, tracked its target, provided maps, monitored vital signs, tracked schedules, and simplified dozens of small tasks to make one's life easier. In adults it interfaced with armor, but Helen was wearing a child's version. It couldn't be removed or turned off by anyone other than a parent.

For the past five years, keeping Helen alive had been the core of Maud's existence. Once they made planetfall, there would be times Helen would have to be on her own. Thinking about it set Maud's teeth on edge. The harbinger didn't take away the anxiety, but it blunted it, and right now she would take all of the help she could get.

"All set?" Maud asked.

"All set," Helen said. "Can I bring my teddy?"

"We'll bring all our things."

They had so little, it didn't take them long to pack. Five minutes later, Maud swung the bag over her shoulder, glanced one final time at the cabin and display, and took Helen by the hand. The door slid open at their approach. Maud squared her shoulders and raised her head and they stepped through it.

Let the games begin. She was ready.

Space crews had a saying, "Volume is cheap; mass is expensive." In space, where air and friction weren't a factor, it didn't matter how large something was, only how much it weighed. It took a certain amount of fuel to accelerate one pound of matter to the right velocity, and then a roughly equal amount of fuel to decelerate it.

House Krahr had taken that saying and run with it. The arrival deck of the ship looked like the courtyard of a castle in the finest Holy Anocracy tradition. Square gray stones paved the floor and veneered the towering walls. Long crimson banners of House Krahr, marked with a black profile of the saber-toothed predator, stretched between the false windows. The gentle breeze of atmospheric circulators stirred the fabric, and the several krahr on the banners seemed to snarl in response.

In the middle of the chamber, a vala tree spread its black branches. Solid, with a sturdy trunk and a mass of limbs that divided and subdivided into a vast crown, the vala reminded Maud of basswood, but unlike the gentle green of linden trees, the vala's leaves were a vivid scarlet. The blood-red heart of the ship, a remnant of the origin world, sacred to vampires. No major ritual took place in vampire society without the vala tree to witness it.

As if all of this wasn't enough, a two-foot wide stream meandered through the smooth stream bed, crossing the deck, winding around the tree in a perfect circle, and disappearing beneath the roots. Maud could've understood if it was part of the water supply that would be later recycled, but there were bright sparkly fish in it. The stream served as a decoration, nothing more. The luxury boggled the mind.

There had to be some way to close it off, if the ship had to maneuver, Maud reflected. Otherwise they would have a mess on their hands. There was nothing more fun than unsecured water in zero-G.

"Can I?" Helen whispered.

"Yes," Maud told her.

Helen ran to the tree, little heels flashing.

Maud followed slowly. She'd walked across stones just like these countless times before when she was married. If she let it, her memory would change their pale gray to a warm travertine beige; the crimson banners to Carolina-blue; and the dark ceiling of the ship to an orange-tinted sky.

She stopped before the vala tree. Every vampire planet had them. If the climate couldn't support them, the vampires built hothouses just to plant them. A vala tree was the heart of the clan, the core of the family, a sacred place. The blossoms of the vala tree had decorated her bridal crown. It was a great honor, appropriate to the bride of the second son of the Marshal of House Ervan.

A hot pain pinched her chest. It's in the past, she told herself. It is over and done with. Let it go.

Careful footsteps approached from behind, trying to sneak up on her. She hid a smile.

"Greetings, Lord Soren."

The footsteps stopped, then resumed, and Lord Soren halted next to her. Vampires aged like their castles—growing bigger and sturdier, as if time itself reinforced them. Lord Soren was the perfect example of a middle-aged vampire: wide in the shoulders, muscled like a grizzled tiger, with a spectacular mane of dark-brown hair and a short but thick beard, both touched with gray. His syn-armor, midnight black with red marks denoting his rank of Knight Sergeant, and the small round crest of House Krahr, bore a few scars here and there, much like Lord Soren himself. A testament to life spent in battle. He looked like a humanoid tank.

He was also Arland's uncle. She had worked hard to get him to like her. Lord Soren wasn't complicated. His worldview came down to three things: honor, tradition, and family. He dedicated his life to upholding all three, and they were never in conflict. He viewed her favorably, but how far exactly his good will extended remained to be seen.

He pondered Helen, who had dropped her bag and was dipping her fingers into the stream. "The child loves the water."

"There is little water on Karhari, my lord." There was nothing on Karhari except miles of dry, hard dirt, and it desiccated those sent there until they hardened and dried as well.

"It's a new experience for her."

"It is."

They watched her in comfortable silence.

"It's good that you joined us," he said.

She hoped he was right.

"Perhaps, with your presence, my nephew will stay put for longer than five minutes before running off on another fool's errand halfway across the galaxy."

The arrival deck was slowly filling up with people waiting to go planetside.

If he does, I'll run off with him. "I understand Lady Ilemina is in residence?"

"She is."

Sooner or later she would have to meet Arland's mother. It wouldn't be a pleasant meeting.

"Has my nephew told you why I had to come to the inn to fetch him?" Lord Soren asked.

"No."

"What do you know of House Serak?"

She raked her memory. "One of the larger Houses. They control most of their planet, which is also named Serak, if I recall correctly. They've never produced a Warlord, but they did come close twice in the past five centuries. After suffering defeat in the Seven Star War, their influence diminished, but they're still formidable. They're also hungry to regain what they've lost and that makes them dangerous."

Lord Soren nodded in approval. "And their sworn enemy?"

It took her a second. "House Kozor. A slightly smaller House, but a great deal more aggressive. They control the second habitable planet in the Serak system."

"They've decided to bury the bones of their fallen," he said.

Interesting. "An alliance?"

"A wedding."

Maud blinked. "Even so?"

"Yes. The son of the Serak's Preceptor will marry the daughter of the Kozor's Archchaplain. They required a neutral location in which the ceremony can be performed."

"Naturally." It was a sword-edge wedding. Nobody trusted anyone, and everyone was waiting for an ambush. "Did House Krahr offer them such a haven?"

"There was no way to reasonably refuse," Lord Soren said. "We dominate the quadrant and Serak is only one hyperspace jump away from us. The wedding is in eight days. It would've been more appropriate for Arland to have been on the planet to assist with preparations, but since he's been otherwise occupied, we'll be arriving about the same time as the wedding guests."

"Correct me, but isn't there another vampire-controlled star system, closer than this one, to the Serak system?"

"There is."

Something was off about this wedding. "One wonders why two Houses with such lack of trust want to be bound."

"Supposedly to end their conflict and form a pact."

"If they are unable to come together for even the most joyous of occasions and require a neutral location and a host to oversee them, their alliance is doomed from the start. There must be willingness from both Houses for the marriage to hold."

Lord Soren studied her.

"How large of a wedding party are you expecting, my lord?"

"One hundred guests from each side."

"And they will arrive armed?"

"They will."

House Krahr could field tens of thousands of troops. Two hundred vampires, no matter how elite, shouldn't have posed a threat. So why did this suddenly make her uneasy?

The door in the far wall slid open and Arland strode through it. She saw his handsome face, framed with a mane of blond hair.

His blue eyes found her. He grinned. Her heart skipped a beat.

Damn it.

Arland zeroed in on them and broke into a march. He moved like a massive predatory cat, deliberately, smoothly, the blood mace at his waist a reminder of his rank. He'd fought for the place at the top and won. All of Krahr's military obeyed him without question. And his mother was the Head of the House, the Preceptor.

Arland was the perfect embodiment of everything a vampire lord should be. Smart, powerful, fearless, and loyal. A paragon of vampire knighthood. It took Maud exactly two seconds to deduce that he was his uncle's pride and joy. He was likely his mother's pride and joy, too. And she was a human nobody.

"Lord Soren," Maud murmured. "Lady Ilemina must be stressed by these preparations. Perhaps it would be wiser not to mention Lord Arland's proposal." And her refusing of it.

"I couldn't agree more," the Knight Sergeant said.

She let out a small breath of relief.

"Unfortunately, my nephew took it upon himself to inform his mother already."

What? She kept her voice calm. "He did?"

"Oh yes," Lord Soren said, his face looking like he'd just bitten into a lemon. "He sent the message two days before we left the planet, by an emergency jump-drone, announcing that he would be bringing a bride and to make sure adequate accommodations were prepared."

Damn it, Arland. "He didn't ask her blessing?"

"No. I believe he commanded the household to make themselves 'presentable.'"

Because his mother would never find that offensive. She closed her eyes for a tiny moment.

"Then he sent a second message, stating that you turned him down but will be joining him anyway."

Arland had accelerated. He was looking at her as if she was the lone light in a dark room.

"Did his mother reply?"

"Yes."

Maud steeled herself. "What did she say?"

"Just five words," Lord Soren said. "'Can't wait to meet her.'"

Great. Just great.

Soren reached over and awkwardly patted her arm. "It could be worse."

She couldn't for the life of her see how.

Arland reached them. "Lady Maud."

His voice sent a soft rumble through her. She hated that. It was a weakness, but she had no idea how to compensate for it. She wished she could be immune.

"Lord Arland."

Lord Soren discreetly stepped away and strolled closer to the arch of the summoning gate. Helen abandoned the fish and the water and brought her bag over. Arland held out his hands, but Helen stayed by her side.

"No hug?" he asked.

"Mommy said to be polite."

"There are certain appearances that must be observed, my lord," Maud said.

"I never cared much for appearances," he said. His eyes were soft and warm. Inviting.

She needed to get her head examined.

"Unfortunately, some of us are not in the position to not care."

The summoning gate turned crimson. Lord Soren stepped into the light and vanished.

"My lady." Arland indicated the gate with his hand.

He reached for her bag, but she shouldered it out of the way. They walked toward the gate.

"What's bothering you?" he asked quietly.

"You told your mother."

"Of course I did. You're not some shameful secret I'm going to hide."

"No, I'm a disgraced exile who had the audacity to turn down the most beloved son of House Krahr."

He considered it. "Not the most beloved. My cousin is much more adorable than me. He is two and his hair is curly."

"Lord Arland..."

His eyes sparkled with humor. "You could always remedy it and say yes."

"No."

Helen was looking at them. Maud realized they were standing in front of the summoning gate and bickering.

"Do you remember this?" Arland asked Helen.

Helen nodded and eyed the gate. "It makes my tummy sick."

"Do you want to hold my hand?" Maud asked.

"We have to do it quick, like charging a castle." Arland reached out, swung Helen onto his shoulder, and ducked through the gate.

"Arland!" she snapped.

He was gone. She was on her own on the arrival deck with half of Arland's crew gaping at her. She clenched her teeth and walked into the crimson glow.

[3]

The red radiance of the summoning gate died behind Maud. She blinked, fighting the vertigo, and walked away from it on autopilot to keep from blocking other arrivals.

To the right, about twenty-five yards away, Arland stopped to speak to three vampires. He'd taken Helen off his shoulders—thank you, universe—and she gaped at the spaceport.

Maud looked around and stopped to gape, too. She stood in a cavernous rectangular chamber. Daylight flooded it through long, narrow rectangular windows cut in the gray stone walls twenty feet above. She turned slowly, trying to take it all in.

To her left, the summoning gate glowed, about to release another traveler into the spaceport. To her right, small craft, sleek fighters and a few light civilian vessels, perched on the floor, and beyond them enormous hangar doors stood wide open, filled with blue sky. Above the hangar doors, a stone relief depicted a snarling krahr. The massive predator, its wide head a cross between a bear and a tiger, roared at the visitors, its maw gaping open, its sabretooth fangs a fatal promise. A thin crack down the krahr's left side had chipped a bit of stone fur from its jaw. Nobody had fixed it.

It hit her. House Krahr was an old House.

Melizard's House, House Ervan, was much younger. Noceen was a prosperous planet, with a gentle climate, colonized only two hundred years ago, and House Ervan had emerged as one of the prominent vampire clans due mostly to sheer luck. They had arrived with the first wave of settlers and the land they'd claimed happened to contain rich mineral deposits. Their wealth bought them weapons, equipment, and infrastructure. Everything on Noceen had been of the highest quality, modern and slick, especially the spaceport, where the traditional vampire stone was a veneer and the wood had been artificially distressed. She'd thought it rather grand when she first saw it. But this...This was the real thing.

All vampire spaceports were castles. Easily defended to allow for evacuation to orbit, easily contained if a threat were to arrive via the summoning gate. The spaceport of House Krahr had been built hundreds of years ago. The weathered stones under her feet, the massive wooden beams above, darkened by time, the thick stone walls, all of it emanated age. This was a stronghold, raised when strongholds had a purpose. Here and there modernization showed, but its touch was subtle and light: upgraded windows of transparent plastisteel, sensors high in the walls, and the massive blast-proof hangar gates. But the stronghold itself breathed an overwhelming sense of ancientness. It spoke to the visitors without uttering a word.

We've built this. It's endured for centuries. Countless generations of us have walked across its threshold and still we own it, for no one is strong enough to take it away from us.

It wasn't about money. It was a statement of power, harsh and brutal. It demanded respect, especially from a vampire, to whom tradition and family meant everything. It commanded awe and took it as its due.

She was so in over her head, it wasn't even funny.

Arland strode to her, Helen at his side. "My lady."

Clipped, formal words. The easy familiarity she'd become accustomed to was gone. She had expected as much.

"My lord."

"I must apologize. A matter requires my urgent attention." He leaned closer to her. "Don't go anywhere. I'll be back in ten minutes."

"As you wish, my lord."

"I mean it," he said. "Ten minutes."

He seemed genuinely worried she would disappear. "Helen and I will wait for you."

He nodded and marched away. The three vampire knights fell in behind him.

To the right, two vampire women followed him with their gazes. Both wore armor with the crest of House Kozor, a horned beast on blue. One was lean and tall, with a waterfall of chestnut hair framed by elaborate braids. The other, curvier, her armor more ornate, left her corn-silk blond mane free. It fell all the way to her butt in shiny waves, and by the way she tossed her head, she was quite proud of it.

Interesting. "Would you like to see the shuttles?"

"Yes," Helen said.

"Let's go look at them."

They drifted closer to the shiny shuttles and to the two vampire women. Helen went to look at the elegant pure white fighter, and Maud watched her, keeping the two women on the very edge of her vision.

"...not the time to satiate your appetites," the taller woman said.

Maud's implant remained silent, but she understood regardless. Ancestor Vampiric. It was an older language, with dozens of regional dialects and variations. A lot of vampires could barely comprehend it, especially if it was spoken by a vampire from a different home world. Speech implants failed to interpret it, and outsiders didn't speak it, but then she wasn't an outsider. A lot of the great epics had been written in Ancestor Vampiric and reciting them in the original dialect had been a point of pride for members of House Ervan. She had tried so hard to be the best wife for Melizard. She was fluent in twelve main dialects and could understand others enough to get by. This particular one was odd, an offshoot of the Third Planet Coastal. They blended their vowels left and right but if she concentrated, she could make do.

"You have to admit, he's a prime specimen," the blond said.

"He's preoccupied with his human toy. That's her over there."

"Toys can be broken," the blond said.

Anytime you want to try.

"That is a beautiful child," the blond said.

"A halfer," the brunette sneered.

"Still, a cute little mongrel. Do you think she's his?"

"No. The woman is an exile from some no-name House. One of the *nouveau riche* from the frontier. She was married to their Marshal's son. He betrayed his House."

"Interesting." The blond stretched the word.

"Apparently Arland found her on Karhari."

"The Marshal gets around." The blond smiled. "You should let me play with him. It really is a shame to lose—"

"Be silent," the chestnut snapped.

"Fine," the blond sighed.

"I mean it. Mind your tongue, Seveline. Too many people have done too much work for you to ruin it with your blabbering. The future of our House is riding on this."

"I said, 'fine.'" Seveline's voice turned sharper.

Short fuse, that one. She could use that later.

Helen moved on to the next shuttle and Maud strolled past the two women.

"My lady," the blond said in Common Vampiric. "Pleasant day to you and your beautiful daughter."

Maud inclined her head a neutral couple of inches. "Greetings, my lady."

"I'm Seveline of the House of Kozor. This is my friend, Lady Onda, also of House Kozor."

They treated her like she was an idiot who couldn't identify crests. Perfect.

"I'm honored," Maud said.

The two women smiled, showing the very edges of their teeth.

"Is this your first time enjoying the hospitality of House Krahr?" Onda asked.

"Yes."

"You're in for a treat," Seveline said. "Their festivities are legendary. Once you are settled, do find me. I see us becoming the best of friends."

"Indeed," Onda said.

Two-faced bitches.

"I'll do my best," Maud promised.

Arland was marching toward her with a grim look on his face.

"I must beg your forgiveness," Maud said. "The Marshal requires my presence."

"We wouldn't presume to keep you," Onda said.

"You are beyond gracious. Come on, my flower."

Maud took Helen by the hand and headed toward Arland. They met halfway.

"Sorry," he murmured.

"Trouble?"

"Inconvenience. Are you ready to depart?"

"Yes."

He led her to a small silver shuttle, a six-seater.

"Am I flying with you in your personal craft?"

"Yes," he said.

"Is that wise?"

"I thought we established that I don't care about being wise."

Flying in his personal shuttle meant she'd face scrutiny at the point of landing, but it also meant she could speak to Arland in privacy.

Maud settled Helen into a soft blue seat and hopped into the passenger spot next to Arland. He touched the controls and the shuttle streaked through the hangar into the sky.

———

ARLAND WAS AN EXCELLENT PILOT. THE TAKE-OFF WAS SO SMOOTH, she barely felt the acceleration. He didn't bother with autopilot.

The landscape rolled under them, a thick forest growth, the massive trees stretching their ancient branches to the sun. A moment, and the dense canopy abruptly fell away. They'd cleared the mesa. Far below, a verdant grassland stretched, rolling to the horizon, like a sea with islands of white mesas that dripped turquoise forests. A wide river wound through it, unrestrained by any dams.

"Do you like Daesyn?" Arland asked.

"It's beautiful," she said honestly.

"It's home," he said.

It could be your home, his glance added.

Too early for that.

He looked straight ahead, his face calm, and she found herself staring at the hard line of his jaw. Imagined running her fingers down its length...

Stop it, she told herself.

"Does it strike you as odd, my lord, that Kozor and Serak decided to bury the hatchet?"

"Alliances are broken and created all the time," he said. His voice held no enthusiasm. He didn't like it either. Her instincts rarely failed her, but it was nice to have confirmation.

"True. But most Houses view such old rivalries as healthy."

"Is that so?" he said.

"It is. Conflict keeps their forces sharp. The strong and talented emerge, weaker people are culled, and there are ample opportunities for heroism and much growling about duty and honor."

Arland smiled, showing a hint of fang. "And speeches. Don't forget the speeches."

"Their feud is generations old. There are dead and wronged on both sides. There must be some mutual advantage for them to set it aside. Are you aware of such an advantage?"

"No."

"Then it must be a common enemy."

Arland sighed.

She raised her eyebrows at him.

"Your reasoning is sound," he said. "I'm not arguing with it. A month ago, I said pretty much the same thing at a strategy session where this wedding request was discussed."

"And?"

"And I was told that there was no graceful way to refuse the request. We are the dominant House in the quadrant. We have no indication that we are being lied to, and we have no excuse to deny it. We aren't at war, and our House is enjoying unprecedented prosperity at the moment. If we denied them, there would be questions."

"'Is House Krahr so meek that they are afraid of allowing a mere two hundred wedding guests into their territory?'"

He nodded.

Hosting a wedding was expensive. Tradition dictated that something had to be offered in return. "What was their offer?"

"Safe haven for the merchant ships."

"House Krahr can't protect its merchant fleet?"

He grimaced. "The sector bordering the Serak system is filled with pirates. Both Kozor and Serak have been fighting them for the better part of the century. There is a four-point warp near that system, just outside of the Anocracy space."

Four-point warps were rare. It meant that a ship could enter hyperspace and choose any of the other three destinations, which meant that stretch of space served as a major shipping artery. A multi-point warp is what made a solar system special. Earth was the only known twelve-point warp in existence.

"Our armada is more than sufficient for the protection of our merchant fleets," Arland continued. "The pirates go after free-lancers, courier ships, exploration and survey crews, and family miners and salvagers."

"Anything too small to warrant an escort by a ship of war."

"Exactly. The crews of these smaller crafts are members of House Krahr and neighboring Houses. It's been an ongoing thorny issue. We've gone after the pirate fleet a few times. They simply scatter. We chase down one or two of their vessels, and meanwhile the rest vanish. Kozor and Serak have the advantage of location and experience fighting them. They offered protection for our smaller craft, and we took it."

To tell him about the two Kozor women or not to tell him?

If he were Melizard, she would've held back until she had something more concrete.

That settled it. "I overheard a conversation in the spaceport. Two knights of House Kozor, Onda and Seveline."

"Anything interesting?" he asked.

"Seveline appraised you like you were a side of beef. In her opinion, you're a prime specimen she wouldn't mind taking for a ride."

He grinned at her. He had a terrible smile. It made him look predatory and slightly boyish at the same time. The combination was devastating.

"They called me a halfer," Helen said from the backseat.

The smiled vanished from his face, as if jerked away. "You're not a halfer," Arland growled. "You're a vampire and a human. Both and whole, not half and half."

Maud could've kissed him. Instead, she plastered a cool expression on her face. "Seveline told Onda that she should be allowed to play with you, because it would be a shame to lose."

"To lose what?"

"I don't know, because Onda jumped down her throat and made her be quiet. According to her, too many people worked too hard for Seveline to ruin it."

Arland's eyes narrowed. "I don't like it."

Maud leaned back in her seat. "Neither do I. Later Seveline made it a point to flag me down and offer me some pleasantries. She believes we will become fast friends."

Arland gave her a calculating look. "Perhaps you should."

If only. She grimaced. "I can't. For me to become her 'friend,' I would have to pretend to be weak and ignorant. Your mother didn't come to greet you at the spaceport. She is displeased."

"My mother is likely too busy with the hassle of arranging the wedding."

She snorted. "Or perhaps, my lord, she is mortally insulted by your instruction to make her household presentable for some disgraced human who turned down your proposal."

"My mother is never insulted. She is far too dignified and refined for that. She has the patience of a saint."

"Lady Ilemina," Maud quoted from memory, "Slaughterer of Ruhamin, Supreme Predator of the Holy Anocracy, Bleeder of Ert, Fierce Subjugator of..."

"Like I said, too dignified to take offense. If someone dares to insult her, she simply kills them, and she isn't going to kill me. I'm her only son. At most, she's annoyed, perhaps slightly irritated."

Maud sighed. "But I'm not her son."

"She won't harm you." He said it like he was swearing an oath. Like he would put himself between her and all danger.

He had no idea how intoxicating it was to hear that. Words are cheap, she reminded herself. Reading too much into them was a dangerous habit and one she couldn't afford. "Your mother will test me. She'll encourage others in your House to test me. I can't pretend to be weak and pass your mother's gauntlet at the same time."

"A fair point," he admitted.

"Perhaps, you should pay attention to Seveline. Just enough to encourage her. Her type gets off on feeling superior. She'd get special pleasure pretending to be my friend while knowing she has your attention."

Arland turned to her, his blue eyes clear and hard. "I proposed to you, my lady. If I treat you with anything but the devotion I feel, my House will dismiss you."

He was right.

Silence fell. The craft zipped over another mesa filled with old growth. In the distance, still a few miles off, a castle rose out of the huge trees, massive and pale gray, so solid and majestic, it looked like it had grown out of the bones of the mountain.

"I *am* devoted to you," Arland said quietly.

"Please don't." The words came out of her before she had a chance to think them over. She felt raw, as if he'd grabbed a bandage on a wound and ripped it off, reopening it.

What the hell is wrong with me?

"I'll wait," he said.

"I may never be ready."

"I'll wait until you tell me to stop. I have no expectations, my lady. If you leave, all you have to do is call on me in the time of need, and I'll be there."

Something in his voice told her he would wait forever.

They reached the castle. The ancestral home of House Krahr defied all expectations. A forest of square towers wrapped in a maze of walkways, parapets, thick walls, and courtyards, greeted her. If she had to run from it, she would never find a way out.

Arland's hands flew over the controls. The shuttle turned smoothly and sank onto a small landing pad on top of a squat tower. People emerged from the taller tower to the left, hurrying across the crosswalk. She had the worst sense of déjà vu. When Melizard came home, the retainers used to hurry to the shuttle just like that.

For a moment she felt like she was drowning.

"Welcome to House Krahr, my lady," Arland said.

She wouldn't lose her future to her memories. It wasn't going to happen. She turned to him and smiled her vampire smile, bright and sharp. "Thank you, my lord."

[4]

A s soon as they exited the shuttle, a young vampire knight with dark auburn hair whose name was Knight Ruin, attached himself to Arland and began rattling things off from his tablet. Arland's face took on the stony expression of a man who was either about to charge the enemy line for the fifth time in a single day, or do his taxes. He marched along the parapet toward the heavy door, with Ruin at his side. Maud took Helen's hand and followed him, and the four other retainers closed in, one next to her and three behind. She could practically feel their stares stabbing her back.

Go ahead. Get an eyeful.

The afternoon sun warmed Maud's skin. She guessed the temperature was somewhere in the mid-eighties, and the breeze was downright pleasant. She had a childish urge to climb onto one of the textured protrusions of the parapets, strip off her armor, and sunbathe for a couple of hours.

Ruin kept spitting out questions, periodically pausing for Arland to bark an answer.

"Third Regiment requests permission to enter negotiations with the architectural guilds to update their Chapel Hall."

"Granted."

"Second and third companies of Fourth Regiment request permission to settle an inter-unit dispute via champion combat."

"Denied. We don't parade our rivalries in front of wedding guests from other Houses. I want the full write-up of this dispute on my tablet within the hour."

"Knight Derit requests transfer out of Second Regiment."

"On what grounds?"

"Irreconcilable differences with his commanding knight."

"Inform Knight Derit that I declined his request and that he has misconstrued the nature of his relationship with Commander Karat. They aren't married. It's not a partnership of equals. Commander Karat says, 'Do this,' and Knight Derit does it, because that's what knights do. It's not a complicated arrangement, and if he has further difficulty understanding it, he needs to hang up his blood mace and look for a different profession more in line with his delicate nature. Perhaps flower arrangement would suit."

Maud hid a smile.

The carved doors swung open at their approach. They walked through them and into the shadowy hall. The air here was cooler. Tall windows spilled narrow blades of light into the hall, drawing golden rectangles on the stone floor. Shadow, light, shadow, light...It reminded her of the north wing of Castle Ervan. The last few weeks before their exile, she'd walked that hall expecting a dagger in her back at any moment.

The male retainer next to her gave her a startled look.

Maud realized she'd switched her gait. She was gliding now, silent like a wraith, each step light and smooth. Next to her Helen desperately tried to imitate her, but her legs were too short, and she ended up gliding two steps and skipping forward on the third.

The hall ended, splitting into a Y-intersection of two hallways. Arland raised his hand. "Enough."

The auburn-haired knight clamped his mouth shut, biting a word in half.

"Dismissed."

The four retainers and Ruin did a 180 and hurried back the way they came.

Arland invited her to proceed down the right hallway with a wave of his hand. "My lady."

"My lord."

She turned right, and they walked side by side to a door at the end of the hallway. It slid aside at their approach.

"Your quarters," Arland said.

Maud glanced inside and froze. A spacious bedroom suite stretched before her. A big arched window in the opposite wall betrayed the true thickness of the walls, a full three feet of solid stone. Delicate glass ornaments, so fragile they looked like they would shatter at the first sign of a breeze, hung from the walls, glowing with gentle light.

On the far left, an enormous bed waited, big enough to lay four vampire adults comfortably, and equipped with an artfully arranged pile of pillows and a soft red comforter. Its legs were carved into tree roots, its headboard was a tree trunk, and the tree's carved branches provided the canopy. A rug spanned the length of the floor, painstakingly depicting an image of a female vampire knight fighting a murr, a massive crocodile-like reptile, in a dozen shades of red, burgundy, and white. Beyond the bed, a door stood wide open, showing her a glimpse of the bathroom with a colossal stone tub. Next to it another door, heavy and plain, waited for someone to open it.

On her right, a fire was laid out but not lit in a fireplace that was tall enough for her to walk into it. A collection of chairs was arranged before it, around a low table. A large banner of House Krahr stirred in the breeze, dripping from the wall next to the window, so if someone sat in the largest chair, the banner would serve as the backdrop. Maud squinted at the chair. A small crest was carved in its back, two stylized fangs.

It was a beautiful room, elegant in its simplicity, and timeless, every line and every angle a perfect blend of function and aesthetics. She couldn't have made a better room for herself back at Dina's inn, if she tried for a week.

"No."

"Are the quarters not to your liking?" Arland asked.

"What are you doing?" she asked through clenched teeth.

"I'm showing you your room."

"This is the room of a Marshal's spouse."

Arland looked into the room, his expression puzzled. "You think so?"

She resisted the urge to punch him. "Yes, I think so. It has the House Krahr banner positioned behind a chair with a Marshal's insignia on it."

Arland blinked and rubbed his chin. "So it does. How peculiar."

"My Lord Marshal."

"My Lady Maud?"

"I'm not your wife. I'm not even your betrothed."

"Where would you like me to put you?"

"Not here."

"I don't know a room suitable to a woman I asked to marry me and who replied with 'maybe.'"

"That wasn't what I said."

"You said, 'Arland, I'm sorry, I can't marry you right now. I need time to decide.'"

It was an exact quote.

"I assure you my recollection is accurate. Your words are branded in my memory. Did I misinterpret?"

She opened her mouth. He had her there. "No." It was a maybe.

"Aside from my mother's quarters, this is the most secure place in the castle. The door is keyed to your harbinger. By assigning these quarters to you, I send a clear signal to everyone within my House. I think of you as my betrothed and I expect you to be treated accordingly."

"It's not an honor I deserve."

"Last time I checked, I was the Marshal of House Krahr," he said, his voice gentle. "Assigning honors to my guests is my prerogative."

And he just reminded her that she was stomping on the most basic rule of vampire hospitality: one abided by the laws of the host's House. It would be a mortal offense to refuse the rooms given to her by the Marshal. From his point of view, no other quarters could be assigned to her either. If he sent her down to the guest rooms, it would look like a dismissal. *Here is the woman who rejected me, I brought her here, and now I don't want anything to do with her...*It made him look bad. It made her look bad. There were no winners in that scenario.

"Would you prefer some other woman takes these quarters?"

There was no point in lying. "No."

"Very well, then."

"This will make things harder," she said.

"Are you unfit for the challenge?"

She glared at him.

Arland grinned and handed her a key. It was a real key; heavy, metal, and cold. "That door next to the bathroom opens into a passageway leading to my quarters. There is a second door there. I left it unlocked. There is only one key, my lady, and you have it.

If you have any need to see me in private, all you have to do is unlock your door and walk down the passageway." He bowed his head. "My lady."

She pictured herself smacking him on the head with that damn key.

"Thank you, my lord," she said. She'd loaded enough steel into the words that even the densest vampire wouldn't miss it.

"Make yourself comfortable," he said and went back down the hallway.

Helen slipped into the room, dropped her bag, took a running start, and leaped onto the bed. She bounced straight up, waving her tiny arms.

"Wheeee!"

Wheee. That was about right. She'd remembered Dina saying Arland had the subtlety of an enraged rhino. Her sister didn't know him at all. Neither did she. Which was why she told him maybe.

Maud stepped into the room, listened to the barely audible click of the electronic lock, and slid the heavy metal bar in place, barricading herself in the Marshal's quarters.

She wasn't unfit for the challenge. This was going to be one hell of a visit. Either way, it was time to unpack and settle in.

Maud made it four feet from the door before a knock stopped her. Maybe Arland forgot something...She unbarred the door and swung it open. A female vampire knight stood in the hallway. Broad-shouldered, sturdy, with a lustrous mane of chocolate-brown hair, she wore the full syn-armor. Her dark eyes stared at Maud, and she felt herself weighed, measured, and judged in a split second.

"My name is Alvina, Lady Renadra, daughter of Soren," she said. "You may call me Karat. That's my battle name. I'm Arland's cousin. His favorite cousin. And you are the human gold digger who rejected his proposal. I think we should talk."

Maud leaned against the doorway and studied her nails. "If I were a gold digger, I would've married him already and come here as his wife. There would be nothing you or your whole House could've done about it."

Lady Karat narrowed her eyes. "You seem so sure that you have my cousin on a leash, ready to do your bidding."

"Nobody in this universe, man or woman, could put Arland on a leash."

"You know what I think?"

"I have no doubt you'll enlighten me."

"I think he wanted to play hero. He found you, an exile living in squalor with your daughter, and he decided to rescue you. You preyed on his noble instincts, manipulated him, and now you're toying with him. It appeals to your pride to have the Marshal of House Krahr pining for you like some lovesick puppy."

And that was exactly the welcome she'd expected. "It's refreshing, Lady Karat."

"What?"

"Your honesty. I'd prepared myself for murmured insults behind my back and ugly glances. I thought perhaps it would take your House a couple of days to build up enough outrage to throw their derision in my face, but you laid it all out in my first hour on the planet. Why, I haven't even had a chance to wash my face after the journey. Truly, you're a credit to your bloodline."

Lady Karat's dark eyes sparked. In that moment, she looked remarkably like her father. "Did you just call me a poor host and insult my family?"

Maud gave her a narrow smile. "Well, clearly."

"And now you call me stupid."

"No. Only slow-witted. Are you going to do something about it, or can I start unpacking?"

Lady Karat stared at her for a long moment and grinned. "My father was right. I do like you."

Apparently, it was a test and she'd passed. Vampires and their games. Nothing was ever simple. Maud sighed and stepped aside. "Come in."

Karat strode into the quarters and saw Helen on the bed. "Cute kid."

Helen bounced off the mattress, flipping in the air, and landed on the pillows. "Are you going to try to kill Mommy?"

"No," Karat told her.

"Good." Helen went back to jumping.

"Does she expect you to be killed by random strangers?" Karat asked.

"That's the way things were on Karhari."

Karat eyed Helen.

Helen gave her a cherubic smile.

"She would attack me if I tried, wouldn't she? She's building up enough bounce to jump across the room."

Maud nodded.

Karat wiggled her fingers at Helen.

"Why do you have so many names?" Helen asked.

"Alvina is the formal given name," Maud explained. "It's used on formal occasions like special dinners or if she gets in trouble with family. Renadra is the title name. It's means all of the people and lands she is responsible for and it's used during government functions when people vote on laws. Karat is her knight name, the one she earned in battle and the one she prefers."

Karat wrinkled her nose at Helen. "My friends call me Karat. You can call me Karat, too. For now."

"You can call me Helen," Helen told her.

"Well met, Lady Helen."

It was customary to offer refreshments when someone visited a room. Where would they have put them? Ah. A faint outline in the wall betrayed a niche. She stepped to it, deliberately turning her back to Karat, and ran her fingers along the crack. A square section of the wall slid forward, revealing a shelf supporting a bowl filled with small pieces of jerky twisted into knots and a big bottle of blue wine. Six heavy tulip-shaped glasses cut from sparkling crystal waited next to the wine.

Maud took the wine and two glasses and offered one to Karat. Soren's daughter landed in the nearest oversized chair. Maud twisted the round stopper out of the wine bottle, breaking the seal, poured them both a glass, and sat in another chair.

Karat sipped the wine. "My father asked me to assist you. He's invested in this pairing. I don't know what you said or did, but that crusty old bastard is singing your praises."

"In the words of your cousin, Lord Soren's 'grizzled exterior hides a gentle heart.'"

Karat chuckled. "Sure it does. He is suffused with warmth and sunshine."

Maud toyed with the wine in her glass.

"Wondering whether to trust me?" Karat asked.

"Yes."

"I'll make it simple for you: you have no choice. You could go it alone, but it will be much harder. Our House is old and complicated."

"Why are you helping me? After all, I manipulated Arland and preyed on his heroic instincts."

Karat swirled the glittering blue liquid in her glass, making the

69

crystal throw a filigree of highlights onto the table. "Arland appears to lack in subtlety and seems easy to influence. In truth he's anything but."

"He very carefully cultivates that image."

Karat nodded. "You noticed?"

"Yes. He told me he was no poet, but a simple soldier, and then delivered a declaration of love that could've come straight from *Of Blood and Honor*." In fact, it could've been included in any vampire saga. It was elegant and beautiful, and she'd memorized every word of it.

Karat raised her eyebrows. "You read."

"I do."

"Oh good. To answer your question, better people than you have tried to manipulate my cousin and failed. He has never proposed to anyone before. He had dalliances, but nothing serious. If he asked you to marry him, he must love you. And you must feel something for him, because you came here without the protection that would've been afforded to you had you accepted his proposal. Right now, you're not his bride. You're not betrothed. You're nothing. I can see you're not naïve and you're familiar with our customs. You knew how you would be received, but you came anyway. There is something here that the two of you have to figure out, and you can't do that if you are expelled out of our territory or killed. I want Arland to be happy."

"That's it?"

Karat nodded. "Yes. And if he marries, my father will start nagging *him* about children instead of reminding me to get married and deliver a host of grandchildren to 'brighten his old age.' A break from his concerned inquiries about my progress in this matter would be most welcome."

"That bad, huh?" Maud asked.

70

A shadow of defeat passed across Karat's face. "You have no idea. Do we have a deal?"

Maud drank her wine. She could trust Soren's daughter, or she could go it alone. She'd known a number of knights who would've come to her room just like that, with sincere offers of help—and would've proudly stabbed her in the back at the first opportunity. Afterward, they would've boasted about their own cleverness.

Karat didn't seem to be one of them. Maud's instincts told her she could be trusted. Her gut had never failed her before.

"Yes, Lady Karat. We have a deal."

Karat sat up straighter. "Good. I'd like to know what we're working with here. What's your status with House Ervan?"

"I was married to Melizard Ervan."

"Yes, Father told me. Marshal's son?"

"Second son." She'd sunk a lot of meaning into that first word.

Karat toyed with her glass. "House Ervan is a young House. Some younger Houses tend to overcompensate by holding fast to the ancient traditions even when they no longer make sense. The times when the heirs were always warriors, no matter their skill."

"My husband was a superb warrior. In personal combat, he knew no equal. But he wasn't as good of a commander as his older brother. Melizard liked to play games. His brother didn't. The knights of Ervan trusted him over my husband."

The troops had sensed something in Melizard that she didn't see until the very end. He didn't value them. They were a means to obtain victory and then serve as adornments when his success was celebrated.

"My brother-in-law was groomed for the position of Marshal, and my husband was to become Maven," she said.

Mavens handled negotiations for the Houses. They served as ambassadors and dealmakers. The position would've conveniently kept Melizard busy and, considering Ervan's trade agreements, it would've frequently taken him and his schemes away from the House.

"Mavens are respected and feared," Karat said.

"He wanted to be the Marshal."

There was so much more she could say. About Melizard's night rages, when he stalked back and forth across their quarters like a caged tiger, ranting about his family, about his brother being handed everything while his talents went unrecognized. About schemes, and petitions, and endless plans to prove he was the better of the two. About the time he marched into his parents' quarters and demanded to be made Marshal only to return like a beaten dog with his tail between his legs. So much more.

"My husband was the youngest son. Admired, babied, and spoiled. Denied nothing except what he wanted most of all. To become Marshal. No," Maud corrected herself, "to be made Marshal. To have the title handed to him."

"What did he do?" Karat asked.

Maud glanced at Helen and lowered her voice. "He tried to murder his brother."

Karat sipped her wine. "Personal combat is a perfectly acceptable way to settle grievances between competing siblings."

If only. Maud leaned back in her chair. "It wasn't personal."

"What?"

"My husband arranged an ambush for his brother."

Karat blinked. "I don't understand. You did say your husband was the better combatant."

"My husband also was told in no uncertain terms that his brother would become the Marshal, and any attempt to sabotage that rise would be unacceptable to his parents and his House. He knew if he challenged his brother, it would enrage the family and House leadership. So, he convinced a group of his knights to jump his brother as he was coming back from an errand. Meanwhile, he and I attended a celebration at his cousin's house. The cousin's older son was granted knighthood. During the celebration, my husband made it a point to overtly flirt with a woman. He must've hoped I would make a scene. I left instead, but that was enough. Everyone had noticed our presence and my exit. He was establishing his alibi."

Karat had forgotten about her wine. "That's highly dishonorable."

"That's what I told him, when he explained all of that to me that night."

"What was his justification?"

Maud sighed. "That he did it for us, for me and our child. That this way we would be more secure, and Helen's future would be assured."

"Did you believe him?"

Talking about it hurt, like ripping off a scab before new skin had a chance to form underneath. "No. A part of me wanted to, very much. I loved him. He was my husband and the father of my child. But even then, I had realized that we were all in service to his ambition. I warned him then it would be the end of everything."

"Was it?"

Maud nodded. "Yes. His brother survived. One of the assailants lived as well. He was interrogated. They came for us that night. We were exiled to Karhari. All three of us."

Karat's expression turned sharp. "Who would exile a child? Especially to Karhari. It's a wasteland. The anus of the galaxy."

"Someone who is desperate to defend their family name." Maud set her glass on the table. "As you've said, House Ervan is young. They are desperate for the respectability that comes with age and history."

"You can't falsify that currency. It must be bought with generations."

"Well, they tried. They would kill you for this castle, if they could. Everything had to be just so. Every tradition followed. Propriety of every detail examined. Appearances kept. They over-compensated. Do you know who doesn't fit into traditions? A human and her daughter."

"She is a child of House Ervan," Karat said. "They had a responsibility to her no matter what her father did."

"They didn't see it that way. We have a saying on Earth: three strikes and you're out. I was strike one, Helen was strike two, and the attempted assassination of my brother-in-law was strike three. I realized this as I begged for my daughter's life on my knees."

Karat winced.

"They wanted to be rid of us, all of us. They struck us from the roster and dumped us on Karhari. It was as if we never existed."

"What happened on Karhari?" Karat asked.

"The planet devoured my husband's soul. It drove him mad. Eventually he betrayed the wrong people and they killed him."

Karat stared at her.

Maud finished her wine. "I know why you came here. You wanted to know what kind of baggage we bring to your House. We have no ties to House Ervan. We are strangers to them. We have settled the blood debt on Karhari. My husband's killers are dead. No one alive has a claim on my life or the life of my daughter. No one is owed. We bring no debts and no allies. We are what we appear to be."

"Oh, I doubt that," Karat said. "You are much more than you appear to be."

You have no idea. "Have I answered your questions, my lady?"

"Yes."

"Then it's my turn. How angry is Lady Ilemina?"

"How angry is a rabid krahr?" Karat slumped against the back of her chair with a sigh. "Arland is brilliant, when he is here. He's almost never here. First, he developed a fascination with Earth and Earth women. Did he tell you we have a cousin whose step-brother is married to one?"

"My sister mentioned it."

"They live on the other side of the planet. She is some sort of scientist that studies insects."

"An entomologist?"

"Yes, that. The other day she was late to her own daughter's birthday because she'd found some new beetle nobody had ever seen before. What good are beetles? They are neither food nor pets. I would've squashed it. You never know when one of them will turn out to be poisonous."

Vampire worldview, condensed into three sentences: If it's not food or a pet, kill it, because it might be poisonous.

"She doesn't get involved in politics, she isn't interested in combat, and if you talk to her for five minutes, your eyes will glaze over, but she is a pretty woman and he loves her, Hiero-phant bless him."

Maud hid a smile.

"Then Arland starts disappearing. 'Where is Arland?' 'He is off on some adventure at some inn on Earth.' Everything is Earth. Broker a peace treaty? Earth. Go shopping for a unique present for his favorite cousin? Earth."

"What did he get you?" Maud asked.

"Coffee. It's of an excellent quality, but when would I ever need ten pounds of it? It's enough to get the entire regiment roaring drunk. The next thing we know, he skips out on the wedding preparations, because someone on Earth needs his help. Because the needs of his House are clearly fisur's kidneys. He goes to Karhari and then there is this footage of him tearing out of some armored hovel with vampires in shabby armor clinging to him and him roaring like he is some hero in a period drama."

Maud lost it and laughed.

"You don't understand." Karat waved her hands. "The damn thing was everywhere. He brained seven vampires singlehandedly. So the Karhari Houses are screaming bloody murder, our relatives twelve generations removed are forwarding the recording to us, our allies are asking why our Marshal is involved in a brawl on some backwater planet and if we sent him there as a plan for some sort of secret offensive and if so, why haven't we told them about it, and we keep getting marriage proposals because half the galaxy decided he is good breeding stock. I saw my father's and aunt's faces when they watched it. They turned a color not found in nature. It's not funny!"

Maud tried to stop laughing, but it was like trying to hold back a flood. It's nerves, she told herself.

"Go ahead." Karat rolled her eyes. "Get it all out. Not only did he make us the focal point of the entire Anocracy for two solid weeks, he then refused to return because he needed a sojourn. He threw this bomb into our House and went on vacation! Then he sent a message: I'm coming home with a human bride. Oh wait, she said no, but I'm bringing her anyway. Prepare the castle!"

Maud made a heroic effort to stop laughing.

"I thought my aunt's head would explode. I honestly did. So no, you won't get a warm reception."

"That's okay," Maud managed. "I didn't expect one."

"I realize it's through no fault of your own, but my aunt will test you at every turn. She made it bloody obvious she is displeased, and we are pack animals."

"When the leader snarls, everyone will jump in to help."

"In essence, yes." Karat gave her a sour smile. "I was going to jump in too, but my father convinced me to keep an open mind. I actually like you now, so my position is complicated. It will be an uphill battle." The vampire woman leaned forward. "Do you want to do this? I mean, do you really?"

"Yes. I'm here. I showed up."

Karat sighed. "That's what I was afraid of. Well, the first step is dinner. It will be held tonight, in about three hours."

"Armor on?"

"Armor on," Karat confirmed. "You have a little time to make yourself presentable, although in your case there's not really enough hair to do anything with. Why short hair?"

Explaining that it was a period at the end of her old life and her bribe to the universe to keep Helen alive would be too complicated, so she said the same thing she'd told her sister. "Very little water on Karhari. It was too hard to keep clean."

"Too bad," Karat said. "Do you need anything?"

"What happens to the children?" Maud asked.

"Helen can stay with the other children or she can remain here in your quarters."

"Helen?" Maud called. "I have to go to a grown-up dinner, and you can't come, my flower. Do you want to play with other children or stay here by yourself?"

"I want to play," Helen said.

Maud swallowed a sigh. Helen would have to integrate into vampire society sooner or later. Maud had hoped to be there. She wanted with every ounce of her being to smooth the way, to make sure nothing bad happened, to help, but she couldn't. She had to let her daughter go. Some lessons Helen had to learn on her own.

"Very well," she said.

"I'll either come myself or send someone by half an hour before the dinner," Karat said. "I would guess Arland will want to escort you, but knowing my aunt, she will make sure he's busy with something vital instead."

And that was exactly what she'd expected. "I'll make do," Maud said.

Karat narrowed her eyes. "I think you will. If I don't see you until the meal, best of luck."

[5]

The door chimed at fifteen minutes till seven.

Maud opened it. A retainer stood in the doorway. She was young, about twenty or so, with long brown hair tamed into a sleek waterfall and secured with an elaborate hairnet of thin knotted chains. A ceremonial garment the color of blood hugged her figure, close cut in the bodice, with relaxed sleeves caught at the wrist and a long skirt, split on the sides up each thigh. The slits betrayed a glimpse of black, skintight pants. Vampires rarely showed skin.

The front and back of the skirt fell in graceful folds almost to the floor, like an artist's rendition of a medieval tabard. The outfit was purely ceremonial, Maud reflected. No sane knight, human or vampire, would run around with a long piece of cloth tangling between their legs, but it was in line with vampire fashion, or at least what Maud remembered of it.

The retainer gave her a quick once-over, her gaze snagging on Maud's jet-black armor with its blank crest. "We will leave now."

That bordered on rudeness. Clearly the news had spread through House Krahr. The human new arrival was out of favor.

Vampires were a predictable lot. There was a time when she found comfort in that predictability.

"Come, Helen," Maud called.

Helen came over. She wore a blue tunic caught with a silver sash over white leggings and an undertunic. Little brown boots hugged her feet. Maud had brushed her hair and worked it into the customary vampire mane. She looked so adorable, Maud snapped a couple of pictures for Dina.

The retainer saw Helen and fought a smile. "Come this way."

They followed the retainer through a long hallway into a round chamber, then into another hallway and to a door. The door slid open as they approached, leading to a narrow stone walkway stretching to another tower. The weather had turned, the dark, furious sky flinging rain at the castle and the plateau beyond, and a transparent roof shielded the walkway from the weather's rage. It was like walking into a storm suspended a hundred feet above the ground. Helen's grip on her fingers tightened. Maud smiled at her and kept walking.

The other tower loomed ahead, a much wider and larger structure.

"How old is the fortress?" Maud asked.

The retainer paused. Maud hid a smile. As a mongrel human, she clearly wasn't worth an answer, but rules of hospitality prescribed courtesy when interacting with guests.

Politeness won. "The core of the castle is twenty-three centuries old. We have expanded it over the generations."

The understatement of the year.

They reached the second tower. The dark door swung open, and they entered another hallway. The stone of the walls here was smoother, newer, cut with greater precision. Lights, soft golden spheres, hung from the twenty-foot ceiling in artful bunches, bathing the hallway in a golden radiance. The blood-red banners of House Krahr spanned the height of the walls. At the far end, double doors stood wide open, offering a glimpse of the feast hall. Sounds of conversation floated over.

The retainer turned left and stopped before an open door. A pair of knights in full armor waited at the entrance, one male and the other female, both middle-aged and thick through the shoulders. A sharp slice of red marked their House crests like a rip of a single claw. Sentinels, the knights trained specifically to guard against an intrusion. Both were armed. Children's laughter rang out behind them.

"The child stays here," the retainer said.

Maud crouched by Helen. "I'll be back soon, okay?"

"Okay," Helen said quietly.

"You will get to play with other kids. Practice rules only."

"Okay," Helen said.

"Repeat it back to me please."

"Practice rules only, Mommy."

"Good girl." Maud kissed her daughter's forehead and straightened.

The male knight stepped aside, and Helen walked into the room. Maud watched her go.

"Your daughter will be safe," the female knight told her. "The keepers of the children watch them closely. They won't permit other children to harm her."

It's not her I'm worried about. Maud nodded and followed the retainer to the feast hall.

———

THE FEAST HALL OCCUPIED A HUGE SQUARE CHAMBER. LARGE rectangular tables, carved from sturdy wood ages ago, filled the room, each seating ten guests. In the center of the hall, the host table stood, marked by a metal pole supporting the standard of House Krahr. The guests were seated in order of receding importance, the higher the rank, the closer to the host table. Servers glided back and forth.

"You sit there," the retainer pointed to the table closest to the wall. A group of tachi had arranged themselves there. "With the insects."

It was customary to walk a guest to her table, no matter how far from the Host table she was seated. That was just about enough.

"They are not insects," Maud said. "They are tachionals. They are warm-blooded, with a centralized brain. They give live birth, nurse their young, and the sharp edges of their arms can slice a vampire's head off her shoulders with a single swipe. You would do well to remember that."

The retainer stared at her, open-mouthed. Maud strode to the table. The tachi appeared to ignore her approach, but their exoskeletons remained a nebulous, bluish gray. Tachi at rest turned darker, revealing their speckled patterns. It was a sign of trust and often a promise of intimacy.

If the tachi stood, they would be slightly taller than her, right around six feet. Their silhouette was vaguely humanlike: two legs, two arms, an elegant thorax that could almost pass for a human chest clad in segmented armor, a very narrow waist, and a head. That's where the similarities ended. Their backs curved backward, the thick exoskeletal plates hiding their wings. Their arms joined to the body not at the sides, like in humans and vampires, but slightly forward. Their necks were long, and their round heads were shielded by three chitin segments, each with slits for a pair of glowing eyes.

They had two main legs with shins that curved too far backward for human comfort, and two short vestigial appendages—

false legs—pointing backward from their pelvises. The vestigial legs had two joints and a very limited range of movement, but when a tachi sat, they gripped the seat, anchoring them in place, which greatly helped them in spaceflight and aerial combat. A tachi was just as comfortable upright as upside down.

Maud swept the table with her gaze. Nine tachi in all. The female in the center wore a crystal bracelet filled with gently glowing fluid. Pale green flecks floated within it, shifting every time the tachi moved. A royal. The rest were bodyguards, likely elite warriors.

They should've never been seated this far from the host table. She couldn't even see it from here. It was an insult and the tachi were sensitive to such slights. Vampires were somewhat xenophobic, especially toward aliens who didn't look like mammals, so the fact that the tachi were permitted here at all meant something significant was on the line. An alliance, a trade agreement. Something of value, which was now jeopardized. This was a tactical blunder. She would have to mention it to Arland.

Where was Arland? She didn't expect him to sit with her—that would be pushing against all the Holy Anocracy's customs—but he could've at the very least strolled by. Just to see that she was actually present.

The tachi had left only one seat open, directly across from the royal. She would be sitting between two sets of bodyguards, with the other four watching her. Maud bowed her head and sat.

"Greetings."

"Greetings," the royal replied, the bottom segment of her face rising to reveal a slash of a mouth.

The ten plates were clean. The vampire cooking utensils, small four-pronged forks, lay untouched. Nobody had eaten. The moment she sat down, she saw why. The two large bowls on the table contained a salad.

They served them *salad*. Maud almost slapped herself.

When on a mission among other species, tachi abstained from consuming meat, so at least House Krahr had gotten that right. But tachi were notoriously fastidious in their presentation of food. It was an art as well as sustenance. Every ingredient had its place. Nothing could touch. The vampires served them a salad. Drenched in dressing. Ugh.

Mom would turn purple if she saw this. Orro, Dina's inn chef, would probably commit homicide.

The tachi would never say anything. They would just sit there and quietly fume. If the royal got up from the table without consuming any food, House Krahr could kiss any hope for cooperation goodbye.

Maud turned to the nearest server. "Bring me bread, honey, a variety of fruit, a large platter, and a sharp knife."

The server hesitated.

She sank ice into her voice. "Am I not a guest of House Krahr?"

The server flashed his fangs at her. "It will be done, lady."

The tachi watched her with calm interest. Nobody spoke.

The server arrived with a massive wooden cutting board bearing a loaf of freshly baked bread. A second server set a large bowl of fruit in front of her and a glass gravy-boat-like vessel of honey. The two servers parked themselves behind her. They didn't bring the platter. No matter.

Maud sliced the crust off the bread, trimming the round loaf into a square shape. At least the knife was sharp. That was one thing one never had to worry about with vampires.

The tachi kept watching.

She cut the bread into precise half-inch cubes, placed five of them together onto the plate, one in the center and four in the corners so they formed a square. She picked up the honey and slowly dripped a few drops onto each cube, until the bread soaked up the amber liquid.

The tachi at the edges of the table leaned in slightly.

Maud plucked the blue kora fruit from the bowl, peeled the thin skin and carefully cut the fruit into even round slices. She managed eight slices, seven perfectly even and one slightly thicker. She placed the seven slices around the cubes. The eighth was a hair too thick. She pondered it.

The tachi pondered it with her.

Better safe than sorry. She reached for another kora.

The tachi to her left emitted an audible sigh of relief and then crunched his mouth shut, embarrassed.

After the kora, she cut the red pear, then the thick yellow stalks of sweet grass, slowly building a mandala pattern on her plate. The kih berries followed, perfect little globes of deep orange. She carefully arranged the berries and took one last look at the plate. It was nowhere as perfect as it should've been, but that was the best she could do with what she had.

Maud got up, lifted the plate, and offered it with a bow to the royal.

"Lady of sun and air, it is my great honor to share my food with you. It is humble, but it is given freely from the heart."

The table was completely silent. The royal looked at her with her six glowing eyes.

Color burst on her exoskeleton, the pale neutral gray turning the deeper azure of the morning sky. She reached out her long elegant arm and took the plate.

"I accept your offering."

Maud exhaled quietly and sat. The color around the table darkened slightly. She could tell the shades of blue, green, and purple apart now.

The two vampire servers behind her took off at a near jog.

She reached for the next fruit and began peeling it.

The royal speared a cube of honey-drenched bread with her claws and popped it into her mouth. "My name is Dil'ki. What is yours?"

"Maud, your highness."

Dil'ki clicked her claws. "Tch-tch-tch. Not so loud. The vampires do not know. Where have you learned our customs?"

"My parents are innkeepers on Earth."

A deeper blue blossomed on Dil'ki's segments. The tachi around the table shifted, their poses less stiff.

"How delightful. Do you speak Akit?"

Thank the universe for dad's insistence on a superior speech implant. "I do."

Maud arranged another, less complex mandala and passed it to the tachi on her right.

"We will speak Akit," Dil'ki declared, switching to the dialect. "Do you understand me, Lady Maud?"

"I do," Maud said.

"Yes." The royal leaned closer and popped a berry into her mouth. "Tell me, what are you doing here, among these barbarians?"

"One of them asked me to marry him."

"No," the green tachi from the right gasped. "You mustn't."

"They can't even make proper seats," another green tachi said. "Some of them are joined into benches."

"You must be very brave to come here," a purple tachi said from the left.

"Did you say yes?" Dil'ki asked.

"I said I would think about it."

The vampire servers arrived, bearing platters of precision sliced fruit and cubed bread. The tachi fell silent. The food was placed on the table and the servers backed away.

"You may serve yourselves," Dil'ki said. "If poor Maud has to feed us all, we will be here all night."

The tachi clicked the mandibles inside their mouths, chuckling. An instinctual alarm dashed through Maud. Every hair on the back of her neck stood on end.

Claws reached for the platters, each arranging their own small masterpiece of fruit on their plate.

"Which one asked you?" Dil'ki asked.

Maud craned her neck. If Arland was anywhere, he'd be at the host table, but she couldn't really see him. "The big blond one. The son of the Lady Ilemina."

Dil'ki leaned in and the other tachi mirrored her movement, as if they had choreographed it.

"Tell me all about it," Dil'ki said.

Maud opened her mouth and saw Seveline walking toward her, two male vampires in tow.

"Enemy?" Dil'ki guessed.

"I don't know yet," Maud said. She realized she had pushed her chair back from the table slightly, on pure muscle memory. When an enemy is approaching, it paid to make sure getting up didn't cost you a precious fraction of a second. "I think she might be."

As one, the tachi went light gray.

"There you are!" Seveline grinned at her. "I was wondering where they hid you."

No proper address. An insult. It would've been fine if they were friends in private, but they were neither friends nor alone.

Maud plastered a smile on her face. "Lady Seveline."

"I expected to have to search, but at this table? Really?"

Another insult. She really was enjoying herself.

"And I see they forgot to bring you meat. Do they honestly think you are an herbivore? Are humans herbivores, Lady Maud? I only ask because of your small teeth."

A third insult. The dark-haired vampire at Seveline's right flashed a quick smile. Couldn't help himself.

A tachi on her right leaned to her and murmured in Akit. "Would you like me to kill her? I can do it quietly tonight. They'll never figure it out."

Oh crap. The last thing she needed was to cause an interstellar incident.

Seveline narrowed her eyebrows slightly. Ten to one, Seveline's implant didn't recognize Akit. It was an internal tachi language. But if Maud replied in English, it would translate her reply. Maud cleared her throat.

"Khia teki-teki, re to kha. Kerchi sia chee." No, thank you. She's a source of information.

Argh, she'd mangled it. There were sounds human mouths just couldn't make.

The tachi clicked their mandibles again, in approval.

"That was very, very good," Dil'ki said in Akit. "Good try."

"Is something the matter?" Seveline asked.

"Not at all," Maud smiled. "Is there something I can help you with?"

"As a matter of fact, there is." Seveline smiled. "These lords with me were wondering if there was some unique aspect to human lovemaking that particularly appeals to vampires. I thought you would be a perfect person to ask, since you have used it to such great effect."

Quarter of a second to get up, another quarter to jump up on the table, half a second to ram her fork into Seveline's neck, piercing the windpipe. She would look so pretty with a bloody fork sticking out of her neck.

Maud smiled and stopped. A sentinel stood at the doorway of the feast hall. A small figure in a blue tunic with a silver sash stood next to him. The beginning of a huge black eye turned Helen's right cheek bright red.

"Please excuse me." She jumped up and hurried through the tables to her daughter.

Helen looked up at her, her face pinched. She was trying not to cry.

"What happened?" Maud asked.

The sentinel, an older male vampire, smiled at her. "Personal challenges are forbidden in the nursery. Lady Helen was warned about the consequences of her actions, yet she chose to continue as did her challenged."

"He called me a liar," Helen squeezed through her teeth.

Fear crushed Maud. Somehow, she made her lips move. "Is the other boy alive?"

"Yes." The older vampire smiled brighter. "His broken arm will serve as a fine reminder of today's events. Unfortunately, Lady Helen must leave us now. She is to report tomorrow to the nursery to atone for her failure in judgement. Should I take her to her quarters?"

"No," Maud said. "I'll do it."

"But your dinner, Lady Maud?"

"I have had my fill."

Maud took her daughter by the hand and walked down the hallway, away from the feast hall.

———

THE LONG HALLWAY OF HOUSE KRAHR'S CITADEL LAY DESERTED. Behind Maud, the noise of the feast hall was dying down, receding with every step. Helen walked next to her, her face sullen.

"What happened?" Maud asked softly.

"They asked me where I came from, and I told them about

how I made my room and Aunt Dina said she would get me fishes. This boy said that houses can't move if you think at them. He said I was lying."

Of course he did. "Then what happened?"

"Then I got mad." Helen bit her lip with her fangs. "And I said take it back. And he said I was stupid and a liar. And then he wagged his finger at me."

"He did what?"

Helen stuck out her hand with her index finger extended and waved it around, drawing an upside-down U in the air, and sang, "Liar-liar-liar."

"Then what happened?"

"Then I said that pointing was bad, because it lets your enemy know where you're looking."

The lessons of Karhari had stuck. No matter how long Helen spent away from it, the wasteland had soaked into her soul and there wasn't anything Maud could do about it.

"And he said I wasn't good enough to be his enemy. And I said, 'I'll punch you so hard, you'll swallow your teeth, worm.'"

Maud hid a groan. "Where did you hear that?"

"Lord Arland."

Oh goodie. "Then what happened?"

"Then the scary old knight came and told me that if I challenged the boy, there would be ripper cushions."

"Repercussions."

"Yes. So I asked if the boy would get repercushions if he fought me, and the knight said yes, and I said I was okay with it."

Maud rubbed the bridge of her nose.

"And then the knight asked the boy if he wanted help and the boy said he didn't, and the knight said 'proceed', and then the boy punched me, and I got his arm. With my legs." Helen rolled on the floor and locked her legs together. "I said, say surrender, and he didn't say anything, he just yelled, so I broke it. If he didn't want me to break it, he should've said surrender."

Maud rubbed her face some more.

Helen looked at her from the floor, her big green eyes huge on her face. "He started it."

And she finished it.

"You weren't wrong," Maud said. "But you weren't wise."

Helen looked at the floor.

"You knew you weren't a liar."

"Yes."

"So why did it matter what the vampire boy said?"

"I don't know," Helen mumbled.

Maud crouched by her. "You don't always meet enemies in battle. Sometimes you meet them during peace. They might even pretend to be your friends. Some of them will try to provoke you so they can see what you can do. You have to learn to wait and watch them until you figure out their weakness. The boy thought you were weak. If you let him keep thinking you were weak, you could've used it later. Remember what I told you about surprise?"

"It wins battles," Helen said.

"Now the boy knows you're strong," Maud said. "It wasn't wrong to show your strength. But in the future, you have to think carefully and decide if you want people to know your true strength or not."

"Okay," Helen said quietly.

"Come on." Maud offered her daughter her hand. Helen grasped her fingers and got up. They resumed their walk down the hallway.

"Mama?"

"Yes?"

"Are vampires our enemies?"

That was to be determined. "That's what we are trying to figure out."

"When are we going to go live with Aunt Dina again?"

An excellent question. *What am I doing here anyway?*

She'd had it up to her throat with all of the vampire back-stabbing the first time. She'd promised herself she was done the moment they landed on Karhari and she'd repeated this promise over and over when she lay on the hilltop, breathing in Karhari dust, watching the blood sword flash and seeing Melizard's head fall to the ground; when she tracked his killers; when she bargained for shelter and water, knowing that if she failed, Helen would die. It became her mantra. *Never again.* Yet here she was.

Arland had abandoned her the first chance he got.

What did you expect? Did you expect he would come and take you by the hand and lead you to a seat at the host table?

Yes. The answer was yes. Maud didn't expect it, but she wanted it.

Stupid.

It was stupid to hope for something that wouldn't happen. It was stupid to come here.

"Mama?" Helen asked.

They could just go home right now. Go back to Dina. Helen would never be able to join a human school or play with human children, because there was no way to hide the fangs, but all three of them, Klaus, Maud, and Dina, had been homeschooled in the inn, and none of them turned out badly.

They could just go home, where nobody would belittle them or punch them in the face. Home to the familiar weird of her childhood, before Melizard. Before Karhari.

But they had come all this way. She had dragged Helen here, because Arland had offered hope for something deeper than

Maud had ever hoped for. A part of her rebelled at giving up without a fight. But was this even a fight worth fighting?

I'll do one more day. One more day. If it's all shit at the end of tomorrow, then I'm done.

"We have some things to do here first."

"I liked it at Aunt Dina's," Helen said. "I like my room."

A short figure turned the corner and was coming toward them, walking upright on furry paws. She was only three and a half feet tall, counting the nearly six-inch lynx ears tipped with tufts. Her fur, full and long like the coat of a mink or a fox, was the color of sand and marked with tiny blue rosettes. Her face was a meld of cat and fox, with a long muzzle and big emerald green eyes that shone slightly when the light caught them just right. She wore a diaphanous apron of pale pink, decorated with black embroidery. Two thin gold hoops twinkled in her left ear.

"A kitty," Helen whispered.

Ha! The universe provided a teaching moment. "No, my flower. That's a lees. Remember how I told you about hiding your strength? The lees hide their strength. They look cute, but they are dangerous and very cunning."

They were also excellent assassins and they would poison their enemies in a heartbeat, but that was a lesson she would deliver a few years down the road.

"See her little apron? She's from a Merchant clan. The markings tell you which one. This one is from Clan Nuan. Remember how I told you that Grandpa and Grandma were innkeepers? They would buy things from Clan Nuan, and sometimes they would take me with them. Your grandpa told me to never bargain with a lees unless I absolutely had to. He was right."

Helen craned her neck, trying to see better. "At Baha-char?"

"Yes, my flower. And every time I visited, Nuan Cee, the great Merchant, would give me candy. It was the best candy ever and it wasn't for sale. He gave me candy because he liked me, but also because he wanted to make a good deal with my parents. It's hard to bargain with someone who made your child happy."

They reached the lees. The little fox glanced at them.

"Greetings," Maud said.

"Greetings," the fox answered.

"Please pass our respects to the Honorable Nuan Cee," Maud said.

"You know our clan?" the fox asked.

"Our family has done business with Clan Nuan. My parents were innkeepers. You may know my sister, Dina. She is an innkeeper also."

The little fox froze.

Maud tensed.

"Dina? We know Dina!"

The little fox grinned, showing all of her tiny teeth, and hopped in place, bouncing like a balloon filled with excitement. "We know Dina! You come. Come with me now. My uncle twice removed will be so happy. Come, come!"

"We are—"

The fox grabbed Helen by her hand. "Come with me now!" She ran down the hallway and Helen dashed with her.

Just what they needed. Maud sprinted after them. They turned right, then left, then right again, and the fox jumped into the doorway, pulling Helen with her. Maud lunged through and slid to a halt.

Veils in pastel colors draped the stone of the vampire walls. Soft, luxurious rugs hid the cold floor. Plush furniture, carved from pale wood and so ornate, Louis XIV would've turned green with jealousy, offered seating by little tables. Glass and metal bowls sat on the tables, offering fruit, sweets, and little pieces of spicy jerky. A dozen lees chatted, snacked, and played games. In the center of it all, on a six-foot-wide floor pillow stuffed to a three-foot thickness sat Nuan Cee. His silver-blue fur darkened on his back, dappled with golden rosettes, and faded to white on his chest and stomach. He wore a beautiful apron of ethereal silver silk embroidered with Clan Nuan's sigils, and a necklace of sapphires, each as big as a walnut.

It was like stepping into a Merchant's shop. Maud almost pinched herself.

The little lees ran into the room, pulling Helen with her. "Dina's sister! And her young!"

Helen froze.

Nuan Cee raised his paw-hands in surprise. "Matilda!"

He remembered her.

The memories came flooding back. Walking with Mom and Dad through the sunlit streets of Baha-char within a current of shoppers from all over the galaxy, while the galactic bazaar hummed with a million voices. Reaching Nuan Cee's shop, a cool oasis in the middle of the desert heat, and hearing Nuan Cee's singsong voice bargaining and chuckling. The taste of ru candy in her mouth. Suddenly she was twelve again. Maud almost cried.

She started moving before she even realized it.

Nuan Cee pushed off his pillow and took three steps toward Maud. She barely registered the honor. She reached him and they hugged.

"There you are, Matilda," the Merchant said.

Somehow, she found her voice. "Yes."

They broke apart.

"And who is this?" Nuan Cee widened his turquoise eyes.

"This is my daughter, Helen."

The lees let out a collective *squee*.

"She is so cute!"

"Look at her hair!"

"Look at her little boots!"

Helen stood in the whirlwind of lees, looking slightly freaked out, like a cat greeted by a pack of overly enthusiastic little dogs.

"I am Nuan Nana," the lees who found them announced. "Come with me. We have the best sweets."

Maud hid a smile as the lees dragged Helen to the nearest table and thrust a dish of candy under her nose.

"Have you seen your sister?" Nuan Cee asked.

"Yes. She is all grown up."

"And an innkeeper!" Nuan Cee raised his hands. "Who would have thought?"

Maud laughed. It was that or crying.

"What are you doing here?" Nuan Cee asked.

"It's complicated."

"Come, come." He led her to a divan by his pillow.

Someone brought her a glass of sweet wine. Someone else delivered a dish of ru candy. She ate one, savoring the taste melting on her tongue, sweet with a slight touch of sour, but so refreshing; it was as if her whole mouth sang.

"Tell me all about it," Nuan Cee said.

[6]

Tell me all about it.

Oh you clever, clever lees. Maud leaned back and laughed.

Clan Nuan watched her. For some reason it cracked her up even more. She laughed until she snorted.

"Did I say something funny?" Nuan Cee inquired.

Maud managed to get the giggles under control, enough to squeeze out a few words. "How long was Nuan Nana waiting in that hallway for me?"

The room was suddenly quiet.

"I mean, it had to be since the beginning of the dinner, since you had no way of knowing if or when I would throw a hissy fit and storm out in a huff. I've been wondering since I came through the door why a Merchant of Baha-char, a distinguished guest, wasn't at dinner. This is so well done, Honorable Nuan Cee. The pillows, the veils, even the candy. Here I am, all alone, a stranger in a strange land, and you're bringing back all of my childhood memories. Such a clever, manipulative trap. I'm primed and ready to spill all of my secrets."

97

For a moment the Merchant just stared at her. Then Nuan Cee raised his paw-hands and dramatically rolled his eyes. "You can't win them all."

The lees around them giggled.

"You're as ruthless as ever," Maud said.

"You flatter me, Matilda," Nuan Cee said.

"Are there jammers active in here?" she asked.

"Please." Nuan Cee waved his left hand. "Of course there are. We jam the audio, but we do give them the video feed. We have to give them something or they will throw us out."

They were being watched, but not heard. Just what she expected. "Did you bug the feast hall?" Maud asked.

Nuan Cee rocked his head side to side, then grinned. "Yes."

Maud chuckled and popped another piece of candy into her mouth.

"You can't blame me, though," Nuan Cee said. "You wield great influence over the Marshal."

"I wouldn't go that far."

"Oh please. Arland is besotted with you."

"Besotted?"

"Yes. I've used that word correctly. If there was a river of fire and you were on the other side of it, he would strip off his ridiculous armor and swim through the flames to get to you."

Maud laughed. "First, the tachi, then you. What is this really about?"

"I doubt the tachi know about your relationship. They are academics," Nuan Cee said. "Which does not mean they won't pounce on you once they know."

"What is this about?"

"Business." Nuan Cee bared a mouth full of sharp teeth. "And a great deal of money."

"I'm listening."

He reached over, took a tall glass of some pink liquid from a side table and sipped it. "You have seen the battle station?"

"I have."

"The battle station changed everything. This is now the safest area of space within this quadrant. There are many trade routes that intersect here, or they could, provided there was a safe haven. A place where a spaceship could dock easily without worrying about burning fuel in orbit. A place of trade and commerce."

The light went on in Maud's head. "You want House Krahr to build a space station."

"Yes. And I'm trying to give them money for it."

"A space station in vampire territory giving access to other species? Dozens of foreign vessels docking in the Holy Anocracy's system? That has never been done."

Maud sipped her pink wine. It tasted like watermelon, strawberry, and sweet grapes rolled into one.

Nuan Cee groaned. "How can a spacefaring species be so close-minded? They already built the battle station. They have made this expensive thing that can guard the whole of the system. It is sitting there and costing them money. I am proposing something that would bring a huge profit for everyone. There is not a docking station for the non-vampire species anywhere within the quadrant."

"Anywhere within the Holy Anocracy's territory, except for the diplomatic space station near the capital star system, as I recall."

"Exactly. Dozens of species desperate for a port facility. They're hanging there like ripe fruit. All I am asking House Krahr to do is to stand under the tree, open their mouths, and let the bounty fall into them. They could recoup the cost of the battle station within two years."

He was right. The space station would earn House Krahr a fortune.

Nuan Cee moaned in genuine distress. "I do not understand. Do they not want to make money?"

"Is that why the tachi are here?"

"Yes. They have an archaeological dig on On-Toru. They have to travel hundreds of light years out of their way around vampire space to get there. A space station here would give them a nearly straight shot to that colony. They're willing to pay top prices."

Maud leaned back. Getting the vampires out of their "by vampires for vampires" mindset would be next to impossible.

"You know vampires," Nuan Cee said. "And you have influence with the Marshal."

"As I said, my influence doesn't go that far. Dina told me that you and House Krahr have reached a settlement on Nexus that made all of you rich. You should be the natural ally for the Krahr. If they are resisting you despite all of your shared history, nothing I say would matter. I am a nobody here."

"You are Matilda Demille."

The family name slashed across her memory.

How would Mom go about this?

"Have you noticed how obsessed with defenses they are?" she asked. "As a species, vampires spend more time in armor than out of it. Take this castle, for example. A smaller structure would've sufficed, yet here it is, a monstrous castle with impossibly thick walls and enough defenses to hold off an assault by an overwhelming force. I haven't been under the castle, but I would bet that below us is a network of tunnels burrowing into the mountain, so deep, it would withstand an orbital bombardment. The chances of such an attack happening are exactly zero. You've seen their fleet. Arland's destroyer alone can hold off a small armada. The system is already as protected as it could be, yet they built a battle station on top of it. You're asking them to allow outsiders into their space, many different outsiders, not just a select few trusted allies. You are forcing them to go against their nature."

"I'm offering to make them wealthy beyond their wildest dreams."

"They don't care. It's not about money." Maud swirled the wine in her glass and took another sip. "It's about the Mukama."

"I have heard about the Mukama," Nuan Cee said, his face thoughtful. "But never from a vampire. You are almost a vampire."

Maud smiled. "Would you like me to tell you about the Mukama?"

"Yes. There is a piece missing that I do not understand."

"Very well. It goes back to the Law of Bronwyn." The galaxy had very few universal laws, but the Law of Bronwyn had proven true again and again, so often that it was simply accepted.

"Once a species is introduced to interstellar spaceflight, it will advance technologically but not socially," Nuan Cee said.

Maud nodded. "Yes. Their individual standard of living may drastically improve, their technological progress will continue, but their social construct mostly stays the same. The ability to travel between the stars removes some of the pressure factors known to drive societal change. Once you get interstellar space-flight, suddenly population density is no longer an issue. Geographical limitations are gone. The competition for natural resources is largely gone, at least in the initial stages. Different splinter groups within the society no longer have to learn to coexist; they can simply move apart from each other."

Nuan Cee nodded.

"Societal change is hard, because a society is made up of individuals. These individuals learn how to be successful in that particular social construct, and they resist change because it threatens their survival. To really implement a change, one must convince the population that their survival as a whole is in doubt unless they alter their course. Because interstellar flight removes a lot of these survival factors, the society in question generally stays as it is once the ability to traverse the stars is achieved. If they were hunter-gatherers, they remain so. If they were a republic, they remain a republic, and so on."

"Yes. It is a known fact," Nuan Cee said.

"The Mukama invaded the Holy Anocracy when the vampires were in a feudal period. The vampiric society, at that point, consisted of powerful clans led by warrior aristocracy and were bound together by a strong religion. The Mukama must've thought the vampires, so technologically behind them, were easy pickings. What do you know of the Mukama?"

"Not much," Nuan Cee said. "They were a secretive species and this conflict happened a long time ago."

"They were a predatory species," Maud said. "They didn't want the planet. They wanted the vampires themselves, particularly the children. The adults were used as the workforce and the children as a food source. The Mukama found children to be tender and delicious."

Nuan Cee grimaced.

"The vampires retreated to their castles. Reducing castles to rubble would have destroyed all of the lovely meat inside, so the Mukama had to commit to ground assault. It was discovered that the Mukama didn't do well in narrow enclosed spaces. They were an aerial species. They hunted from above. It was also found that the Mukama's mass stun weapons didn't work against a vampire in armor. It was a long war."

"How long?" Nuan Cee asked.

"Almost two decades. At some point, about eight years into the conflict, the main Mukama flotilla lost contact with the orbital fleet dispatched to the vampire planet. It took them another decade or so to wrap up their previous engagements. Finally, they bestirred themselves and went to find out what happened. When they arrived, they found the orbital fleet exactly where it was supposed to be, in the system. The ships were intact and filled with vampires."

Maud swirled her wine in her glass and smiled. "Nobody has ever met a Mukama."

"No," Nuan Cee admitted.

"But here we are, enjoying the fresh air of their home world."

Nuan Cee startled.

"House Krahr was one of the original greater houses," Maud told him. "They were entrusted with the planet of Daesyn to make sure no Mukama ever breathed its air again."

She set her empty glass on the table. A little lees ran up and refilled it.

"When we started this story, I told you that a stable society is resistant to change. The Holy Anocracy is stable, Honorable Nuan Cee. They won. Why would they change? Their way of life has worked for them for thousands of years. They never stopped building castles or wearing armor; they just make them stronger. They never abandoned their faith, because it sustained them in their darkest hour. They cherish their children, they guard them like their greatest treasure, and they teach them to fight from a young age, because history taught them that children are both precious and vulnerable. Without children, the Holy Anocracy has no future. Above all, the vampires distrust outsiders. Nothing good ever came to them from beyond the stars. You are an outsider fighting against thousands of years of inertia. A single strange bird flying at a massive flock, trying to change its direction. The kind of change you are seeking can only come from within, from someone deeply respected, someone rooted in their society. Neither you nor I have that kind of clout. But I will speak to Arland the next time I see him. If I see him."

"Oh, you will see him," Nuan Cee said. "He is coming down the hallway now."

Maud took a deep breath.

A moment later, Arland loomed in the doorway, carrying a large gray case. He saw her. "My lady."

Helen waved at Arland. He took a step into the room, but the lees swarmed him, pushing him out into the hallway.

"You left her alone!"

"People were mean to her."

"She was sad!"

Maud glanced at Nuan Cee. He smiled at her.

Arland looked at her above the lees, a pained look on his face, and raised his arms in mock surrender.

"I suppose I should find out where he was." She sighed.

"Come see me anytime, Matilda," Nuan Cee said.

She hadn't heard her real name in years. Only her parents called her that and only in rare moments.

"I will," she promised and meant it.

———

MAUD STEPPED THROUGH THE DOORWAY INTO THE HALLWAY. BEHIND her the door slid shut, cutting off the lees and their outraged cries.

Arland glanced at Helen. His eyes darkened. "Who?"

"It was a formal challenge," Maud said.

"I'm getting ripper cushions," Helen told him.

Arland turned to Maud.

"Lady Helen challenged someone in the nursery, was warned not to fight, and did it anyway. Now there will be repercussions."

"Did you win?" Arland asked.

Helen nodded.

"All is well then. If you go through life never doing anything deserving any repercussions, you'll never know victory."

Helen grinned.

"That is some fine parenting, Lord Marshal." Maud loaded enough sarcasm into her tone to sink a space cruiser.

"I try," Arland said.

The three of them looked at each other. *Awkward.*

"May I walk you to your quarters?" he asked.

"You may." It was that or continue standing in the hallway.

They walked through the keep to the covered bridge, Helen running back and forth, sometimes in front, sometimes behind. The storm still raged and green lightning flashed overhead, ripping through the dark sky.

"I'm sorry," Arland said.

"For what, my lord?"

"For not being there during dinner. It wasn't my intention."

"I don't need your protection or assistance, my lord. I'm not a prisoner. I'm here because I choose to be here. If I felt I couldn't hack it on my own, I would've left already."

They crossed the bridge into the tower and stopped at the end of the chamber where the two hallways branched off, one leading to her quarters, the other to his.

"I know that you don't require my protection, my lady. If I thought you did, I wouldn't have extended the invitation. I'm not looking for a maiden to save. I'm looking for a partner."

She narrowed her eyes at him.

He ignored her and kept going. "However, it was my intention to escort you to dinner and to spend the meal with you. I regret that my duties detained me and that I was unable to make you feel welcome in the feast hall of my home. Please accept my deepest apologies, my lady."

If they got any more painfully polite, they would draw blood simply by speaking.

"No apologies necessary, my lord. It was time well spent. I was fortunate enough to experience the hospitality of House Krahr first-hand."

He waited.

"Nothing to add, Lord Marshal?"

"A wise man knows when to shut up," he said. "I have a mother and a female cousin. I know that tone of voice. Anything I say now will be wrong. I will humbly wait to be banished or forgiven."

"Humbly?"

"Yes."

"Why, my lord, I'm surprised you know the meaning of the word."

He looked at her. She looked back. They crossed stares like swords.

"Are you going to fight?" Helen asked in a small voice.

Oh, for goodness' sake..."What's in the box?" Maud asked.

"Dinner," he said. "I didn't get to have one and from what I understand, neither did you. Join me?"

She considered stomping off to her room in all of her pissed off glory, but it would be childish. Also, she was starving.

"Yes," Maud said.

Arland grinned at her. She nearly raised her hand to shield herself.

"Just a dinner," she said.

"Just a dinner," he said. "Also, I downloaded *The Saga of Olasard, the Ripper of Souls*, onto my viewer. It's animated."

It hit her. Helen had never seen a cartoon before. Then his words sank in deeper. "Umm, there is that one part in the catacombs..."

"Oh, no, they took that out. It's made for children."

"Oh good."

The door to Arland's quarters was identical to hers, heavy, reinforced, old. It slid open and he stood aside, inviting her in. She stepped through the doorway into a mirror image of her suite, complete with doors leading to the bathroom and balcony. Yet nobody would confuse the two spaces. Her chambers were devoid of personal touches, but this place clearly belonged to Arland.

A small alla tree grew in the corner, its branches heavy with white blossoms. It was in good health, so someone was watering it. A stack of actual paper books waited on the table by the massive bed. She saw a copy of a popular YA novel from Earth and bit her lip to keep from laughing. A variety of knickknacks lay here and there; a long, wicked dagger not of vampire make; a piece of misshapen metal; a small wooden figurine carved in painstaking detail, probably by Wing, one of the creatures staying in Dina's inn. If she squinted just right, it sort of looked like her...

Arland swung his hand before a wall. It split open, exposing a linen closet. He grabbed some large floor pillows and tossed them on the rug. A fuzzy blanket followed.

"Viewer," he ordered.

A screen slid from above, covering the opposite wall.

"Saga of Olasard."

An animated vampire knight appeared on the screen, wearing elaborate armor, holding a bloody sword in one hand and a severed head in the other. He raised the sword and roared.

Helen's eyes grew huge. "It's like a book! But it's moving."

"Pause," Arland said. "Helen, I gave you access. You can tell it to pause, rewind, and fast forward."

She looked at the pillows and then back at the screen. "I need my teddy!"

"Let's go get him," Maud said. "We'll be right back."

A couple of minutes later Helen and her teddy were situated

on the pillows. By the time they came back, Arland had opened the box he carried. Ribeye steak, with ribs still attached for the ease of holding. Half a dozen vampire side dishes, thinly sliced meat, roasted vegetables, little tiny pies...The smell alone made Maud's mouth water.

Arland produced a stack of plates. Helen loaded hers up, crawled onto the pillows and started her movie.

Maud made her plate, propped a pillow against Arland's bed, and sat on the floor. Arland sat next to her with his own dinner. Their arms almost touched.

Maud attacked the food. For the first five minutes nobody spoke. Finally, she ate enough to take the edge off the hunger.

"Where were you?" she asked quietly.

"Dealing with an idiot. One of Karat's knights challenged her in direct violation of my orders."

So that's why Karat wasn't at dinner. "How did it go?"

Arland shrugged. "He'll walk again. Some day."

She smiled at him.

"As Marshal, I had to deal with it. And by deal, I mean I had to watch that farce of a fight and then slap him with sanctions."

"'A man who never does anything deserving repercussions will never taste victory,'" she said with a straight face.

"That idiot couldn't find his way out of a boot with floodlights and scout support. Trust me, victory is not in his future."

On the screen, a massive creature charged Olasard, who heroically jumped impossibly high into the air, swinging a sword that was almost as big as he was. Helen clutched the teddy to her and took another bite out of her steak.

"Went a bit overboard with his sword," Maud murmured.

"More dramatic this way," Arland said.

She liked this, Maud realized with a shock. She liked sitting here on the floor with him, watching Helen. It felt almost like a late-night pajama party. Comfortable.

Safe.

It had been so bloody long since she'd felt safe. There was the time in Dina's inn, but Gertrude Hunt had been under assault.

They could've done this in her quarters, just her and Helen, but it wouldn't be the same. It was him. Arland made her feel safe.

Alarm screeched at her senses. To let your guard down was to die. *What am I doing?*

"Is something the matter?" he asked quietly.

The anxiety saddled her and galloped off. This was ridiculous. The simple act of relaxing was so alien to her that her mind went into convulsions, thinking she was in danger.

Maud opened her mouth to lie.

No. She promised herself she wouldn't.

"This is strange," Maud said. "Being safe is strange."

Arland reached behind him, pulled a blanket off the bed, and draped it over her. "It will pass," he said quietly. "Eat a little more. Food will help."

She picked up her plate. Her instincts screamed at her to get out of the room. Instead she moved closer to him. They were touching now.

He draped his big body against the bed, relaxed, calm. Maud took another bite.

"The tachi were on the verge of leaving," she said. "You served them salad."

"They are vegetarians."

"They like meat. They just won't eat it in enemy territory."

"Are we the enemy, then?" he asked, his voice calm and measured.

She took another bite and moved half an inch closer to him.

"They're trying to decide. They like patterns in their food. The more elaborate, the better. Where is your Maven?"

"Dead," he said. "She was murdered just as she prepared to be a Band Bearer for an important wedding. Her name was Olinia. She was my youngest aunt."

"I'm sorry," she said.

"Her assassin is dead. The person who betrayed her is dead as well. That's how I met Lady Dina."

Onscreen, Olasard lopped off three heads from evil vampires in a single swing. Helen waved the ribeye bone around, imitating it.

"Can I ask you something?" Maud asked.

"Of course."

"Why do you have a copy of *Twilight* in your room?"

Arland became completely still. "Um."

"Lord Marshal?" she prompted with a small smile.

"I wanted to know how women from Earth see vampires."

"Why?"

He paused, obviously choosing his words carefully. "Your sister is a fascinating woman."

"You don't ever have to apologize for being attracted to my sister," she told him. "She is amazing."

"She is. To my shame, I must confess that it might have been more than just Lady Dina's fine qualities. A certain rivalry may have played a role."

"Sean Evans," Maud guessed.

"I decided back then that I do not like werewolves," Arland said. "I have yet to change my mind. Ghastly creatures."

They sat together in comfortable silence while she picked at her plate. He was right. Food helped. Of course, if she relied on food to stave off her anxiety, she would soon have to get a new set of armor.

"We do not get many outsiders here," Arland said. "Kacey, my cousin's stepbrother's wife, is the first human I had ever seen. As adolescents, we were all fascinated by her. She was different. When I visited the inn, I had never before met anyone like Lady Dina. Feminine, wrapped in mystery, yet firmly in control of her domain."

"The mystique of the innkeepers," Maud murmured.

"Yes. Sometimes meeting someone so different obscures the real person underneath. One becomes more fascinated with what a person represents than who they are."

"Mmmm." Where was he going with this?

His voice was intimate and sure. "What I'm trying to say is, I see you. I would love you if you were a vampire or a human, because of who you are. You don't need an inn or a broom to fascinate me. You only have to look my way and you'll have all of my attention."

Something fluttered in her chest. Something left over from before Karhari and her marriage.

She tilted her head and gave him a narrow smile. "What if I were a werewolf?"

He sucked in air, pretending to think it over. "I would love you still."

She laughed quietly and rested her head on his shoulder.

T he door chimed.

Maud sat up on the bed, instantly awake, and for a confused moment, tried to open the door with her mind. Then reality sank in: She wasn't back at Dina's inn. She was in her quarters in House Krahr's castle.

She'd dreamt of being small and weak, running for her life through the garden at her parents' inn. Something chased her, something huge and monstrous. She tried to see what it was, but all she could remember were teeth. Enormous teeth as tall as Helen.

The door chimed again.

Maud shook her head, trying to clear the last shreds of the nightmare from her mind. Yesterday she'd stayed in Arland's room way too long. They'd ended up talking about the space station long after Helen had fallen asleep.

"Time?" she asked as she pulled on soft sweatpants.

Glowing red numbers ignited on the wall above the fireplace. 9:30. Daesyn had a thirty-hour cycle, each hour being fifty minutes, each minute fifty moments. It was early. In Earth time, around 6:30 am.

The door chimed once again.

"Open."

The door slid aside, and Karat swept in wearing black armor. Not her best military set, either. When a military set suffered damage, it was often repaired while in battle or shortly after. Fixing syn-armor required a quiet environment, a lot of time, and a steady hand. Under battle conditions all three were frequently in short supply, which was why war armor showed scars and imperfections. The black set Karat wore now looked like it had just come from a nanite forge. Whatever damage it had suffered had been mended without a trace.

Karat dropped into the nearest chair. "How was my cousin?"

Maud blinked at her.

"You spent most of the night in his rooms."

"You're spying on me."

"Of course we're spying on you. We know you went back to your room with Helen. We also know that the current usage in his room was elevated until well after midnight, which is atypical of him, so we deduced that you dropped off your child and returned via the private passageway. I trust everything went well?"

Vampire cousins. "The armor stayed on."

"What? Why?"

"We're not to that stage of the relationship."

Karat stared at her. "Have you ever?"

"No."

"That's absurd. How do you know you're compatible? How could he ask you to marry him without first verifying this?"

"You would have to ask him," Maud growled.

"What were you doing all that time in his rooms?"

"Helen watched a movie. We talked. It was sweet."

"So, you took the child with you...Wait." Karat paused. "Did you just say my cousin was sweet? Arland Krahr? The Bloodmace? The Bone Crusher? The Ravager of Nexus? That Arland?"

"Yes. He was sweet and there was no ravaging." The way he looked at her last night gave her no doubt he wanted to. She wanted to as well, but something held her back. She was like a bridled horse. Every time she thought about it, something tugged on the reins and made her stop.

Karat leaned back and laughed. "That is so not like him. Poor, poor Arland. So far gone."

Maud sighed. "The problem isn't your cousin. The problem is me. He's giving me time."

Karat sobered up. "Yes, of course."

"Is there a point in you coming here and waking me up?"

"Yes." All mirth drained from Karat's face. "Lady Ilemina requests your presence at the Ladies' Communal this morning."

Figured. Maud squared her shoulders. She knew it was coming and here it was. There was no escape.

"Do you have practice armor?" Karat asked.

"I'll wear my usual set."

"Probably for the best. You'll need it. You have about twenty minutes to get ready. We'll need to collect Helen as well. She has labor duty."

"We'll get dressed," Maud said.

———

"Here we go." Karat stopped by the doorway to a large chamber. The older sentinel who'd brought Helen to the feast hall waited in the doorway. Beyond the doorway children played on floor.

114

The sentinel's blue eyes sparkled slightly with hidden humor. "Lady Helen."

Lady Helen squared her tiny shoulders. "I'm here for repercussions."

"Indeed." The older vampire produced a small brush and a tube filled with blue gel. "You will squeeze some gel on the floor and scrub it with your brush until all the dirt is removed. You will clean ten stone squares of the floor. You will remain here until your task is complete."

Helen took the little brush and the tube, held her head high, and went inside.

Behind her Maud saw another figure on the floor with an identical brush, his left arm in a plasticast. Vampire justice knew no mercy.

"She will be fine," Karat told her. "Come."

They strode ten yards down the hallway to the large wide-open doors. Beyond the doors lay a lawn of turquoise grass flooded with golden sunshine and bordered by ornamental trees. A three-foot stone wall encircled the lawn, clearly part of a parapet. Beyond the wall, across the stretch of empty air, towers and castle walls rose. They were on top of a mid-level tower.

Vampire women sparred on the grass with practice weapons. Several others watched the sparring. To the side a table stood with refreshments. A typical Ladies' Communal. They would beat up on each other for an hour or so, then drink and gossip. Maud had quite enjoyed Communals before she became a pariah. Once she had proven herself, they were a nice way to catch up with everyone. Today wouldn't be pleasant. Today they would throw her to the dogs, expecting her to cringe and submit. It was a test, one she had to pass.

Tradition dictated that both genders stayed away from each other's Communals. She was on her own.

Karat stopped by the rack of practice weapons.

"We're going to do this nice and easy," she said under her breath. "You and I will spar, then we will drink some fruity drinks and go back. Don't worry."

They really didn't think much of her.

Maud tried the first sword. Too heavy. Too long. Too short. Weighted wrong. The polymer weapons resembled their counterparts down to every minute detail, but they couldn't cut armor. The main danger lay in being bashed with one. A skilled thrust could also cause internal injury despite the armor.

Strikes with practice weapons did leave a red mark, which would fade with time or cleaning. It was an easy way to keep score and many Communals resulted in a long examination of red marks and whether or not the wound would be fatal if a live weapon had been used. The edges of the practice swords weren't exactly sharp, but you could draw blood with one. She'd done it before, just three days ago, when Arland and she had sparred aboard his destroyer. The Marshal had been fascinated with the concept of the buckler and they had spent a good three hours slicing at each other.

There. She found a blade similar to her own. Karat selected a longer, heavier sword, then eyed Maud's choice and went for a shorter blade. Really, now.

Karat strolled to a spot in the grass and hefted her blade. "Don't worry."

Maud positioned herself. "I don't see any vampires from the other Houses here."

"This is a Krahr affair."

"I feel so flattered to be invited."

Karat swung her blade and took a deliberately slow lunge.

Maud looked at her. "I'm not going to dignify that with a parry."

Karat straightened and hissed, "I'm trying to help you."

A red-haired vampire marched toward them, green eyes blazing.

"There is a vampire walking toward us and she looks like she's about to run us over."

Karat glanced over her shoulder. "Faron's piss."

"Is she here for you or me?"

"You." Karat stepped into the vampire's path. "Lady Konstana. You're interrupting."

"Lady Maud!" Konstana pointed her sword at Maud. "Your mongrel child broke my son's arm."

Oh. That.

"I wonder if you would be so kind as to demonstrate to me how she did it." Konstana bared her fangs.

Around them other people stopped sparring and moved aside, clearing the space. They had an audience now.

"Konstana," Karat growled under her breath. "She is human and a guest."

"As you wish," Maud said.

"Step aside, Karat," Konstana ground out.

A muscle jerked in Karat's face. "Do not presume to order me."

"Alvina," a female voice said.

Karat froze.

To the right of them, behind Karat, under a copse of trees, four older vampire women stood. The one who spoke was tall, with broad shoulders and a mane of blond hair cascading all the way past her waist. Her plain practice armor hugged her figure. Her gray eyes were cold. Maud looked into them and saw ice.

"Let our guest partake of the Communal," Lady Ilemina said.

Karat moved out of the way.

Maud walked a few steps farther to the right, giving herself room.

"After I break your arms, you will apologize to me," Konstana said. "For taking up my valuable time."

She was about two inches taller, probably thirty-five pounds or so heavier than Maud, and the way she held her sword indicated the South technique, which meant she would favor slash attacks. Right or left, that was the question. Strike from the left would be better. It was a more powerful attack.

Maud tipped her sword up and checked the point. "Is it a habit of House Krahr to waste time with empty threats?"

Konstana charged, slashing from left to right, aiming for a cut across the chest. It was a good slash, fast and deadly. Maud parried, letting the force of the attack slide off her blade, caught the woman's wrist for a second, yanking her arm into the perfect position, let go, thrust her own sword under Konstana's forearm, and rolled her sword arm up and over Konstana's, trapping the vampire's sword in her armpit. It happened so fast, Konstana had no chance to react. The redirected momentum of her own strike twisted her, and she went down to one knee, Maud's right hand on Konstana's wrist, her left flat against the elbow, locking it.

"You asked me how my daughter did it," Maud said. "She did it just like this."

She hit the elbow. The elbow capsule popped with a loud crack as the sheath around the joint tore. Konstana cried out. The women around them winced and made sucking noises.

"Exactly like I taught her." Maud let go and stepped away.

The vampire woman struggled to her feet, her arm hanging useless, and swiped the sword from the ground with her left hand.

"Well fought, Lady Konstana," Maud said.

The vampire woman unhinged her jaws. "Well fought, Lady Maud."

"Well," Lady Ilemina said. "That was quite stirring. I feel myself in need of some exercise. Lady Maud, perhaps you would indulge me?"

Crap, crap, crap. Maud bowed. "I'm deeply honored."

"Of course you are." Lady Ilemina walked forward.

Six feet six at least. Close to two hundred pounds. Like watching a tank approach.

Thoughts skittered through Maud, running too fast. There was no way to back down from the fight. Throwing the fight wasn't an option either. They had too many eyes on them, and Ilemina would definitely view it as an insult. Winning the fight wasn't an option, even if it was possible, which it wasn't. She couldn't humiliate Arland's mother. She couldn't let herself be humiliated. It would kill any chances she had for being accepted, and after last night she wanted Arland more than ever.

What to do? How do I handle it?

Arland's mother was the Preceptor of House Krahr and she got there because she was the best leader. Vampires led from the front. That and the two-page list of titles behind her name meant she would be a superior fighter. Her strength would be overwhelming.

Maud tested the sword one more time, warming up. She was well trained, but in a contest of pure strength, especially against a vampire knight with decades of experience, she would lose. She relied on surprise and dirty tactics, but thanks to Konstana, the cat was out of the bag and the open grassy lawn presented no opportunity for ambush, which meant she had only two things left in her corner: speed and endurance.

I have to outlast her. That's my only chance. Outlast her and exit the fight with some grace.

Ilemina turned sideways, the blade of her sword held parallel to the grass, raised her hand, and motioned with her fingers.

Oh great.

Maud thrust, light on her feet. Ilemina parried and struck from above. Maud spun around, avoiding the blade by a hair, and slashed at Ilemina's chest. The point of her blade grazed the armor, drawing a bright red line for everyone to see.

"First blood!" Karat announced.

Crap.

Lady Ilemina laughed. It was the sound of pure menace.

Maud went cold.

You've got this. You can do this. Arland's been the Marshal for the last six years, with Nexus being his first major command, which means it's been six years since Ilemina really had to get her sword dirty.

Arland's mother charged. Her blade came crashing down, impossibly fast. Maud dodged. Before she had a chance to counter, Ilemina reversed. It was a beautiful move, but Maud had no time to admire it. She dodged again, dancing around Ilemina.

Strike, dodge, strike, dodge.

Thrust. Maud parried, angling her blade, directing most of the force downward. The kinetic punch reverberated through her arm all the way into her shoulder. Ow.

A direct hit would break her bones. Maud was sure of it.

Ilemina thrust again and smashed her shoulder into Maud's.

There was no place to go. Maud barely had time to brace. The impact took her off her feet. She flew, spun her legs, and rolled to her feet in time to jump away from Ilemina's sword.

Arland's mother chased her.

Dodge, dodge, dodge.

Maud slid between the blows and sliced a diagonal gash across Ilemina's chest. The tip of the sword caught Arland's mother's neck. A drop of blood swelled.

Oh no.

Ilemina charged.

The flurry of blows came too fast to dodge. The blade connected with Maud's ribs. Pain cracked in her side, dull not sharp—the armor held. Ilemina struck again and again. All semblance of restraint was gone from her face. She tore at Maud with single-minded intensity.

Ilemina's blade came in a wide horizontal arc. Maud leaned backward, so far she almost toppled to the ground. All of the hair on the back of her neck stood on end. If that sword hit her unprotected skull, she would be dead.

This is no longer a practice fight.

Ilemina's slash caught her left arm. Pain hammered into Maud. She had to survive. She couldn't abandon Helen.

Hold on, baby. Mommy won't die.

The same sharp heat that always drowned her when their lives were in danger swallowed Maud. She lunged forward. Ilemina's sword whistled past her. Maud reversed her grip and thrust the heavy pommel into Ilemina's throat.

Arland's mother made a gargling noise and backhanded her. The punch spun Maud around. The sharp tang of her own blood wet Maud's tongue. She whirled and sliced at Ilemina.

They clashed across the field, cutting, striking, snarling, turning into a whirlwind of blades. People scrambled out of their path. One of the refreshment tables loomed at Maud's back. She jumped onto it and kicked a glass pitcher at Arland's mother. It took Ilemina a second to bat it away with her sword. Maud used it to jump aside and dash, opening the distance.

Arland's mother bore down on her, attacking, tireless, like a machine. Another hit. Another.

The world went slightly fuzzy. Maud shook it off and cut another red useless wound across Ilemina's side. Ilemina shoved her back. Maud stumbled, dodging a thrust with nothing to spare.

I can't take much more. I have to end it or she'll end me.

Ilemina delivered a vertical cut, followed it with another. In a split second, Maud recognized the pattern. Arland's mother reversed her blade again. Instead of dancing away, Maud dropped to the ground, planted her hands, and kicked at Ilemina's left knee. The knee cap cracked.

Ilemina snarled and kicked at her with her injured leg. *Sweet universe, did she even feel pain?* Maud saw the boot coming, curled up, took it, and wrapped her legs around Ilemina, trying to take her to the ground.

Arland's mother roared, bent down, and grabbed Maud's arm, dragging her up. It was like being lifted by a bobcat. Maud dropped her sword.

Ilemina jerked her up and Maud smashed both hands against Ilemina's ears. Ilemina screamed and flung her away, like she was a feral cat. Maud sprinted to the practice rack and grabbed a sword. It was too heavy, but there wasn't time to be picky.

Arland's mother stomped across the field, unstoppable, her eyes fixed on Maud. Maud bared her teeth.

Helen dashed between them, her back to Maud, holding her daggers, and snarled, right into Ilemina's path.

"No!" Maud screamed.

Lady Ilemina stopped.

Maud almost collapsed with relief.

Rational thought returned to Ilemina's eyes. "Oh my," she said.

Helen raised her daggers. "Don't hurt my mommy or I'll kill you."

"It's okay, my flower," Maud managed. "We were just practicing."

Ilemina laughed. "That is beyond adorable. No need, little one. I surrender. Your mother and I are quite finished, and you're very frightening."

She glanced up and Maud read her eyes. Ilemina knew they had gone too far. The fight was over.

"This is Lady Ilemina," Maud said. "Lord Arland's mother. We must give her every courtesy."

Helen lowered her daggers, put her legs together, and bent her knees in an ancient vampire bow.

Ilemina laughed. "My goodness."

Helen straightened.

"Are those your daggers?" Ilemina asked.

"Yes."

"Are they sharp?"

"Yes."

"Do you think they are sharp enough to cut a cookie in a half?"

Helen paused. "Yes."

"Come show me."

Helen turned to Maud.

"Yes," Maud said. "Be polite."

Ilemina offered Helen her hand. Helen put her daggers away, took Arland's mother's hand, and walked away with her. "What kind of cookies..."

Maud slumped over. Suddenly Karat was there, holding her up. Maud retched, spat out blood, and wiped her lips with the back of her hand.

People were staring at her.

"Everything hurts," she murmured.

"No shit," Karat said. "Look at yourself."

Maud glanced down. Cuts and slashes crisscrossed her armor, so many of them, it was no longer black. It was blood red. Across the field, Ilemina handed Helen a cookie. Her armor was crimson as well.

Karat gently lowered Maud to the grass. "The medic is coming. Just sit here and rest a bit."

Konstana thrust into her view with field med unit. "Here."

"Are you going to poison me?"

"Shut up and take the pain killer." Konstana held the unit up. Maud pressed it against her neck. A stab and then a cool rush flooded her body, lifting the pain.

"Drink this." Karat stuck a glass pitcher under her nose. Mint cordial. Of course. Maud gulped.

"Where the hell did you learn to fight?" Konstana asked.

"At my parents' inn."

"Humans don't fight like that."

"I couldn't let her kill me," Maud said. "I couldn't leave Helen."

Karat stared at her.

"You'll get it when you have your own," Konstana told Karat.

Maud leaned back against the stone. She didn't win. But she didn't lose either. The day was looking up.

———

EVERY STEP HURT. MAUD WALKED DOWN THE HALLWAY, TRYING NOT to wince, aware of Karat hovering by her side.

The medic had arrived and quickly confirmed three cracked ribs. He offered a stretcher. Getting onto that stretcher and being carted off would undo everything she'd just fought for. She had sparred with Ilemina. She hadn't lost. She had to be seen walking away from the fight without any help.

It took another agonizing quarter of an hour before Lady Ilemina retired, and the older sentinel had come to collect Helen, who still had some scrubbing to do. Maud made it through by sheer will, but walking hurt like hell, and her will was quickly growing thin.

Two middle-aged women strode past them, eyeing her red armor. An awful lot of people had found an excuse to either cross or walk through the hallway. Word of her match with Ilemina had gotten around. They probably filmed it, Maud reflected. When it came to violence, the vampires filmed everything.

The harbinger on her wrist chimed. She glanced at it, and the harbinger tracked her eye movement, projecting a holoscreen over her wrist. It flashed and focused into Arland's face. The beginning of a spectacular shiner swelled around his left eye. A long, ragged cut crossed his right cheek. His eyes blazed. He bared his teeth. She'd seen that look before on his face and recognized it instantly. Battle rage.

"Are you alright?" he growled.

"Are you?" she asked.

"Yes."

Karat grabbed her wrist and raised Maud's arm so she could look at the screen.

"Don't you dare show up here," she hissed. "She's walking on her own power and we have an audience. What the hell happened to you?"

"Otubar," Arland snarled.

What?

Karat swore.

Maud took her arm back. "You had a fight with your mother's consort?"

"We had a spirited practice," Arland said. "I'll find you as soon as I'm done speaking with my mother."

"Don't say anything stupid," Karat barked, but the screen went dark. Karat rolled her eyes. "What is happening in our House?"

They made another turn and walked into a room filled with medical equipment and curved cots surrounded by metal and plastic arms bearing an array of lasers, needles, and what surely had to be tools of torture. The door blissfully hissed shut behind them. The room tried to crawl sideways. Karat grabbed her arm and steadied her.

The medic, a lean male vampire with dark gray skin and long mane of dark hair pulled back from his face, pointed at her. "Out of the armor."

Maud hesitated. The armor was protection. In enemy territory, it determined life and death. Taking it off would make her vulnerable and she was feeling vulnerable enough already.

"Do you want to walk out of here in two hours or do you want to be carried out?" the medic asked.

She couldn't afford to be carried out.

Maud hit her crest. The armor split along the seams and peeled off her, leaving her in the under-armor jumpsuit. The sudden absence of the reinforced outer shell took her by surprise. The floor rushed at her, yawning, dangerously close. Strong hands caught her, and the medic carried her to a cot. A scalpel flashed and then her jump suit came apart on the right side. The cot's arms buzzed and hovered over her, as if the bed was a high-tech spider suddenly come to life. The cushion supporting her rose, curving, sliding her into a half-seated position. A green light stabbed from one of the mechanical arms, dancing across her bruised ribs in a hot rush.

"How bad is it?" Karat asked.

The medic met Maud's eyes. "You'll be fine. If you get to me in time, I can heal almost everything. Except stupid. You're on your own with that one."

"What are you implying?" Karat demanded.

"Going toe to toe with Ilemina was stupid," the medic said.

Karat fixed him with her stare. The medic swiped across his harbinger. A huge holographic screen flared in front of them. On it, Ilemina kicked Maud across the lawn. The memory of the foot connecting with her ribs cracked through Maud. She winced.

"Stupid," the medic said.

Maud sagged against the bed. The cushion cradled her, holding her battered body gently. The bed's upper left arm pricked her forearm with a small needle. A soothing coolness flooded her.

For some inexplicable reason, she missed her father. She missed him with all of the desperate intensity of a scared lonely child. She would've given anything to have him walk through the door. Heat gathered behind her eyes. She was about to cry.

A sedative, she realized. The medic must have given her a mood stabilizer or a mild relaxant with her cocktail of painkillers. It was probably standard practice for vampires. Once the pain was gone, most of them would decide that they were fine now and likely try to dramatically kick free of the medical equipment and destroy the door to finish the fight.

Gerard Demille wasn't her biological parent, but he was the only father she ever knew. He came from a time when knowing how to use a sword meant the difference between life and death. His wasn't the modern sword fighting as a sport or an artform, but a brutally efficient skill, a way to survive. When she was six years old, she'd picked up his saber and swung it around. He'd watched her for a couple of minutes, stopped what he was doing, got up, and delivered her first sword lesson. The lessons came every day after that, and when she beat him, he hired others— some human, some not—to teach her.

Maud sighed. Mom always thought it was part of her magic, her particular brand of power. That's why Mother spent most of Maud's adolescence worrying that an ad-hal would come to the door.

The ad-hal served as the Innkeeper Assembly's enforcers. While the innkeepers were bound to their inns, capable of almost unlimited power on the inn's grounds and able to do almost nothing outside of it, the magic of the ad-hal came from within them. They served the Assembly. Safeguarding the treaty that guaranteed Earth's protected status, they investigated, apprehended offenders, and punished them. Seeing an ad-hal was never a good thing. The last time she saw one was just a few days ago, when he walked into the battle for her sister's inn and paralyzed every fighter on that field.

I could have ended up just like that.

There was a time when becoming an ad-hal hadn't seemed so bad. She didn't have Klaus' encyclopedic knowledge of every species and custom in the galaxy. He was exceptional even by innkeeper standards. She didn't have Dina's green thumb, either. Her sister could plant a broomstick in the yard, and next summer it would bear lovely apples. All Maud had was an ability to read people and an innate understanding of violence and its degrees and uses. Within seconds of meeting an opponent, she knew exactly how to provoke or calm them and how much force she would have to use to stop, cripple, or kill them. Person or animal, Maud could take its measure and push them to the desired result. That's what made her so good at navigating vampire politics.

She always thought that Klaus would inherit the inn, and Dina, who always wanted to live a normal life, would end up as a gardener or botanist somewhere, while Maud became an ad-hal. Motherhood and marriage hadn't been on her radar.

Now her parents were missing, Klaus was lost, Dina was an innkeeper, and Maud lay in a vampire hospital bed after getting the living daylights beat out of her by a prospective mother-in-law.

The door chimed.

Now what?

The medic glanced at the screen to his left. "The Scribe is outside the door," the medic said. "Do you want to receive him?"

Scribes kept vampire histories. Every genealogical quirk, every victory and defeat, every scheme gone wrong or right, they recorded it all. But she wasn't a part of House Krahr. There was no reason why he would want to see her.

Delaying wouldn't accomplish anything and refusing the meeting would be unwise. The Scribe held enough power to force

130

a meeting if he wanted and she had precious few allies as it was. No reason to alienate him.

Maud fought through the relaxant's fog. "Yes."

The door hissed open, and the Scribe walked in. Tall, broad-shouldered, with a mane of chestnut brown hair, he was older than Arland, but not by much. He had a long intelligent face and his eyes, pale green under a sweep of thick eyebrows, were sharp.

"Lady Maud," he said. "My name is Lord Erast."

"To what do we owe the honor?" Karat asked.

"It seems Lady Maud and I have gotten off on the wrong foot," the Scribe said.

"That's impossible, my lord," Maud said. "We haven't met."

"Precisely. I labored under the assumption that as a human, you would be exempt from our traditions." Erast nodded at the recording playing on the screen. "I was in error. We know exactly nothing about you, which makes it awkward at formal functions."

He flicked his fingers at his crest. "This session is now being recorded. What is your lifetime kill count?"

"I don't know."

Erast's eyes bulged. "What do you mean, you don't know?"

"I haven't kept track."

"You were the wife of a Marshal's son. Was the importance of keeping a personal record not impressed upon you?"

Maud sighed. "In the three years I was with House Ervan, they had no major conflicts. I had several personal bouts, but none of them were to the death. Afterward, on Karhari, it didn't seem important."

"Did you have any titles?" Karat asked.

"Maud the Eloquent."

Karat and Erast looked at each other.

"House Ervan put great emphasis on the knowledge of ancient sagas," Maud explained.

"Can she use that?" Karat asked.

Erast pinched the bridge of his nose. "Technically, no. They struck her from their records, so any titles or honors earned while with House Ervan are forfeit. They are subjective, bestowed upon an individual by others to highlight certain deeds. The kill count is different because taking a life is an irrefutable fact."

"What about Maud the Exile?" Karat asked. "Could we do something with that?"

Erast frowned. "My lady, answer honestly. What was the most important duty in your life before your exile?"

"Taking care of Helen."

"What about on Karhari?"

"Taking care of Helen."

"And now?"

"Helen."

"Do you desire revenge on House Ervan?"

"I wouldn't mind punching a couple of them, but no. I was mad at my husband, and I buried him long ago."

Erast sighed. "The Exile won't work. A title like that implies an element of rebirth. Lady Maud hasn't permitted the act of being exiled to affect her worldview. There was no seismic shift in her personality as the result of being sent to Karhari."

The two vampires stared at her. The frustration on Erast's face was almost comical.

"They did call me something on Karhari."

"What was it?"

"Maud the Sariv."

"What does that mean?" Karat asked.

"On Karhari there is a summer wind that comes from the wastes. Nobody knows how it forms, but it comes out of nowhere and it picks up thorny spores from local weeds. When you inhale sariv's breath, the spores enter your lungs and cut you from the inside. There is no escape from this storm. If you are caught in it without protective gear, it will kill you. They called me that because I paid the blood debt I owed to my husband's killers."

Erast perked up. "Do you have any proof of that, my lady?"

"Would you hand me my crest?"

Erast picked up her breastplate. His eyes widened at the mess of red. He offered it to her, and she pulled the crest off. She'd transferred all of her recordings to it as soon as Arland gave it to her.

"Play all files tagged Melizard's Death in chronological order," she said.

The crest lit with red, projecting onto a wall. She knew every frame of the recording by heart. It played in her head for months. The view of a fortified town from a dusty hilltop. A crowd dragging Melizard through the street, faces contorted with fury and glee, rabid. Melizard's bloody face as they took turns punching him, while he stumbled, caught in the ring of striking arms and legs. Him crawling on the ground while they kicked him. The stone bench they dragged out of the nearest house. The flash of a rising axe. Melizard's head rolling as they cut him apart. The greasy smoke rising from his burned body. Melizard's head on a pike rising above the gates, his empty dead eyes staring into the distance.

Silence claimed the room.

A light ring singled out a face in the crowd and zoomed in. A huge dark-haired male vampire with a scar across his face. A caption appeared. *Rumbolt of House Gyr.*

The recording zoomed in on his face, turning dark, then blossoming into bright daylight, filmed by a camera attached to her shoulder. Rumbolt's face, skewed by rage, as he swung a blood mace at her. One, two, three blows, all whistling past her. Her own stab, fast and precise as it slid into his throat and opened a second bloody mouth across his neck. Rumbolt collapsing on his knees then face down into the dirt, his blood spilling onto the dust. Her blade again as she sliced across his neck and kicked his head across the dusty street, sending it rolling and bouncing off the hard dirt.

The recording blinked and a woman resembling Rumbolt stared up at her as Maud smashed her face with a rock. A caption popped up. *Erline of House Gyr.*

"His sister," she explained. "The relatives came after me at first, but they stopped after the first few kills."

The freeze frame of the crowd gripping Melizard flashed again. The light circle picked out a new face, a woman with gray hair, screeching, her fangs bared. The caption read *Kirlin the Gray.*

The recording zoomed in, turned dark, and then a vampire in heavy scarred armor was coming at her, her neck and face hidden by a full helmet.

"Is that an antique space-rated unit?" Karat asked.

"Yes. She preferred to fight in it. It made her slow, but the armor is so thick, the blood weapons can't penetrate."

On the recording, Maud dodged the swings of Kirlin's blade and thrust herself against the woman. Kirlin's arm came up, then the recording shook and rocked as Maud reeled away after taking the blow. Kirlin raised her sword, about to charge. A small dot of crimson flared on her neck. It blinked and Kirlin's throat exploded in a gush of gore, taking the head with it.

"Mining charge." Maud smiled.

The image of the crowd appeared again, singling out a new target. Zoom, darkness, then a lean vampire backing away up the hill from the wild swings of Maud's mace, moving closer and closer to the drop. She kept hammering at him, her voice a guttural snarl echoing every blow. He planted himself, aware he was almost out of ground, and slashed at her with his sword. She dropped her mace, spun out of the way of his blade, and kicked him. It was a front kick, driven not up, but down, almost a stomp. She'd sunk all of the power of her body into it. Her heel landed on the vampire's leading knee. His leg gave out and he dropped down to compensate. She punched him in the face and rammed her shoulder into his chest. He sailed off the cliff. She bent down, and the camera caught his body impaled on spikes below. The recording blinked, and a second body joined the first. Then a third. And a fourth.

"He had three brothers," she explained. "They kept coming after me, so I told them that if they tried to fight me, they would die in the same spot their brother did, and they followed me to the cliff. Worked every time. I already had the spikes set up. It seemed a shame to waste them."

Erast, Karat, and the medic were looking at her like she had sprouted a second head.

The next target loomed on the screen, an older vampire, his hair shot through with gray.

"This one isn't mine," she grimaced. "This is my worst failure."

The recording zoomed in. She was on the ground, her breath coming out in sharp pained gasps. The camera was splattered with blood. The vampire stood several feet away, his armor a mess of cuts. He gripped Helen by her hair. She dangled from his hand, screaming, her high-pitched shriek so sharp. Every time Maud heard it, it felt like her heart was breaking.

"I've got your whelp, bitch! I'll slit her throat so you can watch," the vampire roared.

He jerked Helen up. She spun in his grip, pulling her two daggers out, and drove them into the vampire's face.

He dropped her. Maud surged off the ground, drove her sword into a cut in his breastplate, and twisted. The armor cracked, contracting, and locked on the vampire, paralyzing him. The vampire collapsed, and Helen stabbed his exposed neck again and again, screaming.

"This one is hers," Maud said.

It was so quiet, she could hear herself breathing.

"How many are there?" Erast asked.

"I don't know," she answered. "I never counted."

"Then perhaps we should do so," he said.

[8]

"Mama?"

Maud opened her eyes. Two pairs of eyes stared at her, one Helen's green and the other golden brown.

She must've fallen asleep. In enemy territory. Alarm shot through her in a chemical jolt. Instantly she was awake.

The pale walls rushed at her, the only room she'd seen in the castle so far that was made with a sterile polymer instead of ancient stone. She was still in the med ward. The medic must've added a mild sedative to her medications. Combined with the additional strain on her body, exhausted from the fight and healing at an accelerated rate, the medication had put her under. She wasn't sure how long she'd slept, but the sharp pain in her ribs was gone. Fatigue wrapped around her like a soft straitjacket. Her head was fuzzy.

"Mommy?"

"Yes, my flower?"

"This is Ymanie."

Ymanie blinked her big round eyes and gave a little wave. She was about Helen's age, although a little taller and more solid, with dark brown hair and dark-gray skin.

Maud's mouth was dry, but she made it move. "Good to meet you, Lady Ymanie."

"She also had repercussions," Helen said.

"I did," Lady Ymanie confirmed.

"They have a place," Helen said. "There's a big tree and it's on a tower and you have to climb to get to the top and then there is a thing and you grab the handle and go whoosh."

What?

"You go whoosh," Helen repeated. "Down the rope."

"Are you talking about a zipline?"

"Yes!" Ymanie and Helen said at the same time.

"They won't let me go unless I have permission," Helen added. "Can I please go?"

"Is Lady Ymanie going too?"

Both girls nodded.

Helen had made a friend and wanted to go play. "Um...sure. You have permission."

"Thank you!"

The two girls scurried away.

Maud pushed from the cushion and sat up slowly. The medic looked up from his post near the console.

"How do you feel?"

"Tired, but the ribs stopped hurting."

"Good. The ribs should be completely healed by tomorrow morning. The damage to your internal organs was slight, but it required some repair as well, so treat yourself well for the next twelve hours. No strenuous activity today. No fighting, no training, no sex. A nice satisfying meal, early to bed, and a full night's sleep. You may soak to lessen the body aches, but do not take any stimulants, medications, or supplements.

If you do something stupid, and come back to me again before tomorrow, I won't be as kind. Do we understand each other?"

"Yes."

"Good. I'll help you with your armor."

Five minutes later, Maud walked down the breezeway back to the tower. The transparent shield that had guarded the bridge from the elements yesterday was gone. Sunshine flooded the world and wind stirred her hair. It was late afternoon. She'd slept most of the day. Who knew what happened in the last few hours? Logic said she should be worried about it and taking some steps to find out, but she felt too groggy.

A piercing squeal whipped her around. Hundreds of feet above, a tiny body shot down a nearly invisible rope across the open gap between two towers at breakneck speed. Maud's heart tried to jump out of her chest. She sagged against the parapet.

The child disappeared from view behind a forest of towers.

It was too late to do anything about it. She tapped her harbinger. Helen's life signs read normal, except for elevated heartbeat. She would just have to hope her daughter survived the vampire zipline.

It took Maud a full thirty seconds to haul herself off the stone wall and start walking. If they were in the inn, she would've sworn her sister stretched the distance between Maud and her quarters, artificially elongating it into a never-ending trek. But they were in House Krahr, so she just had to keep moving. She would get there eventually.

Finally, the door of her suite loomed before Maud. She waved at it and it slid open. She went straight into the bathroom. A square tub big enough to comfortably soak six vampires sat in the middle of the room, a dozen different bottles and canisters waiting on the shelf for her selection.

"Water at 105 degrees Fahrenheit, fill to six inches from the rim"

Jets opened along the tub's rim, gushing water. She sorted through the bottles. Mint, mint, more mint. There. Soothing blend. The scent reminded her of lavender.

She tossed a couple handfuls of the powder and dried herbs into the tub, stripped off her armor, bodysuit, and underwear, and slid into the water; positioning herself on a shelf, she submerged all the way up to her neck. The hot water swirled around her.

Water. Wonderful hot water. All the water she ever wanted.

She could grow her hair out again and then she could wash it with every shampoo available.

A small sound escaped her mouth, before she could catch it, and Maud wasn't sure if it was a giggle or a sob.

She was about to close her eyes when she saw it, a small transparent sphere sitting on the edge of the sink. It wasn't there when she and Helen had left the bathroom this morning.

Maud slipped out of the tub and padded to the sink. The sphere was barely a quarter of an inch across. On Earth it would've passed for a tiny glass marble or a stray bead.

A high-storage datacore, likely encrypted to her. Someone left her a present.

She picked it up, leaned forward, and blew on the mirror. Faint words appeared, written in the glyphs of the Merchant clans.

With compliments from the Great Nuan Cee.

The lees. Of course. And so sleek, too. A little message to her— we can slip into your quarters anytime we want.

Father always said dealing with the lees was like juggling fire. You never knew when you would get burned.

Maud returned to the tub and sat back on the shelf, rolling the datacore between her fingers. To look or not to look? She wasn't sure she could take bad news right this second. But then if it was bad news, the sooner she found out, the better. Maud set the bead on the tub's rim.

"Access," she whispered.

A light flared within the bead, the silver glow sweeping her. The light shot out in a new direction. An open window framed by long gauzy curtains. Whoever was filming this had to be hanging just outside of it. Knowing lees, they were probably upside down.

The recording zoomed in through the window. Lady Ilemina reclined on a sofa.

Ha!

Arland's mother was out of her armor and wearing a long blue tunic. Her arms were bare and covered with swollen patches of red. Maud smiled. She had worked Ilemina over more than she realized. A portable med unit that looked like some nightmarish robotic spider shone green light at the largest bruise. Ilemina grimaced.

Her quarters were beautiful. The furniture was soft, carved from some cream-colored wood, and upholstered in deep blue that verged on turquoise. Two crystal vases dripped flowers. It was an elegant, uncluttered space, simple, peaceful, and surprisingly feminine.

The door in the far wall slid open and Arland marched through, his face battered, his eyes blazing, looking like he couldn't wait to rip something with his bare hands.

"Hello, Mother," he growled.

Ilemina sighed. "Took you long enough."

Arland shrugged his massive shoulders. "I was detained."

"By whom?"

"Lord Consort."

Ilemina raised her eyebrows.

"He approached me at Communal," Arland said. "We had some words."

"What kind of words?"

"He said, 'You're upsetting your mother.' I asked him if he was planning on doing something about it, and here we are."

"Is Otubar alive?" Ilemina asked, her voice flat.

"Yes. Although I did dislocate his shoulder. I expect he'll make a full recovery by evening."

"I wish you would reach an understanding," Ilemina said.

"We understand each other perfectly well, Mother. He doesn't care about anything except making sure you're safe and happy. I, however, can't afford such a delightful luxury. I have to worry about the stability of our House, the readiness and commitment of our troops, and our reputation. Normally Otubar and I strive to get along with each other, because it makes things simpler. However, I'm the Marshal and I won't allow him to take me to task like I am a child. Especially in front of witnesses. He knew this would only end one way when he started it."

"He knows," Ilemina said. The medical robot moved on to her leg and she winced. "He holds back."

"Perhaps the next time he could hold back enough to conduct his inquiries in private and use words so I don't have to break my stepfather's arm in front of the entire House!"

"Do not raise your voice at me," Ilemina snapped.

"Was this planned, Mother?"

"Yes, Arland, I planned for you to break my husband's arm."

"Did the two of you conspire to give me and my fiancée a beating?"

"She is *not* your fiancée. She turned you down."

They glared at each other.

"I'll say this," Ilemina said. "She isn't a pushover."

"What were you thinking attacking her, Mother? What was the plan?"

"There was no plan." Ilemina sighed. "You're my only son. I want only the best for you. I wanted to see you married to a strong House. To someone worthy of you. With a lineage and a legacy. Someone who would walk with you into Cathedral and the entire House would be in awe."

"I see." Arland furrowed his eyebrows. "And was my happiness ever a consideration in this glowing picture?"

"Of course! I want you to be happy! I want that most of all for you. I could have handled you marrying down, but a human, Arland? A human! And she doesn't even want to marry you! Does she not understand who you are? Did you not properly explain your station in life? Your achievements? How dare she!"

Water touched her nose. Maud realized she was sinking deeper into the water to hide and caught herself.

"She knows exactly who I am, Mother. She wants to marry me. She loves me."

"Then why did she turn you down?"

He ran his hand through his hair. "It's complicated."

"Enlighten me."

"No. That's between me and her."

"I waited years for you to find someone. I should be knee-deep in grandchildren by now. Instead you're off, running back and forth to Earth, to Karhari, to Hierophant alone knows where. And you come back with this...this...woman. A woman exiled in disgrace! You have the audacity to demand I ready our House for her as if she is worthy of the honor. You don't talk to me. You don't talk to your uncle or your cousin. You don't talk to anyone."

"I spoke to Uncle Soren at length," Arland said. "He approves."

"What?" Ilemina jerked up, and the medical robot screeched in disapproval. "Why?"

"Because he is my uncle and I sought his counsel."

"No, foolish child. Why does he approve?"

"You would have to ask him."

Ilemina shook her head. "Both of you have lost your minds. You brought this woman here. She didn't introduce herself. You didn't even talk to me about her. You didn't seek my counsel."

"And for that you decided to kill the woman I love?"

Maud shivered in the water. *He said he loves me.* For a second, she simply glowed in it and then reality intruded, and she put her hand over her face. *What am I, twelve?*

"I wasn't trying to kill her. I was…frustrated. And there she was, wearing armor as if she knew what to do with it."

"She does," Arland said.

"Well, I know that now." Ilemina waved her hand. "It went too far. I admit it."

"If that had been a real fight, you would be dead."

Ilemina laughed, a low wolfish sound that raised the hair on the back of Maud's neck. "You presume too much."

Arland smiled. "You assume she would meet you in a duel. She wouldn't. One day you would travel somewhere, step out of the vehicle, suspecting nothing, and there she would be with her blade. If she didn't cut your head off with the first strike, she'd let you win until you got close enough to her, spit poison gas into your face, then run you through and be gone before anyone was the wiser."

"So, she's an assassin," Ilemina said.

"No. She's a woman who was dumped on Karhari with a three-year-old child and a husband who was a snake. She is a survivor. She doesn't fight for fun or glory. She fights to eliminate the threat. Every time she draws her sword, it's life or death. She gives it everything, because her child's life hangs in the balance. Of all people, I thought you would relate."

144

Ilemina fell silent. "I'll say this, sparring with her was an illuminating experience."

"It is."

"And the child is adorable." Ilemina smiled. "The daggers were so cute."

"I've seen her kill with those daggers," Arland said.

"The baby, Helen?"

He nodded. "She cut a Draziri assassin's throat in the middle of a battle. She did it the right way, mother."

Ilemina recoiled, shocked.

Maud ducked her head under the water and wished she were a better mother. Helen shouldn't know how to kill. Sitting under water wouldn't change that fact, but she would have given everything to take that back from her daughter.

She surfaced.

"But why?" Ilemina asked.

"Karhari," he said. He was right. That was the only explanation needed.

"What sort of House exiles a child?" Ilemina growled.

"The kind of House that's beneath our contempt."

Ilemina sighed. "You really love her?"

"Yes."

"But are you sure, Arland? Are you sure she would make you happy?"

"Yes, Mother. Give her a chance. At least find out who you're dealing with before you reject her."

"And if I do reject her? If I reject this union?"

"I'll go with her," he said.

Maud fell off the shelf and splashed, scrambling back onto it.

"Arland, you wouldn't dare!"

"You walked away with Father. I don't see any reason why I can't do the same."

145

She opened her mouth, closed it, and opened it again. "You're the Marshal."

"So were you. You'll just have to replace me with another."

"What if she rejects you?"

"I'll respect her wishes."

Ilemina threw her hands in the air. "This is blackmail, Arland."

"No, it's a boundary. Your blessing isn't necessary, Mother. But I would like to have it. I know she would, too. She respects you a great deal. She's a daughter of innkeepers. She has vast knowledge and understanding. She will be a great asset to the House."

Ilemina held up her hand. "I'll give her a chance. But only a chance, Arland. I will make up my own mind. If she stumbles, if she endangers you in any way..."

Arland bowed his head. "Thank you, Mother."

The recording faded out.

Maud leaned back against the tub. He would leave with her.

She wouldn't ask for that sacrifice. She had no right. If she wanted him—truly wanted him—she had to make sure not to stumble.

[9]

The door chimed. *Arland. Finally.* They had things to discuss. She planned to open with "The Lees are spying on your mother and here is the recording of that conversation you had with her." If her prior experiences with vampires in general and Arland in particular were anything to go by, it would take her at least twenty minutes to talk sense into him and convince him not to do something drastic like kicking Nuan Cee and his furry clan out of the castle.

Maud checked the time. After her bath, she'd tracked Helen down through their linked harbingers. Helen and Ymanie had charmed some dessert out of the kitchen staff and were eating it on the balcony of one of the towers. Helen begged for more time and Maud had given her another hour. That was twenty minutes ago. Plenty of time left for a private conversation with Arland.

Maud paused before the door, trying to compose her thoughts. Things refused to line up in her head. Words like "love" and "leave" buzzed around in there, muddying things up. *Get a grip.*

The door chimed again, then again. Not Arland.

"Show the guest," she said.

A screen opened above the door, showing Karat. The vampire knight tapped her foot on the floor, her arms crossed.

What now?

"Accept."

The door slid open and Karat stormed inside.

"What is it?" Maud asked.

"I have urgent news."

"I'm beginning to wonder if you bring any other kind."

A careful knock echoed through the chamber. It came from the side door, from the passage connecting her rooms to Arland's. Maud crossed the chamber and opened it. Arland stepped inside. He must've stopped by the medic as well, because the bruises on his face had faded to almost nothing.

"Lady Maud."

"Lord Marshal."

He saw Karat. Something snapped in Arland's eyes. It might have been his patience.

"Why are you here?" he growled. "Why are you always here? Do you not have any other duties, cousin?"

Yes, definitely his patience.

Karat's eyes narrowed. "I'm sorry, did I frustrate your intentions? Were you about to make an awkward love pronouncement? Perhaps follow it with a sonnet you'd composed?"

Arland's expression turned ice cold. "The nature of my conversations with my fiancée are none of your business."

"One would think that a man in your position would be grateful that a female relative is trying to safeguard his not-fiancée."

"A man in my position would be grateful for a bit of privacy!"

"You can have privacy when you're dead!"

They glared at each other.

Right. She'd been in enough sibling battles to know exactly where this would end.

"My lady!" Maud said.

"What?" Karat snarled.

"Urgent news?" Maud prompted.

"Go ahead," Arland said. "The sooner we hear this, the faster you can leave."

"I came here to tell your not-fiancée," Karat said, looking at Arland, "that the bride just invited her to the Lantern Vigil."

Arland swore.

"When?" Maud asked.

"We leave in thirty minutes."

Arland swore again. Clearly, this whole situation was getting to him, Maud decided.

"What in the icy plains do they want with her?" Arland asked.

"I don't know," Karat said. "You have to go, Maud. If you refuse..."

"It will be an insult. I know. I had the Lantern Vigil for my wedding."

It was an ancient wedding ritual, born from myth and love. A thousand years ago, a vampire knight had gone to war against interstellar invaders. His fiancée, who had been crippled in battle, had to stay behind. Every week, despite her injury, she made a long journey to the sacred vala tree high on the mountain and hung a new lantern on its branches, praying that her fiancé would come home. When he returned, years later, triumphant, he saw the vala tree out of the window of his shuttle. It glowed with lanterns, a symbol of his beloved's devotion.

Nobody remembered the couple's names, but countless vampire brides made the journey to a vala tree carefully planted somewhere in the wilderness, preferably on a mountain trail. They were accompanied by the young women from the bridal party. The journey had to be made on foot. No armor. No weapons. No men.

"Can you get her out of it?" Arland asked.

"They specifically asked for her by name. It came directly from the bride." Karat grimaced. "The bridal tree is five miles up the trail. The terrain is steep and the path is narrow, bordering a cliff. We'll end up walking single file half of the way. The order in which we walk is predetermined by the bride. Maud will be walking between Onda and Seveline. I'll be three women ahead. If something happens, I won't even know."

"You think they could push her off the path?" Arland's eyes blazed.

"I wouldn't put it past them."

"To what end?"

Karat waved her arms. "To piss you off. To upset the wedding. For their amusement because they are evil bitches."

Maud cleared her throat. The two vampires looked at her.

"I'll be fine," she said. "I'm hard to kill. Better people have tried and failed. Besides, it's unlikely they would bump me off. I'm an honored guest. If I die, Arland would withdraw from the wedding to mourn me and they have a particular interest in him."

"That sounds thin to me," Karat said.

"I'm better out of armor than they are. I'll need a booster," Maud said. Walking five miles to the tree and five miles back would definitely count as "strenuous activity." Under normal circumstances, she could hike it in her sleep, but considering everything her body had been through in the last few hours, she would need help.

"No problem."

Arland locked his teeth. The muscles on the corners of his jaw stood out. She kind of liked it.

"A penny for your thoughts, Lord Marshal?"

He unhinged his jaws. "There is nothing I can do to remedy this situation," he said, his voice so calm, it was almost eerie. "To refuse the invitation is a grave insult. The only acceptable excuse would be physical incapacitation. If we were to tell them that you were injured, there would be questions. First, how did you get injured? Why would House Krahr let a human guest come to harm? And if I were to disclose the true reason for your injuries, I would be throwing away the element of surprise, which may be the only advantage you have should your life be in danger."

He looked so put out, she had to needle him. "Not the only advantage," Maud told him. "There is also my sexy human allure."

Karat choked on a laugh.

Arland shut his eyes for a long moment and then fixed her with a glacial stare. "I implore you to take this seriously."

"Never underestimate the impact of a strategic hip roll." Where was she even going with this? It was like she couldn't stop. "I'm sure some of the ladies within the bridal party would be intrigued if properly motivated. If I get in trouble, I'll just bite my lip seductively and twirl my hair…"

"Maud!" he snapped.

"You know I have to go," she told him. "They are planning something, and they think I'm both too stupid and too weak to be a threat. They count on me being a source of information."

"I'm going to keep a shuttle on standby," Arland said. "If something happens…"

"I will call you for assistance. Meanwhile, it would put my mind at ease if you would keep an eye on Helen."

"I will," he said.

"Thank you," she told him.

"A human goes off to walk the Lantern Vigil, while my cousin the Marshal stays home to babysit," Karat said. "I realize now why

I have never fallen in love. I'm entirely too sane for that nonsense."

—————

THE STEEP PATH CLIMBED ALONG THE SIDE OF THE MOUNTAIN, barely a foot wide. Maud shifted her grip on the slender staff in her hand. The lantern hanging from the staff's forked end swayed, the orange flames dancing behind the translucent glass. To the right of her, the mountain rose, the gray rock scarred by rain and stained by patches of green and turquoise vegetation that somehow found purchase in the near-sheer cliff face. To the left, a dizzying drop to the rocks and trees far below promised a few seconds of terror before a gruesome death. Back on Earth there would have been guardrails and signs at the bottom of the path warning visitors to be careful and that they ascended at their own peril. Vampires didn't bother. If one of them was dumb enough to fall off the trail, they would consider their death natural selection.

In front of Maud a procession of women walked, each carrying a lantern on a staff. More women followed. They stretched along the path, twenty in all, anonymous in their identical white robes, their heads hidden by wide hoods. The gentle tinkling of the bells from the bride's staff floated on the breeze. Invisible insects buzzed in the crevices, reminding Maud of the cicadas from Dina's garden back home, at their parents' inn that no longer existed. The air smelled of strange flowers and potent herbs.

Maud kept walking, her body unusually light and slightly jittery, as if she'd had too much coffee. She had to fight the urge to skip. The booster Karat brought her had worked wonders. She would have at least four, maybe five hours of this excited state, and then she would crash. They had been walking for the better part of an hour. Since the tree was about five miles up the trail, they had to be getting close. Plenty of time to finish the hike and get off the mountain.

Maud stared at Onda's back in front of her. She had expected them to make some sort of move by now. Conversation in low voices was permitted during the Vigil, but so far, they made no move to engage her.

As if on cue, Seveline cleared her throat behind her, the words in Ancestor Vampiric soft, barely a whisper. *"We could just push her off this path."*

Maud kept walking. If Seveline did push her, she didn't have many options.

Ahead Onda sighed. *"And how would we explain that?"*

"Clumsy human fell."

"No."

"I can make it look like an accident."

"Seveline, find another way to amuse yourself. We can't risk him withdrawing from the wedding to mourn her."

Figured. Maud hid a smile. They needed Arland for something. The question was, what?

"How far is this damn tree?" Seveline murmured in Common Vampiric.

"Seveline," Onda hissed. "Be respectful. Kavaline is your cousin."

"Second cousin," Seveline murmured.

This called for a snicker. Maud made a light coughing noise.

"Did you have a Lantern Vigil for your wedding, Lady Maud?" Seveline asked.

Dangerous territory. She didn't just have the Lantern Vigil, she had the Flower Lament, and the Cathedral Fasting, and every other archaic ritual House Ervan could dig up. Admitting all that would make her appear less clueless, which Maud couldn't afford.

"To be honest, I barely remember any of it," Maud said, trying to make her voice sincere and slightly sad. "It was very different from human weddings. I lost track of it all at some point and it became a blur."

"Sounds like a typical wedding," Onda said.

"I'm not planning on getting married for a while," Seveline announced.

"Who would be fool enough to marry you?" Onda muttered.

"She's so mean to me," Seveline whined.

Maud obliged with another snicker. They were putting on a show for her benefit. She hated to disappoint.

"Are you going to marry the Lord Marshal?" Seveline asked.

"It's complicated," Maud said.

"I say don't do it," Seveline said. "Live free."

"She has a child to think about," Onda said. "Has the Lord Marshal made any assurances as to the child's future?"

They were definitely fishing, but for what? "We haven't entered into any formalized agreement."

Onda's voice floated to her. "But Lord Arland knows he is the Marshal and Krahr is an aggressive House. They love war. He must've acknowledged his life is frequently in danger."

"Onda is right," Seveline added. "To not have a contingency plan would be irresponsible. Men often are, but not where a spouse and children are concerned."

What were they after? "I'm aware of the dangers," Maud said, letting just enough sadness through.

"But of course you are," Onda said. "You've been widowed."

"Husbands don't always last," Seveline said.

"I cannot believe that, with your history, the Marshal hasn't made at least some arrangements to reassure you," Onda said, a slight outrage vibrating in her voice.

"He has to have done something," Seveline added.

"Has he mentioned anyone?" Onda asked. "Someone who might take care of you and your daughter in case of an emergency? Someone who would accept that noble responsibility?"

It hit her like a lightning bolt. They were after the Under-Marshal. Of course.

As a Marshal, Arland led the totality of House Krahr's armed forces. He commanded every fighter, every war animal, every military vehicle, no matter if it was a two-seater land runner or a space destroyer. If it could fight and belonged to House Krahr, it answered to Arland. He was in possession of codes, passwords, and command sequences. If Arland was incapacitated, House Krahr's military would find itself adrift. To avoid that, every vampire House large enough to have a Marshal also had an Under-Marshal, a secret second-in-command who possessed a duplicate of everything that gave Arland power and access. If anything happened, the Under-Marshal would step in, the transfer of power would be seamless, and House Krahr would continue to fight until the threat passed and a new Marshal could be appointed. Until then, the Under-Marshal would assume all of Arland's responsibilities, including his obligation for the safety of his spouse and children.

The identity of the Under-Marshal was a closely-guarded secret. It was never revealed to outsiders. It could have been anyone, Karat, Soren, Ilemina, her consort. Had Maud been trusted with that knowledge, letting another House in on it would be treason.

They really thought she was a complete idiot.

"Lord Arland didn't mention anyone," she said. "But you're right, this is worrying. I'll ask him."

"You should," Onda said. "Just for your peace of mind."

"She's totally useless," Seveline murmured in Ancestor Vampiric. *"Let me trip her."*

"No."

"She would scream all the way down. It would be funny."

"We might still get something out of her."

The path widened and turned, following the mountain. A massive gorge opened before them, the trees at its bottom so far below, the expanse of empty air had taken on a slight blue tint. Another mountain cliff formed the other side of the gorge, a sister to the one they'd climbed. A mess of narrow stone arches and breezeways bridged the gaps between the two cliffs, as if some chaotic giant had carelessly tossed a bundle of stone sticks into the gap. The stone formations crossed over each other, some spanning the distance, some ending abruptly, crumbling into nothing, turning the gorge into a maze. They looked completely natural, as if time and weather had whittled the living rock, but their placement was too deliberate. No geological phenomenon would produce slender crisscrossing bridges like these. Someone must've made them; how, she had no idea.

On the right, atop one narrow stone protrusion, a vala tree spread its branches. It was ancient and massive, its thick roots wrapping around the stone and burrowing deep into the mountain, as if challenging the gorge. Between the two cliffs the setting sun painted color onto the evening sky, turning it yellow, rose, lavender and finally, high above, a beautiful purple. Against this backdrop, the red leaves of the vala all but glowed.

The view took Maud's breath away. She stopped. The other women halted too.

"Behold," a woman's voice rang out from ahead. "The Mukama Roost."

Nothing more needed to be said. Once, the ancient enemy made their home here. Now the sacred vala tree ruled the cliff.

The procession resumed. Maud stared at Onda's back. They wanted the identity of the Under-Marshal. That could mean only one thing. She would have to warn Arland as soon as she could.

She was painfully aware of Seveline behind her. In Seveline's place, Maud would push herself off the cliff. There was always that chance that she would say something to Arland to alert him.

The world turned sharp. Maud moved forward on her toes, straining to catch every noise, alert for any hint of movement.

The bride was almost to the tree.

Maud hadn't seen Seveline lunge, she couldn't have, but she felt it. Her ears caught the faint scrape of a foot on stone, her eyes glimpsed a hint of movement on the very edge of her vision, and her instincts, honed by the wasteland, jerked her out of the way. She pressed her back against the cliff. Seveline stumbled past her and Maud caught the vampire woman's arm.

Shock slapped Seveline's face. One push, and Seveline would tumble to her death.

Maud opened her eyes as wide as she could. "My goodness! You have to be careful here, my lady. See how the edge has crumbled? That's why I walk by the wall."

Seveline blinked.

"Seveline!" Onda hissed. "You're embarrassing us."

Maud released Seveline's arm. The vampire woman frowned.

Maud resumed her walking. She might have given away too much, but there was no way around it. She was safe now. Stumbling once and knocking her off the path might be an accident. Stumbling twice would be seen as a deliberate attempt on Maud's life. Even Seveline with her poor impulse control understood that.

Still, Maud's best defense, at least for now, was to be seen as a non-threat.

She deliberately stumbled, catching herself on the cliffside, and kept walking. There. Clumsy human almost fell. No need for alarm. Everything is as it appears to be.

Ahead the bride reached the bridge of the vala tree and solemnly walked along its curved length to the enormous trunk.

The women lined up on the ledge before the bridge, where the path widened to a luxurious ten feet, and began to chant the words to an old poem in low voices. Maud knew them by heart. Her memory superimposed an image of another time and place on the present. Another vala tree, a lantern in her own hand, and her voice soft and earnest, as she recited, and back then, believed every word:

> Night has fallen, sky has opened,
> Ancient stars have no mercy,
> In the Void and cold darkness,
> Find my light and feel my hope.

> You will never stand alone,
> You will never be forgotten,
> Time will never make me falter,
> Find my light and feel my hope.

> I will wait for you forever,
> You won't lose your way, beloved,
> Find my light and feel my hope,
> And my love will guide you home.

Sometimes even the strongest love wasn't enough.

The bride raised her lantern and hung it on a tree branch. The lantern swayed gently. The bride stood to the side, her hand on the tree's dark bark. One by one the women moved forward to add their own lanterns to the branches, then walked back off the bridge to the ledge.

The sound of a flyer tore through the serenity of the gorge. A slick fighter, all gleaming metal, narrow like a dagger, plummeted from the sky at a dead fall. At the last moment the pilot pulled up. The fighter shot through the gorge at breakneck speed, threading through the maze of arches like a needle, buzzing so close by, the branches of the vala tree shivered. The bride's robe fluttered from the wind. Maud gasped.

Kavaline shook her staff at the retreating craft. "Tellis, you idiot!"

The fighter streaked toward the setting sun.

Seveline leaned back and laughed.

"I changed my mind!" Kavaline growled. "I'm not marrying him!"

"Was that the groom?" Maud asked.

"Yes," Onda said, cracking a smile.

"That was beyond reckless," Maud muttered.

"There was no danger," Seveline waved her hand. "Tellis is an exceptional pilot."

"He is," Onda confirmed. "He has over three thousand hours in a small attack craft."

Seveline chuckled. "We need to get a move on. If he comes back for a second pass, Kavaline might explode. Your turn, Lady Maud."

Maud stepped onto the bridge and took her lantern to the tree.

[10]

When the procession descended the trail, Maud saw two figures waiting for her on the edge of the bridge leading to the upper levels of the castle. Both were blond. The first, huge and made even larger by his armor, leaned against the stone rail that shielded the patio from the drop below. The second, tiny, sat on the said stone rail with her legs crossed.

Maud fought the urge to speed up. Like it or not, she wasn't going anywhere until the women in front of her exited the trail.

"How adorable," Seveline murmured behind her, her voice sickeningly saccharine.

It took all of Maud's control to not spin around and punch the other woman in the mouth. Seveline was a threat and the wasteland taught her to eliminate threats before they had the chance to blossom into full-blown danger. *Spin around, kick Seveline off the trail, spin back, lock an arm around Onda's throat, and choke her until she passed out and she could crush her windpipe...*Maud shook herself. She had bigger fish to fry.

The women in front of her veered left, toward the bridge,

while Maud turned right and headed for the two people waiting for her.

A long brown smudge crossed Helen's face. On closer examination, the smudge appeared to be sticky, decorated with tiny bits of bark, and smelling faintly of pine resin. Maud slowly shifted her gaze to Arland. A series of similar smudges stained his armor.

"Do you want to tell me what happened?"

"No," Arland and Helen said in the same voice. Maud compared the expression on their faces. Identical. *Dear universe, she could almost be his child.*

Something green peeked from between the strands of Arland's blond mane. Maud reached over, plucked it, and pulled out a twig with three leaves still attached. She held the twig between them. Arland stoically refused to notice it.

Right. She let the small branch fall. "Are the others watching us?"

"Mhm." Arland's face remained relaxed.

"I need some information," she murmured. "About the Kozor and Serak."

"What sort of information?" Arland asked, keeping his voice low.

"Rank and power structure."

"Is it urgent?"

"It might be."

Arland offered her his arm. She rested her fingers on his elbow and together they strolled to the bridge, letting the last of the bridal party go before them.

They crossed the bridge leisurely, Helen walking in front of them.

"Where are we going?" Maud asked.

"To see my dear uncle. I so miss him."

Maud hid a smile.

The last robed woman disappeared into the nearest tower. They followed, but where the women went left, they went right. As soon as the bend of the hallway hid them from the view of the departing bridal party, both she and Arland sped up as if they had planned it. Helen ran to catch up. Arland bent down, picked Helen up and carried her, and Helen let him, as if it was a thing he did every day.

They took a lift up three floors, crossed a breezeway, then another, until they came to a solid, almost square tower secured with a blast door solid enough to take a hit from an aerial missile. The door slid open at Arland's approach, and Maud followed him inside, through yet another, blissfully short, hallway to a large room.

If they had shown her twenty different rooms and asked her which was Soren's, she would immediately pick this one. A thick rug, looking as old as the castle, cushioned the floor. The skulls of strange beasts and arcane weapons decorated the gray stone walls between the banners of House Krahr and antique bookcases. The bookcases were made with real wood and filled with an assortment of objects and trophies, chronicling decades of war and dangerous pursuits: odd weapons, maps, rocks, data cores of every shape and size, uncut gems, an otrokar charm belt—Soren either made friends with an otrokar shaman or killed one, and knowing the history of the Holy Anocracy and The Hope-Crushing Horde, the latter was far more likely. Money from a dozen galactic nations, daggers, dried plants, shackles, several Earth books, one of the them probably Sun Tzu's *Art of War*, unless she read the golden Hanzi logograms incorrectly, and a Christmas ornament in the shape of a big blue ball with a sparkling snowflake inside rounded up the bizarre collection. Here and there padded chairs and a couple of sofas offered seating. In the middle of the room a large desk held court, so massive and heavy, Maud doubted Arland could lift it alone. Behind the desk, in an equally solid chair, sat Lord Soren, carefully studying some document on his reader.

The room screamed Veteran Vampire Knight. It was so classic, it hurt.

The door slid shut. Lord Soren raised his head and regarded the three of them with his dark eyes. He scowled at Arland, nodded to Maud, smiled at Helen, and resumed scowling at his nephew.

"What?" Arland asked.

"Did you have to break his arm?"

Arland made a noise deep in his throat that sounded suspiciously like a growl.

Lord Soren sighed. "To what do I owe the pleasure of the visit?"

"I need to understand the structure of House Serak," Maud said.

Lord Soren nodded and flicked his fingers across his desk. A giant screen slid out of the ceiling on Maud's right and presented two pyramids of names connected by lines. The one on the left read Serak, the other Kozor.

"Who are you interested in?" Lord Soren asked.

"Tellis Serak," she said.

Helen crawled onto one of the sofas, curled up on the big blue pillow, and yawned.

"Ah. The dashing groom." Soren flicked his fingers, and Tellis' name near the top of the pyramid, ignited with silver. "His father is the Preceptor; his mother is the Strateg."

"Who is the Marshal?" she asked.

Another name ignited in the column to the left. "Hudra. She is the Marshal in name only."

"Why?" Arland asked.

"She has five decades on me," Soren said. "She was fierce in her day, but time is a bitter enemy, and it always wins."

Interesting. "Are they grooming Tellis to become the Marshal?" Maud asked.

"He is the most obvious choice," Soren said. "His ascension to Marshal would cement the family's hold on the House. They have been preparing him since childhood. Not that he is ready, by any means. Too young, too reckless. Tonight is the perfect example. What sort of fool requests permission for a fighter flight just so he can fan his bride's hair while she is standing on a cliff?"

Of course. If Arland had buzzed his bride in the fighter, he would be dashing. But since this was the scion of Serak, Tellis was reckless. "Correct me if I'm wrong, but Marshal candidates must be well-rounded in their military education?"

"Indeed," Soren said. "They are trained to lead. They spend a certain amount of time with every branch of the House's military to familiarize themselves with the people under their command, but the bulk of their education centers on the effective deployment of these forces and military strategy."

"A Marshal usually has a specialty," Arland added.

"Yes," Soren confirmed. "Typically they concentrate on whatever aspect of warfare presents the greatest threat to the House in the foreseeable future."

Maud turned to Arland. "What's yours?"

"Ground combat," he said.

"Arland was trained to lead us into battle on Nexus," Soren said. "We had anticipated being embroiled in that conflict several times over the next few decades, but thanks to your sister, it's no longer a concern."

It was just as she thought. "How likely is it for the Marshal to have other pursuits?"

Arland's thick blond eyebrows rose. "What do you mean?"

"If you wanted to devote a lot of your time to something not vital to the House, could you do it? For example, if you enjoyed target shooting, could you spend a significant chunk of your time practicing it?"

"Would I have time to devote to hobbies and leisurely pursuits?" Arland frowned, pretending to think. "Let me ponder. Two weeks! I took two weeks off in the last six years, and my uncle came to fetch me as if I were a wayward lamb. Because the great House of Krahr cannot endure without my constant oversight. My job, my hobby, my off time, my 'me' time, all my time consists of taking care of the never-ending sequence of mundane and yet life-threatening tasks generated by the well-honed machine that is the knighthood of House Krahr. I haven't had a moment to myself since I was ten years old."

Lord Soren stood up, took a small blanket off the back of the nearest chair, walked up to Arland, and draped it over his nephew's head like a hood.

Okay. She hadn't encountered that before.

"He is giving me a mourning shroud," Arland said and pulled the blanket off his head. "Like the mourners wear at funerals."

"So you may lament the tragic loss of your youth," Soren said.

Arland draped the blanket over Helen, who'd fallen asleep on the pillow. "To answer your question, my lady, no. A Marshal has no time for any significant pursuits outside of his duties."

"Tellis of Serak has logged over three thousand hours in a small attack craft," Maud said.

Both men fell silent.

Years ago she watched a science fiction epic with its fleets of small attack crafts spinning over enormous destroyers. The reality of space combat vaporized that romantic notion about as fast as an average warship would vaporize the fleet of individual fighters. Even if the fighters somehow managed to make it through the shields, the damage they would inflict would be insignificant. It would be like trying to attack an aircraft carrier with a fleet of row boats. They could spend their arsenal, resupply, spend it again, and still the capital vessel wouldn't be disabled.

"It's my understanding that small attack crafts are used only for one thing," Maud said.

"Boarding," Arland said, his voice a quiet snarl. "Once a ship surrenders, the fighters deliver the boarding crew to take charge of the vessel and secure its cargo."

"Explains the flying acrobatics," Soren said, his face grim.

Maud glanced at Arland.

"After the battle, there is usually a debris field," Arland said. "Chunks that used to be escorts flying in all directions. The pilot needs a maneuverable ship and quick hands."

"Is there any reason House Serak would ever board pirates?" Maud asked. The question sounded ridiculous even as she said it, but it needed to be voiced.

"No," Lord Soren said.

"Pirate ships are glass cannons," Arland said. "They're modified to inflict maximum damage and rapidly scatter when necessary. Most of them are held together by hopes and prayers. The vessels have no value, and the crews have even less. I wouldn't waste time or resources on boarding. I'd simply blow them out of existence."

"So, who is he boarding?" she asked.

Silence reigned. All three of them were thinking the same thing. There were two kinds of vessels in the vicinity of Serak system: pirates and traders. And if Tellis wasn't boarding the pirates…

"This is a hefty accusation," Soren said. "We have no proof. We might even be mistaken."

"I heard it quite clearly," Maud said.

Soren raised his hand. "I don't dispute that. But we don't have all the facts. Perhaps Tellis is indulged and he simply likes to fly around Serak dodging asteroids."

"Three thousand hours?" Arland asked.

"Stranger things have happened."

"There may be a way to obtain confirmation," Maud said. "I would need an untraceable uplink that could reach beyond this system."

Arland walked over to Soren's desk and placed his palm on its surface. A red light rolled over the desk. The screen blinked, and the blood-red symbol of House Krahr appeared on it. Maud blinked. Arland had just taken over the entire communication node. The power of a Marshal on display.

Arland recited a long string of numbers. The screen went black and winked back into existence, a neutral gray.

"What did you do?" she asked.

"Bounced the signal off the lees' cruiser," he said. "They encrypt their communication origins, so they can't be traced. I'm hitching a ride on their encryption system. If the call's recipient tries to trace it, the signal will look like it's bouncing around from random spots in the galaxy."

Wow. "Impressive."

Arland shrugged. "Nuan Cee spies on us every chance he gets. I'm simply balancing the scales."

She was suddenly acutely aware of the data sphere hidden in the inner pocket of her robe.

"Whom would you like to call, my lady?" Arland asked.

"Someone from my other life." Maud walked over and sat on the other of the two couches, away from Helen. "It might be best if you stay silent and remain offscreen."

Soren grimaced but stayed by his desk. Arland dragged his fingers across the desk's controls, turning the screen toward her.

A second screen appeared in the wall, showing a duplicate image, a one-way feed. They would be able to see what she saw but they would be invisible to the other person. Which was just as well. The last thing she wanted was to introduce everyone to each other.

"I need the names of two cargo ships," she said. "One from your House and one from Serak."

The names popped into her harbinger.

Maud pulled up a long sequence. Not a call she thought she would ever make.

From where she sat, she had an excellent view of both vampires and the screen. This would suck.

The screen remained blank.

She waited.

A long minute passed.

The screen flared into life. The bridge of a spaceship came into view. Renouard sprawled in the captain seat. He looked the same—older than Arland by about a decade and a half, long dark hair spilling over his back and shoulders onto jet black armor without a crest, a ragged scar chewing up the left side of his face. The bionic targeting module in his ruined eye focused on her. From this distance, it looked filled with glowing silver dust.

Renouard leered at her. A familiar shiver of alarm gripped her. Ugh.

"The Sariv," he said. If wolves could talk in the dark forests, they would sound like him. "Karhari's gentle flower. So you managed to get out after all."

Arland narrowed his eyes.

"No thanks to you."

"I made you an offer."

Yeah, there wasn't a mother alive who would have taken him

up on it. "You told me my daughter would fetch a good price on the slave market."

"I was joking. Mostly. I heard you bagged yourself a pretty boy Marshal."

The pretty boy Marshal went from annoyed to furious in an instant.

"The word is, you haven't managed to seal the deal yet." Renouard leaned forward. "Does he not do it for you? I could give him some lessons."

Arland's face went stone hard.

"I see the scar on your groin wants a twin," she told him.

He bared his teeth and laughed.

"I have a job," she said.

"I'm all ears."

"I need cargo retrieved from two ships. They'll be passing through the quadrant at the following coordinates." She tagged the section of the quadrant near the Serak system and sent it to him. "Not a large volume, two crates off the first vessel, one off the second, less than three cubic meters and roughly one hundred and twenty kilos of mass."

"Who is hauling this precious cargo?"

"The first ship is the *Silver Talon*."

Renouard checked his screen. "House Krahr. So the rumors are right. You're playing the Marshal. I always knew you had it in you." He winked to make sure she got it.

Ugh. "Can this be done or not?"

"It can be done," he said. "For the right price. I won't do it, but I'll act as an intermediary. What's in the crates?"

"That's not important."

He smiled. "Second vessel?"

"*Valiant Charger*."

"No."

169

He hadn't even bothered to check the screen this time.

"It's a barge," she said. "You can do it with your eyes closed."

"I told you, that's not my territory and my contact won't go after that ship."

"Get someone else."

"There is nobody else. That playing field is a monopoly."

"The deal's off," she said. "I'll find someone else."

She flicked the screen blank, severing the connection, and looked at Arland and Soren.

"House Serak is pirating that quadrant," Arland said. "Independent pirates are too fragmented and too weak to monopolize a star system. Of course, they wouldn't pirate their own traders."

"And Kozor is in on it," his uncle added. "Alone, neither House has sufficient resources to pirate and to hold the other at bay. They are evenly matched. If they were still at war and either Kozor or Serak devoted part of their fleet to piracy, the other would seize the opportunity to attack."

"I wonder how long ago they formed an alliance," Arland said.

"At least ten years," Soren said. "That's when they had their last serious battle. They bad-mouth each other at political gatherings in front of other Houses and they have small skirmishes from time to time, but nothing serious enough to really bloody each other's noses."

"Their combined fleet isn't enough to get close to our nose, let alone bloody it," Arland growled.

"So why House Krahr?" Maud asked. "Wouldn't it make more sense to go for a smaller House?"

"They're pirates," Soren said, "and we are the richest prize."

"If they're going to expose themselves as pirates and allies, they want to reap the greatest benefits," Arland said.

"How?" Maud asked. "There are only two hundred of them."

"I don't know," Arland said. "But I will find out."

"It's a fun game they're playing." Soren bared his sharp fangs. "I welcome the challenge."

———

TEETH. RUNNING. RUNNING SO FAST. BIG UGLY SHAPE BEHIND HER. *Footsteps stomping.*

Dad stepping into her path, his innkeeper robe solid black, his eyes and the broom in his hand glowing with turquoise fire.

Teeth. Right behind her.

Maud opened her eyes. Another nightmare, the same one, muddled and odd, as if it were less a dream and more a memory.

This place is driving me crazy.

She turned to check on Helen.

Her daughter's bed was empty.

Panic stabbed her. Maud bolted upright and saw the open door to the balcony. Sunlight sifted through the pale gauzy curtains, painting bright rectangles on the floor. As they parted, coaxed by the breeze, Maud glimpsed a small figure sitting on the stone rail.

Maud picked up a robe off the chair, pulled it on, and walked onto the balcony. It stretched along the entirety of their quarters, thirty feet at the widest part. On the right, a fountain protruded from the wall, shaped like a flower stalk with five delicate blossoms that reminded her of bell flowers. A man-made stream about a foot wide stretched from the fountain's basin, meandered in gentle curves along the perimeter of the balcony and disappeared into the wall. Both the stream and the fountain had run dry. A couple of benches had been set up, inviting a quiet conversation. The balcony begged for plants. It seemed almost barren without them.

Maud crossed the parched stream and leaned on the stone wall of the balcony next to Helen. The ground yawned at her, far below, hidden by the breezeways, towers, and finally trees. A normal mother would've pulled her daughter off the rail, but then there was nothing normal about either of them.

Helen had found a stick somewhere and was poking the stone wall with it. Something was bothering her. Maud waited. When she was little, she used to sit just like that, sullen and alone. Eventually Mom would find her. Mom never pried. She just waited nearby, until Maud's problems finally poured out of her.

For a while, Maud just stood there, taking a mental catalogue of the aches and pains tugging at her. Her ribcage hurt. It was to be expected. She should've spent yesterday in bed, not hiking up a mountain and dodging vampire knights who tried to throw her off the path. The booster had taxed her body further and exacted its price. She'd slept like a rock for over twelve hours. The sun was well on its way to the zenith. Soon it would be lunchtime.

She had to have missed breakfast. There were probably messages on her harbinger. She would check them, but not yet.

The breeze stirred her robe. Maud straightened her shoulders, feeling the luxurious softness of the spiderweb thin fabric draped over her skin.

Seeing Renouard last night had dredged up the familiar paranoia. It had hummed through her like a low-level ache, a wound that bled just enough to make sure you couldn't ignore it. She fought it for a while, but eventually it won, as it always did, and she'd excused herself, picked up Helen off the couch, and carried her to their room, driven by the urgent need to hole up behind solid doors.

Arland seemed to sense that she needed it and he hadn't offered to take Helen from her. Instead they walked in comfortable silence to her room.

Feeling Helen's weight draped across her chest and shoulder

172

and the familiar scent of her hair had soothed her a little. Helen was safe. They were both safe.

Once at her door, Maud had stepped inside and carefully put Helen on her bed. She put her daughter's daggers next to her, tucked her in, and straightened. She'd left the door open and Arland waited at the threshold.

Last night, she turned and saw him standing there, in the doorway, half hidden in shadows, tall, broad-shouldered, his armor swallowing the light. His hair had fallen over his face, the line of his chiseled jaw hard against that backdrop, and when the light of the two moons caught his eyes, they shone with blue green. He took her breath away. He looked like an ancient warrior, a wandering knight who somehow found his way out of a legend and into her room, except he was real, flesh and blood, and when she looked into his eyes, she saw heat simmering just under the surface.

She had forgotten what it felt like when a man looked at her like that. She wasn't sure Melizard even had, although he must have. Every nerve in her body came to attention. Her breath caught. All she wanted to do, all she could think of in that moment, was closing the distance, reaching up, and kissing him. She wanted to taste him. She wanted to drop her armor, to see him abandon his, and to touch him, body to body, skin to skin. Even now, as she remembered it, her heartbeat sped up.

Helen had fallen asleep. Arland's quarters were only a short hallway away.

One step. One word. That was all it would've taken. A tiny, minute sign, the faintest expression of desire.

She wanted to. Oh, how she wanted to. Instead she stood there like a statue, as if she had been frozen. He told her good night and she just nodded.

He'd left.

The door slid shut.

She let him go. She let him slip away and then she had stripped off her armor, pissed off, and climbed into bed. The booster kept her up for another half hour and she lay on the covers, mad at herself, trying to figure out what happened and failing.

She'd never had problems with intimacy. Melizard wasn't her first, and whatever problems they had in their marriage, sex wasn't one of them. Bodies spoke their own language, in love and in war, a language Maud innately understood. A blind woman could've read Arland last night, and if Maud told herself she didn't know what she wanted, she would be lying.

What's wrong with me?

"Am I a mongrel?"

Helen's question caught her off guard. Maud blinked, trying to switch mental gears.

"It's fine if I am," Helen said. "I just want to know."

"Did someone call you that?"

Helen didn't answer. She didn't have to.

"Did they use that word?"

"They called me *erhissa*."

Maud's hands curled on the stone wall. Helen must've plugged the word into her harbinger, and the translation software spat out the closest equivalent: mongrel. They called her that, those assholes. In that moment, she could've hurt whoever said it and she didn't particularly care if it was an adult or a child.

Maud gripped her anger with her will and bent it until she was sure her voice would sound calm and measured. She had to explain. Hiding the truth wouldn't serve either of them well.

"Touch this." She held out the sleeve of her robe. Helen brushed her fingers over the smooth material.

"The vampires breed a special creature, a type of strange-looking snake. The snakes secrete long threads of silk and spin

174

their nests from them. The vampires collect these nests and make them into fabric. There are two main types, *kahissa*, which make very thin, light fabric like this one, and *ohissa*, which make stronger fabric that's warm and durable. Both are useful. Sometimes *kahissa* and *ohissa* breed and they make a third kind of snake, *erhissa*. *Erhissa* don't make nests. They're poisonous and they bite."

Helen flinched.

"To vampires, *erhissa* have no purpose," Maud said. "But the *erhissa* knows the world doesn't revolve around vampires. It doesn't care what vampires think. It just keeps doing its own thing."

"So, I'm a mongrel."

"On Earth, that's a word people use when they don't know what breed a dog is. You know who you are. You are Helen."

Helen looked down and dragged her stick across the stone, her jaw set.

"Each of us is more than just a human or just a vampire. There is only one you. Some people realize that, and others refuse to see it."

"Why?"

Maud sighed. "Because some people have rigid minds. They like everything to be clearly labeled. They have a box for everyone they meet. A box for vampires, a box for lees, a box for humans. When someone doesn't fit into their boxes, they panic."

"But why?"

"I don't exactly know, my flower. I think it's because they lack confidence. They think they figured out the rules of their world and when something falls outside those rules, it scares them."

"So, I'm scary?"

"To those people? Yes. If the rules they made up don't apply anymore, they don't know how to act, and it makes them feel like their survival is in doubt. Instead of adapting to a new situation and coming up with a new set of rules, some of them will fight to the death trying to keep the world the way it was. Do you remember when we lived in Fort Kur? What was written above the door?"

"Adapt or die," Helen said.

"It's impossible to stop change," Maud said. "It's the nature of life. Those who refuse to adapt will eventually die out. But before they do, they will get nasty. They might even hate you."

Helen looked up. Her eyes flashed. "I'll hate them back!"

"Hate is a very powerful tool. Don't waste it. People who don't like you because of what you are may change their minds when they get to know you. But some people will hate you because of who you are. If they were honest with themselves, they would admit that they don't like you because something about you makes them feel inferior. They might think you're a better fighter, or you're smarter, or prettier, or you're taking up attention they think should be going to them. Those people are truly dangerous. If they get a chance, they will hurt you and those you love. Save your hate for those people. Never hurt them first, but if they hurt you or your friends, you must hurt them back harder. Do you understand?"

Helen nodded.

"Do you want to go back to Aunt Dina's inn?"

Helen's shoulders sagged. "Sometimes."

Maud stepped close to her daughter and hugged her. "We can go anytime. We don't have to stay here."

"But sometimes I like it here," Helen said into her shoulder. "I like Ymanie. Aunt Dina's inn doesn't have Ymanie."

"No, it doesn't."

If they went back to Dina's inn, Helen would have to be home-schooled. Even if Maud could alter her daughter's outlook on life, there was no way to disguise the fangs, or her strength, or the way her eyes caught the light at night. Growing up at the inn was interesting and fun, but it had its lonely moments. All three of them, Klaus, Maud, and Dina, had dealt with it in their own ways. Klaus left the inn every chance he got. He and Michael, his best friend and another innkeeper's son, went on excursions, to Baha-char, to Kio-kio, and every place they could possibly reach from either of the inns. Maud had burrowed into books and spent way too much time practicing martial arts with their father and then various tutors. And Dina went through phases when she tried to pretend to be just human and attempt to go to public school to find friends. Friendships built on lies never lasted.

Maud hugged Helen tighter. There were no perfect options.

She wanted to fix it. If she could wave a magic wand and streamline the galaxy for the sake of her daughter, she would do it in a heartbeat.

"It doesn't have to be here or the inn," she said. "We can try living somewhere else. We can open a shop at Baha-char. We can get a ship and travel the galaxy."

Helen's harbinger chirped. She poked at it with her finger. "Ymanie says there are baby birds on Tower 12."

Maud sighed. In the end, Helen was just five years old. "Would you like to go and see baby birds?"

"Yes!" Helen jumped off the wall onto the balcony.

"Go ahead. No heroics, Helen. No touching the birds, no climbing up dangerous high places, and no—"

"Yes, Mommy!"

Maud closed her mouth and watched her daughter sprint inside and to the door.

Right now, baby birds fixed all of Helen's problems. But she wouldn't be five forever.

What do I do? What's the right thing here?

In this moment, Maud would've given ten years of her life to be able to call her mother.

She went inside. Her harbinger glowed. Great. A high priority message, ten minutes ago. At least it didn't sit there for too long.

Maud touched the screen. Lady Ilemina's face appeared.

"Lady Maud," Arland's mother said. "Do join me for lunch."

[11]

L ady Ilemina had decided to take her lunch in the Small Garden. Small, Maud decided, as she walked down the stone path, was a relative term.

The Small Garden occupied roughly four acres atop a tiny mesa that thrust out of the living rock of the mountain. There were many such mesas on the grounds and the castle simply grew around them, incorporating them into its structure. Some supported towers, others provided space for utility areas or other parks. Her harbinger informed her that there was a larger garden, imaginatively titled the Large Garden, almost twice the size of the small one; also the High Garden, the Low Garden, the Silver Garden, the River Garden...she stopped reading after that.

Vampires loved nature, but where on Earth a garden meant a carefully cultivated space, organized, planned, and often offering a variety of plants from all over the planet, a vampire garden was basically a chunk of preserved wilderness. It was a carefully tended wilderness, pruned, managed, and well loved, but every plant in it was native to the area. The vampire gardeners planted extra flowers and encouraged picturesque shrubs and native herbs, but it would never occur to them to transplant flowers from one continent to another. If they saw a Chinese butterfly bush in a British garden among the native bluebells, they would've pulled it out as a weed.

The exception was the vala tree. The Holy Anocracy brought them to every planet it colonized.

The garden around Maud showcased the best this biozone had to offer. Tall trees with narrow turquoise leaves and pale bark rose on both sides of the path. Their roots lay partially exposed and knotted together as if someone had taken cypress trees and decided to try their hand at macramé. Under the roots delicate lavender and blue flowers bloomed in clusters, with five petals each and a spray of long stamens. The flowers glowed slightly, their leaves shimmering with a nacre sheen. A frilly emerald shrub, its leaves tinged with brighter green, crowded around the roots. Between the trees, where more sun penetrated through the canopy, other flowers bloomed. Tall stems supported narrow blossoms shaped like rose-colored champagne flutes stuffed to the brim with a wealth of white stamens. Translucent flowers, as big as her head, spread their tissue-thin petals, each petal a faint blue marked with a bright red vein running through its middle and meeting in the flower's glowing golden center. Long spikes, shivering with yellow tendrils, dripped glittering pollen on to their neighbors' leaves. The air smelled of spice and sweet perfumes.

Dina would have a field day here.

The path ended in a large circle. A stream ran in a ring, sectioning off the center of the path into a round island. A single vala tree grew in the circle, not one of the massive thousand-year-old giants, but a more recent planting, its trunk barely four feet wide. It spread its dark branches bearing blood-red leaves over the water of the stream and the small stone table with two chairs, one empty and the other occupied by Lady Ilemina in full armor.

Here we go. Maud walked across the stone bridge. The older woman looked at her.

"So, you've made it after all. Excellent."

Maud bowed and took her seat. A plate was already set in front of her. A large platter held an assortment of fried foods, meats, and fruit on small skewers. Finger foods. A tall glass pitcher offered green wine.

Ilemina leaned back in her chair, sitting sideways, one long leg over the other, her left arm resting on the table. Up close, the resemblance between her and Arland was unmistakable. Same hair, same determined look in the blue eyes, same stubborn angle of the jaw. A lunch with a krahr.

"Your face was thoughtful as you walked the path," Ilemina said.

How much to say? "I was thinking about my sister."

"Oh?"

"When the three of us, my brother, my sister, and I, were growing up in our parents' inn, each of us was responsible for a specific area of the inn in addition to our general chores. Dina's was gardens. She would love it here."

"What was yours?"

"Stables."

"I would've never guessed. You have no mount or pet."

"There weren't many opportunities for pets on Karhari."

"And before that?" Ilemina asked.

She had to set some boundaries. "That's in the past."

"My brother told me of your findings." Ilemina picked up the pitcher and filled their glasses.

Maud lifted the glass to her lips and took a small sip of wine. The older woman was watching her carefully.

181

"We've suspected Kozor and Serak of collaborating with the pirates, but to stoop to piracy themselves is base."

"It's not unheard of," Maud pointed out and wished she had bitten her tongue.

"You're right. But the Houses of the Holy Anocracy never prey on each other without a declaration of war." Ilemina took a swallow of her wine. "It's a hefty accusation. I need proof."

"I understand," Maud said.

They sipped their wine. The pressure was mounting inside Maud with every passing second.

"You didn't ask me here to talk about Kozor," Maud said.

"You're not very good with silences," Ilemina said. "Something to work on."

Maud reached out, took a skewer of small yellow berries and slid one into her mouth.

"What are your intentions toward my son?" Ilemina asked.

Maud considered the question. What the hell were her intentions? She settled on honesty. "I don't know."

"What's there to know?" Ilemina fixed her with her stare. "You have feelings for him. You followed him across the Void. He has feelings for you. He brought you here. What's the holdup?"

"It's not that simple."

"But it is. You're both adults. I see the way you look at him when you forget to guard your face."

What?

"He asked you to marry him. You said no. What are you waiting for? What is it you want? Wealth? Power? Marry him and you'll have both."

She thought Maud was a gold digger. A familiar irritation stabbed at her, like a burr under her foot. "I don't need Arland to earn a living. I'm the daughter of innkeepers. I speak dozens of languages, I'm trained for combat, and I'm at home at any trade hub. If I wish, I can return to my sister's inn anytime I want."

She could. Given that Dina's inn had access to Baha-char, the galactic bazaar, if she wanted to take jobs, they would be plentiful, and the pay would be great.

A small triumphant light sparked in Ilemina's eyes. "And yet here you are. Subjecting yourself to the humiliation of being a human in a vampire House and bearing a blank crest."

Maud almost bit her tongue.

"Clearly, a strong bond pulled you across space."

Maud said nothing.

"Do you love my son?" Ilemina asked.

"Yes." The answer came with surprising ease.

Ilemina stared at her. "Then do something about it."

Maud opened her mouth and clicked it shut.

"It's a problem that has a straightforward solution. There is no need to make a *hissot* out of it."

Fantastic. Her might be mother-in-law just compared her feelings to a ball of wriggling venomous snakes.

"It's not just me," Maud said quietly.

Ilemina leaned forward. "Do you honestly think your child would fare better on Earth? She has killed, Maud. She has fangs. She's a vampire child if I ever saw one. We can do so much with her. Humans can do nothing. You will have to hide her for the rest of her life. Can you do that to your daughter?"

"What do you want from me?" Maud growled.

"I want to get to the bottom of this. Stop pretending to be an idiot and tell me what's holding you back, because my son is miserable and I'm tired of watching the two of you dance about each other."

"I've been on the planet for three days!"

183

"Three days is plenty. What is it you want, Maud of the Innkeepers?"

"I want Helen to be happy."

Ilemina sighed and drank her wine. "My parents had no use for me when I was growing up. Their House was a war House. There was always a battle they were fighting or preparing to fight. They didn't notice me until I grew enough to be useful. I exerted myself to my fullest, I excelled, I volunteered for every action, just to get a crumb of their attention. When I met my future husband, I was the Marshal of their House. I talked to Arland's father for less than an hour, and I knew I would walk away with him if he asked. For the very first time in my life, someone saw me as I was."

The words sank deep. She'd shown Arland exactly who she was and he'd admired her for it.

Ilemina smiled. "I did walk away with him and then I fought a war against my parents' House when they tried to punish me for finding happiness. It was the ultimate act of selfishness on their part. So when my daughter was born, I swore that I wouldn't be my mother. I paid attention to my child. I was involved in every aspect of her life. I nurtured her, supported her, encouraged her. I trained her. So did my husband. Some might say that my husband and I neglected our own union for the sake of our daughter and they wouldn't be wrong."

Ilemina paused, tracing the rim of her glass with her finger. "When my daughter was twenty-two years old, she met a knight and fell in love. He was everything I could ever wish for in a son-in-law. My heart broke anyway, but I didn't want to stand in her way. She married him. She lives halfway across the galaxy and visits once every year or two. Arland was ten years old when she left. He barely knows her. I have grandchildren I almost never see."

Maud had no idea what to say, so she stayed silent.

"Children leave," Ilemina told her. "It is the greatest tragedy of motherhood that if you have done everything right, if you have raised them in confidence and independence, they will pick up and leave you. It is as it's meant to be. One day Helen will leave."

Anxiety pierced Maud. She swallowed, trying to keep it under wraps.

"If you try to hold and restrain her, you'll be committing an irreparable sin. We shouldn't hobble our young. We do not cut their teeth. One day it will be just you, Maud."

"I understand," Maud murmured. Thinking about it hurt.

"Where do you see yourself when that day comes?" Ilemina asked.

She knew where she wanted to be but getting there was so complicated.

"So I'll ask again. What is it you're afraid of? Are you trying to out-vampire us? It's futile. Nothing you do will change the circumstances of your birth, and if my son had wanted a vampire, he has a veritable crowd of women with ancient bloodlines falling all over themselves to love him. Are you ashamed of being a human? Do you hate your species?"

Maud raised her head. "I have no desire to pretend I'm a vampire."

"Then what is it?" Ilemina raised her voice.

Something inside Maud snapped like a thin glass rod breaking.

"House Ervan threw me away. They threw my daughter away like we were old rags. We had no value to them outside of my husband. All the time we lived among them, all the things I'd done in service of the House, all the friendships I forged, none of it mattered. They didn't fight to keep us. They wanted to be rid of us."

The words kept pouring out of some secret place she'd hidden them and no matter how hard she tried, she couldn't stop them. "I lived a lie. I can't take that chance again. I won't. I don't want Arland to marry an outsider who is barely tolerated. I want him to marry someone who is valued by his House. Someone who is indispensable. I want that marriage to be seen as a boon for House Krahr. I don't trust any of you except Arland. I want to ensure that you will never turn on me. That my daughter will have a place here not because of your son, but because of me and eventually because of herself."

She'd said too much. Where did it even come from? She'd had no idea that's what she wanted until the words came out of her.

Silence lay between them. A light breeze stirred the vala tree.

Ilemina arched her eyebrows and took a sip of her wine. "Now this? This I understand."

———

MAUD MARCHED ACROSS THE BRIDGE, FUMING. SHE'D LET ILEMINA get under her skin. It was a strategic error. Understanding your opponent was the most important advantage one could have in a conflict. Numbers, strengths, and luck mattered, but if you knew how your opponent thought, you could predict her strategy and prepare.

She'd given Arland's mother enough ammunition to manipulate her. Stupid. So stupid.

What the hell was she thinking, baring her soul to a damn vampire?

The memory of kneeling before Stangiva and begging for Helen's life stabbed her, hot and sharp. If only she could get her hands on that bitch, she would've snapped her former mother-in-law's neck. And to think she spent years trying to mold herself into a perfect vampire wife for the sake of Melizard, and his mother, and their whole damn House. She twisted herself into a pretzel to become exceptional in every way, all so she could be paraded before the visitors with an unspoken context of "Look what an exemplary House we are. We have taken a human and shaped her into a vampire. Listen to her recite the ancient sagas. Watch her perform for your amusement."

And she, she was the idiot who had willingly put on that bridle and dragged the cart forward. For what? For love?

She laughed at herself, and the sound came out sharp and brittle.

Love. How could she have been so young and stupid?

Ugh. Rage coursed through her. Maud wanted desperately to punch something.

A sharp chittering sound made her turn. She'd come to a T-shaped junction. On her right, another bridge branched from the first at a perfect right angle. The end of the bridge led onto another garden plateau. Trees and shrubs obscured her view, but Maud was absolutely sure of what she just heard. The high-pitched, short bark of a lees backed into a corner.

She turned and jogged down the bridge into the garden. Nuan Cee's Clan were invited guests of the Krahr. No harm could come to them on Krahr's watch.

Voices carried from up ahead. She couldn't quite make them out, but she heard the intonation well enough: male, vampire, arrogant. She rounded the bend. In front of her a straight stretch of the path led to a round plaza with a small fountain in the center. In the plaza, closest to the entrance from the path, stood a small, blue-furred lees and a tachi. The lees was on her toes, ready to bolt. The tachi had gone so gray, it looked desaturated. Across from them four male vampires stood. Two leaned forward slightly, the third one stroked the hilt of his blood hammer, and the fourth crossed his arms on his chest, clearly the leader. She'd been studying the files on the wedding guests, and she had no trouble recognizing him. Lord Suykon, the groom's brother. Big, red-haired, and aggressive.

They were about to get violent. The tachi would retaliate and relations between the tachi and House Krahr would drown in blood. She had no authority to stop it. She was just another guest. If she were attacked, the tachi would jump in. She was sure of it. She'd served food to their queen and was looked on with favor. The tachi would be honor-bound to assist her against a mutual threat.

She had to avoid violence and delay. It would be near impossible. She was a human, and in the vampire's eyes, she belonged to Arland but had no status. If anything, her presence would only provoke.

Maud tapped her crest. The thin stalk of a communicator slid from her armor and split in two. One tendril reached into her ear, the other to her mouth. The crest pulsed with white light, letting her know the camera was activated.

"Arland?"

There was a slight pause, then he answered. *"Here."*

"Tap into my feed."

There was another tiny pause. Suykon said something. The vampire next to him laughed. Maud picked up speed.

The lees screeched, the sharpness in her voice making her sound like a pissed off squirrel.

Arland's crisp voice spoke into her ear piece. *"Backup is on the way."*

Her harbinger chimed, announcing an incoming message. Maud tapped it. A contract that made her an official retainer of House Krahr. She scrolled, spot searching for the right words.

... military service, to be performed as is deemed necessary by the Marshal...

He'd just hired her, giving her the same authority as any knight of the House.

"Accept," she said.

Dizziness punched her as her updated crest interfaced with the armor. It only took a moment. Arland must've preloaded the House interface onto the crest before he'd given it to her and now it was activated.

Her crest flashed with red. A third tendril sprouted from the stalk, projecting a screen over her left eye. On it the icon of House Krahr glowed dimly in the far corner. Next to it, another icon, a tiny banner, waited.

This man. For this man, she would put up with Ilemina. He was worth it.

Maud marched into the clearing. Her eyepiece tagged the lees, displaying her name above her head in pale letters. Nuan Tooki. The tachi was Ke'Lek.

"Behold, a human comes!" a dark-haired vampire declared. Her eyepiece tagged him with a name. Lord Kurr. Now that she was a retainer, the internal files were at her fingertips.

Nuan Tooki ducked behind her, stuck her paw-hands into the pockets of her apron, and came out with a handful of darts in her left hand and a small dagger in her right. Monomolecular edge on both, likely poisoned.

Ke'Lek's color darkened slightly, but only a shade, a barely perceptible green.

Suykon smiled.

Maud moved in front of the tachi, looked at the banner icon and deliberately blinked to activate it.

The crest tolled like a bell. A bright red spark blinked on her left shoulder, projecting a holographic image of the banner of House Krahr. She gripped her blood sword and it whined in her hand as red light dashed through it, priming the weapon.

The banner glowed slightly brighter.

"And what have we here?" Suykon asked. "Adorable, is she not?"

Anything she said would give them an opportunity to claim she provoked them. Any word would be presented as an insult and used as a pretext for violence. She simply said nothing.

"Are you mute, human?"

Maud waited.

Suykon's eyes narrowed. "Lord Kurr."

"Yes?" the dark-haired knight asked.

"I think our lady is in distress. Look at her being menaced by those two outsiders. You should go and rescue her."

The tachi moved forward.

Maud activated the banner again. Her crest projected a red line onto the ground and tossed the prewritten warning onto her eyepiece. She read it. "You are guests of House Krahr in the presence of a knight of House Krahr. Any violence against other guests of House Krahr will be met with immediate retribution. Cross this line and die."

Ke'Lek clicked his mouth in disappointment and stepped back. The line cut both ways.

Lord Kurr chuckled.

Her eyepiece scanned him, highlighting a long, slightly glossy streak on the left side of his armor. A recent patch job, and not a very good one. Patching armor was as much of an art as science, and it took a light touch. He'd been heavy-handed with the tools. He should've let someone who knew what they were doing repair it, but armor maintenance was a point of pride. It was a small target, less than a quarter of an inch wide. She would've missed it without the eyepiece.

"This is the only warning you will receive."

"My fair maiden," Kurr roared, pulling out a massive blood sword. "I shall rescue you."

I can't wait.

Kurr charged.

The moment his foot crossed the line, she dropped to one knee. His blade slid over her shoulder, screeching against her armor. She thrust her sword into the patch and twisted. The armor cracked with an audible snap. The nanothreads contracted, ripping themselves apart.

She freed her blade, pushed to her feet, and hammered a kick into Kurr's exposed side. The impact knocked him back over the line. He stumbled and doubled over, clutching at his side. Blood dripped between his fingers. Half of his breastplate hung down, crawling and shifting as the individual nanothreads attempted to reconnect.

For a moment everyone forgot to posture and just stared. She had pried Kurr out of his armor. The humiliation was absolute.

The prompt flashed on her eyepiece again.

"You are guests of House Krahr in the presence of a knight of House Krahr. Any violence against other guests of House Krahr will be met with immediate retribution. Cross this line and die."

Kurr gripped his sword. "I'll kill that bitch."

"Kurr!" Suykon barked.

Kurr charged.

A shadow fell from the sky. She barely had a chance to shy back. An enormous male vampire landed in front of her in full combat armor, his broad back blocking her view. His gray hair was cut human short.

The new vampire swung his blood hammer. It ripped the air with a hair-raising whine and connected.

Maud lunged to the side, trying to see.

Kurr was twenty feet away, flat on his ass, trying to breathe.

The other two vampires knelt by him, struggling to activate his crest. Only Suykon remained standing.

The new vampire opened his mouth, displaying his fangs, and bent his head forward, exhaling menace, like a bull ready to charge. He was a giant even by vampire standards. Her eyepiece tagged him, identifying his name.

Maud blinked.

"Our apologies, Lord Consort," Suykon said. "We meant no harm. We clearly misinterpreted the situation."

Lord Otubar unhinged his jaws and said in a deep voice. "Leave."

The two knights picked Kurr up like a child and the four of them took off down the path.

Lord Otubar turned to the lees and the tachi. "What were the two of you doing here without an escort?"

Nuan Tooki ducked her head, fluffing her tail, and clasped her little paw-hands together, looking almost terminally adorable. "Please forgive us, Lord Consort. It's all my fault. I was lost. This brave tachi came to my rescue and then these mean vampires came and menaced us. You are not like them. You are a good vampire. I was so frightened and helpless, and you have saved us. I am so sorry."

"Go back to your quarters."

"Thank you."

The lees scampered off. Ke'Lek looked at them, hesitated for a moment, and followed the lees down the path.

"Dismissed," Lord Otubar said.

Her legs carried Maud down the path before her brain had time to process what happened.

"My lady," Otubar called to her back.

She stopped and pivoted to face him. "Lord Consort?"

"Good strike," he said.

[12]

Maud sat on the barren balcony. Her quarters projected a screen in front of her and she scrolled through the files of the wedding party, trying to make some sense of it. Her new status gave her access to more detailed dossiers, and she was speed-reading them while she could. The wealth of additional information made her brain buzz. She was in a rotten mood.

Wind stirred her hair. Maud glanced up, and her gaze lingered on the distant mesas. She liked being high up, but the breathtaking view failed to pull her out of her unease. The Kozor and Serak were planning something, but what? They had only two hundred fighters, while the Krahr had thousands.

She'd tried to find Arland after her encounter with the overly enthusiastic best man and his yipping escort, but he wasn't anywhere she could go. She sent a message to his harbinger, but he hadn't responded.

She'd been spoiled. For the last few weeks, he'd been at her beck and call. She only had to say his name and there he was, ready to help. Now she wanted to talk to him, and he was out of reach.

He is a Marshal. I've been taking his availability for granted.

Maud missed him. It ate at her.

Maybe he got bored.

It was a definite possibility. She could just be a brief infatuation. He rescued her, got to be the hero, and it was exciting with the inn under siege, and now, regular life returned and the novelty faded. Maybe she was a travel romance.

The recording of Arland facing his mother replayed in her head. No. He loved her.

The only way to have constant access to Arland was to marry him. That's what marriage was, at the core—the exclusive right to spend as much time with someone you loved as they were willing to give.

Her screen chimed, announcing someone at the front door. Her heart beat faster. She touched the screen and there he was. She shot out of the chair as if she'd found a scorpion in it and dashed through the room to the door. She took a deep breath to steady herself.

"Open."

The door slid aside. Arland looked at her. To the casual observer, he would have looked fine, but she'd spent too much time studying his face. She saw distance in his eyes and it chilled her. Something had happened. She frantically cycled through the possibilities. Had she embarrassed the House? Did she somehow hurt his feelings? Did he read her message and it pissed him off?

"My mother requests your presence at the picnic in the groom's honor, my lady."

"I'm honored, my lord. Weapons?"

"Not permitted."

"Allow me a moment to check on my daughter."

"No need. Lady Helen and the rest of the children have been taken to the lakeshore."

And Lady Helen had failed to check in with her. They would have to have a talk tonight.

He stepped aside, letting her pass. They walked side by side.

"Lord Kurr?" she asked.

"He lives. Barely."

"I apologize if I caused any offense."

"You didn't. Your conduct was exemplary. You exhibited remarkable self-control, my lady. House Krahr is fortunate to have the benefit of your service."

Nope, he hadn't read her message.

They entered a long breezeway leading to a tower which, in turn, allowed passage to another small mesa rising on their left. According to her harbinger, the picnic was being held there. Even without the harbinger, the clumps of vampires spread across the green lawn would've been a dead giveaway. Once they reached the mesa, they would be in public and she'd have to kiss any chance at a private conversation goodbye. She had to clear this up now.

"Is something the matter, my lord?"

"Everything is well," he said.

Okay, that was all she was willing to tolerate. "Then why are you impersonating an icicle?"

He glared at her. She matched his stare. She was reasonably sure they were being watched from the mesa, but she didn't care.

The look in his eyes got to her and she slipped into English despite herself. "Did a cat get your tongue?"

His face iced over. "No. Lions didn't injure my mouth. You and I have a complex relationship, my lady. These complications notwithstanding, in public you must conduct yourself in accordance with your place in the chain of command."

"Are you pulling rank?"

"Yes."

She laughed and walked off. They were almost to the tower.

"My lady." Unmistakable command suffused his voice.

"You should read your messages, Lord Marshal."

She made it another three steps before he snarled, "Maud!"

Maud pivoted on her foot. "Is something the matter?"

He bore down on her. "You resigned. Why?"

"What do you mean, why?" It was painfully obvious. Maybe he really did have second thoughts.

"You should have at least given me the courtesy of telling me face to face," his voice was quiet and icy.

"I tried but you were busy. The message was my only option."

"When?" he asked, his eyes dark.

"I don't follow."

They definitely had an audience now. Their voices didn't carry that far, but just about everyone on the lawn was looking their way.

He forced the words out. "When are you leaving?"

It stabbed at her. "Do you want me to leave?"

"Do you think this is funny? Because I fail to see the humor. I've given you a place in House Krahr. You're throwing it in my face. That can mean only one thing. You're leaving."

He thought that she resigned because she wanted to quit him and his House. He'd honored her with trust and a position within the House and he thought she was throwing it back in his face.

Oh, you idiot.

Arland kept going. "You almost married Betin Cagnat on Karhari. You were in negotiations, with the contracts being drawn, and you haven't even entertained my proposal."

I wonder when he learned that tidbit.

"I told you that I'm content to await your decision. But if you have feelings for another from your past, it is only fair that you tell me."

Oh. He thought she was having second thoughts because last night she'd talked to Renouard. Maud almost laughed.

"Being a knight of Krahr would have allowed you time to make your decision. It was the best option available under the circumstances."

"Is that why you offered it to me?" she asked, keeping her voice mild.

"No. I offered it to you because you were in a dangerous situation without any authority to intervene. But after you accepted it, it felt like the best solution."

He was trying to keep her close any way he could. He must've been worried she would leave and offering her an in-House position was his way to ensure she stayed.

Behind Arland, Knight Ruin stepped out of the doors, a tablet in his hands. He saw Arland and broke into a run, heading toward them.

"Now you're leaving," Arland ground out. "I just want to know why. What is it about me you find lacking? What is it?"

"Are you done?" she asked.

"Lord Arland!" Knight Ruin called out. "I have an urgent message from Lord Soren."

"I deserve an answer. Surely, you can give me that much."

"The Writ of Command, Part Seven."

He frowned. "Prohibition of fraternization between knights separated by more than three ranks? What does that have to do with anything?"

She stepped closer to him, raised her hand, and gently popped him on the forehead.

The young knight reached them and thrust a tablet at Arland.

Maud turned around and walked away.

"Maud, wait!"

The change in his tone told her he finally got it.

She sped up. He couldn't outright run after her. He would look like an idiot to the audience below.

"Get this infernal tablet out of my face! Maud, wait!"

The moment she entered the tower, she sprinted down the stairs. As soon as he untangled himself from Knight Ruin, he would chase her to inquire about the exact nature of fraternization she had in mind, and she didn't want to have this conversation in the tower. She wanted to have it in her quarters or his, after they had been swept clear of Nuan Cee's bugs. She needed to get down to that lawn as fast as she could.

———

MAUD EMERGED FROM THE TOWER INTO THE SUNSHINE. DIRECTLY in front of her, a stone path led to a wide-open lawn ringed by trees. She strode forward to where stone benches and small tables had been placed to accommodate small groups, offering a clear view of the lawn. Many of the benches were occupied; vampires in full armor lounged, snacked on finger foods presented on large platters, and drank refreshments. The air smelled of charred meat, fresh bread, and honey. A banner marked each sitting area, announcing the allegiance of its occupants. Most of the seats directly in front of her, spread out in a crescent, were taken by House Krahr, the line of black and red pennants familiar and almost welcoming. House Kozor curved to the right, its colors red and green. House Serak lined the left side. Their banners, blue and yellow, waved in the breeze.

On the lawn, two teams, one red and black, the other comprised of both Kozor and Serak, clashed with practice weapons. Krim, Maud realized, the Holy Anocracy's favorite sport. One team had drawn a circle roughly fifty feet wide. In the middle of the circle a fifteen-foot pillar about eighteen inches across supported a white flag. The defenders positioned themselves around the pillar, guarding it, while the attackers tried to break through and grab the flag. It wasn't a complicated game, but what it lacked in complexity, it more than made up for in sheer brutality. This time, Krahr defended. Everyone wore full armor, carried practice weapons, and sported headbands equipped with sensors. The headbands analyzed input from the armor and flashed when the wearer sustained enough damage to die.

"Lady Maud!" a familiar voice called.

Well, look at that. She managed not to cringe. "My Lady Ilemina?"

The Preceptor of House Krahr sat at a table to her right. The Lord Consort loomed in the chair next to her like an immovable mountain of vampire knighthood.

"Join us," Lady Ilemina said. It didn't sound like a request.

Great, just what she wanted, to be on display next to her possible future mother-in-law.

Behind her the door of the tower slid open and Arland stepped onto the path.

On second thought, joining Lady Ilemina was an excellent idea. Maud walked over and took a seat on Ilemina's left. Out of the corner of her eye, she saw Arland stalking down the path toward them.

Yes, yes. Stalk all you want. There was no way he would be discussing any kind of fraternization in front of his mother and stepfather. She'd outmaneuvered him. For some odd reason, it made her feel ridiculously accomplished.

On the lawn, House Krahr, led by Karat, formed a dense ring of bodies around the pillar. Houses Kozor and Serak split their forces, preparing to attack from opposite sides. A familiar blond mane caught Maud's eye on Kozor's side. Seveline was leading their assault.

"They're using the Pincher attack," Ilemina said.

"Seems badly thought out," Lord Otubar said. "There aren't enough of them to effectively break through, and she knows they're coming. Too crude."

The maneuver seemed painfully blatant. Karat was shifting her forces to compensate, but she was doing it slowly, waiting for the other shoe to drop.

Arland strode over. The only open seat was next to Otubar. Arland picked it up, moved it next to her, and sat down.

"Opinion?" Ilemina asked him.

He studied the field. "Nothing in either Kozor's or Serak's tactics up until now indicates a preference for direct assault."

"It's a feint," Otubar said.

"The question is, where are they going with this?" Ilemina murmured. "Did you finish the comparative analysis?"

Arland grimaced. "There was not enough data for a definitive conclusion. What data we have from the known pirate assaults is consistent with the known tactical patterns of our cherished guests. Similarity isn't proof, however."

"What about the lees' data?" Otubar asked.

"Nuan Cee is stalling," Arland said.

"Perhaps something can be done to persuade him to share." Lady Ilemina glanced at Maud.

They were speaking in front of her as if she was already part of the House, and more, they were asking for her advice. She wasn't sure if she should be flattered or upset that everyone at the table viewed her joining House Krahr as a foregone conclusion.

"Give me something to trade," she said. "It is a common misconception that the lees love money above all else. That's not exactly true. They love a bargain; they love getting a good deal. Getting more for less is the foundation of their society. Let me take something to them they will find irresistible."

"I find haggling distasteful." Ilemina frowned. "Mostly because I'm terrible at it. I prefer a fair price, which I can pay without any negotiations."

"And they think you weaker for it." Maud shrugged.

When you bargained with a lees, the first price they quoted you was always outrageous. It was a test and you had three options: first, you could pay the price and be known as a fool by their great-great grandchildren; second, you could walk away and be judged too rigid to become a business partner or an ally; and third, you could bargain. Only the third option brought respect.

On the lawn, House Serak engaged Karat's left flank. She'd shifted her formation into a rough oval ring, with two ends facing Serak and Kozor. Karat stood in the middle by the pillar, her practice blade ready in her hand.

The Serak's assault hammered the Krahr, but the left flank held. On the right, nearly twenty-five yards away, the Kozor formed a wedge with Seveline as the tip of the spear. The two vampire knights directly behind her looked like they had jumped out of a production of an ancient saga, each of them almost as large as Otubar.

The wedge charged. The knights thundered forward, picking up speed, like a herd of enraged rhinos.

"Hold!" Karat's voice rang out. The defenders braced themselves, doing their best impersonation of an immovable object about to meet an unstoppable force.

Now the plan made more sense. If it wasn't for Serak, Karat's forces could scatter, leaving only a few defenders in the middle to slow the charge as it penetrated the circle while the majority of her knights cut at the mass of invaders from the sides. Maud had seen that maneuver before. Done correctly, it absorbed the kinetic energy of the charge like a sponge. But with Serak at her back,

Karat had no opportunity to maneuver. The steady pressure at her back left her only one choice—to hold.

The Kozor were almost on them. Maud held her breath, bracing herself as if she were in the line of defenders.

The wedge parted slightly, Seveline slipping through the ranks to the back. The final row of the wedge swept her off her feet and up. Seveline dashed across the armored shoulders and backs of Kozor knights and leaped. For a moment she flew, her lean form silhouetted against the blue sky, sunlight gleaming from her armor, then she landed in the circle. Karat shied to the right, avoiding getting knocked down by a hair.

Seveline struck at her, spinning fast like a dervish. Karat blocked, backing up, straight into the back of her own armored line. Seveline was a whirlwind. Her strikes pierced Karat's defense in a flurry, so fast Maud could barely follow. *Damn.* Karat blocked and dodged but she had nowhere to go. Red streaks slashed her armor, the blows of Seveline's practice sword leaving their mark.

Damn it.

Karat's headpiece flashed white. Seveline had scored a mortal wound. Karat swore and threw her sword to the ground. Seveline laughed and fell onto the Krahr's defensive line.

"Interesting," Otubar said, watching Seveline massacre the knights from the rear.

"What could we offer the lees?" Ilemina sipped blue wine from her glass, her tone relaxed.

"They want the trade station," Maud said.

Ilemina smiled. "Only that?"

"The idea of a trade station has some merit," Arland said, his gaze fixed on the crumbling Krahr line.

Otubar made a low rumbling noise that may have been agreement or disdain. Maud didn't know the Lord Consort well enough to tell.

Ilemina's eyebrows rose. "You too?"

Otubar gave a barely perceptible shrug.

"We can take the fleet to the Serak system, and I can reduce their fleets to space garbage," Arland said. "We have military superiority in both numbers and the caliber of our ships. However, we can't hold the system indefinitely. Lady Maud is a student of vampire history. Tell us, my lady, what do we know about occupying the territory of other houses?"

Thank you for that bus that just rolled over me after you threw me under it. Felt lovely.

"Nobody in the history of the Holy Anocracy has ever won a partisan war. Anytime an occupation of another House was attempted, it either failed or the weaker House ceased to exist."

"If you count both Serak and Kozor, there are almost a million beings between the two planets," Arland said. "We cannot occupy their territory, so the only recourse would be annihilation."

Arland's destroyer flashed before Maud's eyes. Stationary targets, like planets and defensive installations on moons, had no chance against space fleets. They followed a fixed orbit and they couldn't dodge. Launching a kinetic projectile or a barrage of missiles when the computers could calculate the precise position of your target was child's play. House Krahr could simply sit back and bombard the two planets until nothing alive remained on the surface. An icy needle pierced her spine. They were sitting here discussing the potential death of a million beings. It wasn't an abstract discussion on the morality of it; it wasn't hypothetical. They really could do it. Whatever was said here in the next few minutes would determine if the next generation of Kozor and Serak children would ever grow up.

"Some would see it as the only option," Ilemina said.

"We are not a House that would stoop to genocide against our own kind," Arland said.

Ilemina smiled.

Seveline was climbing the pillar.

"Lady Maud?" Ilemina asked. "Do you have any thoughts?"

Maud sipped her wine. Her throat had suddenly gone dry. "It seems to me that since Serak and Kozor found themselves resorting to plundering trade vessels, they are short on funds."

"They are stuck in a remote system with no means to expand their military," Otubar said.

Seveline waved the flag from the pillar's top.

"So, there is very little gain to be had from wiping them out," Maud said. "Financially, it's a loss. It would cost a fortune in fuel and munitions. From a military standpoint, it's also a loss. House Krahr would gain no territory, resources, or strategic advantage. If one considers it a matter of honor, there is little of it in a victory over an opponent who never had a chance. It would do nothing to enhance the already stellar reputation of House Krahr."

Ilemina chuckled into her wine. "Such flattery, Lady Maud. They have raided our ships. Satisfaction must be achieved."

"And I'm sure Lord Arland would crush them so completely that by the time he finished, the only space-worthy vessels in the system would be escape pods." Maud drank more wine. "It seems to me that once the pirating adventures of our esteemed guests become public knowledge, the trade would shift. The two systems will wither and rot without their main source of income. The trade will have to go somewhere."

"It will go to Sarenbar," Arland said. "Or it can come here. Bringing it here via a trade station would allow us to control the terms of engagement and give us a unique opportunity to bypass foreign trade ports by receiving shipments from other species. Placing the lees in a key role will ensure the station's profitability."

"And using the tachi would ensure its technological superiority," Maud added.

"You would allow strangers into our secure space." Ilemina's face hardened.

Arland faced her. "Eventually we will have to interact with the rest of the galaxy by means other than invasion and war. We can't kill everyone, Mother."

Otubar cleared his throat. "We have a visitor."

Tellis, the groom, was walking toward the table.

"A bit of swagger in his step," Ilemina observed. "Do something about it, won't you, dear?"

"Yes," Otubar and Arland said in unison.

Maud braced herself.

———

TELLIS STOPPED ABOUT EIGHTEEN INCHES TOO CLOSE.

When she was a child, one of the first lessons her father had given her concerned the importance of tradition to vampires. An aggressive and predatory species, vampires fought at the slightest provocation and their interactions had to be strictly regimented. All of the rules and ceremony ensured that nobody would be casually offended. A vampire would have to actively ignore customs to cause offense, and when they did so, it was always deliberate.

An appropriate distance between two potential enemies was about five feet, far enough for both to draw weapons if necessary. Allies stood a little closer, three and a half feet, just out of arm's length. Friends stood within touching distance, and family members often allowed for only a few inches of personal space.

Tellis had come close enough to brush against the table, which put him within three and a half feet of Ilemina and Otubar but only two feet away from Maud. He could reach out and touch her, and he was smiling. When vampires bared their teeth like that, it was done for one reason only: to impress. It was the grin of an apex predator demonstrating the full splendor of his fangs.

It was also an obvious insult whichever way you spun it. Either he didn't consider her belonging to House Krahr and, therefore, not worthy of basic courtesies, or he was deliberately being overly familiar with another's fiancée. A human equivalent would be to put his arm around a woman celebrating her engagement to another man and smirk while doing it. Tellis couldn't have been more obvious about it if he'd had leered and asked her if she was free tonight.

Out of the corner of her eye, Maud could see Arland's face. His expression was thoroughly relaxed. In fact, she had never seen him so tranquil. He looked a hair away from a dreamy smile.

Oh crap.

"Excellent game," Tellis said, "Our deepest compliments."

Lord Otubar smiled. It was enough to give human children nightmares. "Interesting tactics."

"Yes," Lady Ilemina said. "We quite enjoyed this informative glimpse into the minds of House Kozor and House Serak. Truly, the cooperation between your two Houses is praiseworthy. Don't you think so, Arland?"

"An example to us all," Arland said.

Tellis' eyebrows rose slightly. He wasn't an idiot, and he had just realized they had overplayed their hand, revealing more than they intended. He had two options now: he could beat a graceful retreat, or he could barrel on ahead. Given that he was a male vampire knight, he valiantly chose the second and threw himself into the assault with all the subtlety of a battering ram.

"Speaking of examples, we were all in awe of Lord Arland's escapades on Karhari."

Maud drank her wine, killing a wince before it started.

Tellis was still smiling. "How many attackers did you take on? Was it four or five? I can't remember."

"I was a little busy and I didn't have time to make them count off. In a real battle, things get a little hectic." Arland was still floating on his own private cloud of Zen.

"Would you care to give us a demonstration, Lord Marshal? I'm afraid the game didn't quite last as long as we would've liked. We still need a bit of exercise. If you don't mind, that is."

He did not just say that. Apparently, House Krahr was so weak that Tellis hadn't broken a sweat.

Arland looked bored. "I haven't finished my wine. If I take the time to engage in a demonstration, it will be warm by the time I return."

Tellis blinked. Maud hid a smile. *Yes, he did just tell you that his wine getting warm was more important than you.* Tellis would have to abandon all pretense of propriety to goad Arland into action.

"Of course, if the Lord Marshal is too fatigued from chasing his unwilling human bride to redeem the honor of his House, I understand completely. We have all enjoyed your noble pursuit, however, I do believe the lady finds you wanting." Tellis looked at Maud and smiled.

Yes, that would do it.

Arland sighed and rose to his feet, looking put upon, as if someone had asked him to take out the trash in the middle of a good movie.

"I'll have your wine refreshed, dear," Ilemina said. "Go and have some fun."

Arland turned to Tellis. "If you insist. Full armor, primed weapons, first down?"

Tellis' grin didn't die all the way, but it definitely faltered. Under normal circumstances, vampire weapons had the same limitations as Earth weapons. They were made of an advanced alloy that provided greater durability, and the vampire metal-smiths had developed weapon making into an art, but if one tried to chop a large tree down with a vampire sword, the sword would break before the tree did. Priming a weapon flooded it with rathan rhun, the shining blood. Not even her father knew exactly what rathan rhun was. It was red and glowing and it flowed through the weapon, emitting a telltale whine, spreading through the metal just like its name suggested it would. Once you heard a blood weapon being primed, you never forgot it. A blood mace wielded by a strong vampire knight would knock down a telephone pole.

Blood weapons were not used for practice. Arland had just suggested a fight under battle conditions, to the point where combatants were out when they were unable to continue.

"Primed weapons?' Tellis asked.

"You are the one who wanted exercise." Arland looked at Tellis. "Was my lord under the impression that the fight at the Road Lodge was an exhibition bout? You asked for an accurate demonstration. I have honored your request."

Tellis opened his mouth and clicked it shut.

Arland raised his head and bellowed, "Bring our guests their weapons!"

[13]

This was stupid, Maud decided. In fact, this was one of the dumbest things she had seen Arland do, and he was, by no means, a stupid man.

Arland eyed the two Serak knights that stepped forward to join Tellis. Both held themselves with the seasoned confidence of veterans. They had fought before, they had won, and they didn't find Arland's presence or his reputation especially intimidating. In a word, they seemed ready, and Maud didn't like it one bit.

Arland raised his voice. "Are these the only brave knights House Serak has to offer?"

What is he doing?

He looked around, spreading his arms. "Is there no one else?"

Two more knights stood up from their tables on House Kozor's side, Onda and a grizzled male knight who looked like he would knock a charging bull out with one punch. *Great, just great.*

"We are up to five," Arland said. "Fantastic."

Maud grabbed her glass and drank.

"The Road Lodge offered me seven, but if five brave souls is the best your two mighty Houses can scrounge, I'll make do."

What? The wine went down the wrong way, and she choked.

Four more knights stood up, two from Serak, two from Kozor.

"That's more like it," Arland declared.

Nine opponents. He'd gone insane. That was the only explanation.

The weapon racks were being brought onto the lawn. The knights armed themselves. The sharp whine of blood weapons being primed sliced the quiet. Arland hefted his mace. Their stares crossed and he grinned at her.

"He's gone mad," she muttered.

"Nexus," Otubar said.

She glanced at him. "I don't follow, my Lord."

"We have advanced quite far from the days when this castle was built," Ilemina said. "These days, the conflicts between Houses are decided in space. Ground battles are precious few. I doubt either Kozor or Serak has ever truly fought in one."

"Nexus permits no air battles," Otubar said. "On Nexus, ground is fought for and won inch by inch, watered with blood and fertilized with corpses."

"I knew I would have to send my son to Nexus twenty years ago." Ilemina smiled. "His father and I did everything we could to make sure he came back alive. This is what he does best. Trust him."

A young knight ran up to Arland and held out a round shield, about eighteen inches across, made of the same dark alloy as the syn-armor. A half-moon indentation had been cut out on one side, just large enough to trap an arm. He planned to use her buckler.

She had shown him the buckler and blade technique during one of their practice sessions at Dina's inn. He had asked about Earth sword fighting and she had gone through several different styles with him. At the time, he'd scoffed at the buckler. Vampire shields were obsolete. The syn-armor offered superior protection without encumbering and the only shields still in use were massive and designed to protect the wielder during bombardment. Vampires either dual-wielded or favored enormous two-handed weapons that made the most of their strength and stamina. Why defend when you can attack? After she'd stabbed Arland a couple of times, he had changed his tune. They had sparred with bucklers the entire time they'd spent in space on the way here.

Arland gripped the buckler with his left hand. The shield whined, priming. Veins of red streaked it, and as he turned the buckler, Maud saw its red tinted edge. It was razor sharp.

Aww. He'd built a vampire version of it.

Tellis, carrying twin blades, laughed. "My Lord, are you so poor that you couldn't afford a proper shield, or so stupid that you think that little toy will protect you?"

"All in good time," Arland said. "Wait, and I'll show you."

Ilemina leaned forward, focused on Arland. "A shield. Interesting. But why so small?"

Otubar grimaced. "Because it's lively."

The nine vampires spread out, encircling Arland. Suddenly she understood. Because there were nine of them, arranged around him in a rough circle, each knight only had a forty-degree angle to work with. The ideal distance for combat was about the length of your weapon plus a step. If they had stayed at the ideal distance, they would be nearly touching. They needed room to work, so instinctively they backed up, giving themselves space, but now they were so far away from Arland, they might as well announce their attacks before launching them. He had more than enough time to react, and they could only come at him two or three at a time, or they would get in each other's way.

The knights realized it too, but there was no time to plan any kind of strategy. The longer they just stood there, the more it looked like they were afraid, and their plan to humiliate Arland was going belly up.

"Today!" Arland bellowed.

An older knight on his left charged, the huge two-handed sword slicing through the air in a vicious arc. Arland dodged. The vampire's momentum carried him past Arland, who smashed his mace into the back of the other man's helmet. The force of the blow knocked the knight to the ground. He rolled and lay still.

Onda and a blond knight to her right charged at the same time and collided. A leaner red-headed knight dashed in at Arland, thrusting his sword. Funny thing about bucklers: held close to the body, they offered very little protection, but when held out at arm's length, not only did they protect most of you, they also cut your opponent's view down to nothing. Arland let the blow glance off the buckler, directing it to his right, and brought his mace down like a hammer on the knight's exposed right shoulder. Bone crunched as the armor failed to fully absorb the force of the hit. The red-headed vampire dropped his sword, but Arland was already turning to meet Tellis, who was attacking him from behind.

Tellis' left sword met Arland's mace, his right glanced off the buckler, leaving Tellis wide open for a fraction of a second, and Arland sank a vicious front kick into his stomach. Tellis stumbled back.

A broad-shouldered female knight leaped at Arland from the left, while a tall male knight charged from the right. Arland stepped back, and the female knight plowed into the male, both collapsing in a heap. Arland smashed the woman's back with his mace. She screamed and rolled off the knight, who was flailing under her. The knight tried to rise and got a face full of buckler.

Onda smashed her hammer into Arland's back. He must've sensed the blow but with no way to avoid it, he simply hunched his shoulders and took the hit. Onda must have expected him to go down, because she stared at him for half a second. Maud knew from experience that giving Arland half a second was a lethal mistake. He spun around, putting all of his weight behind a horizontal strike. His mace connected with Onda's ribs. The hit swept her off her feet. It was almost comical—one moment she was there, brandishing her hammer, and the next she was gone, lying somewhere on the grass.

The six knights still standing attacked. Arland worked through them with methodical precision, crushing limbs, smashing bone, ramming his buckler into their joints. They swarmed him, and he broke them one by one, until they could no longer move. It was a cold, controlled rage, harnessed and channeled into carnage.

Finally, only Tellis and Arland remained standing. Arland bled from a cut on his left temple. Gouges and dents marked his armor. The right side of his jaw swelled. Maud feverishly tried to remember all the hits he had taken. There was no way to tell if he was okay or bleeding inside that damn armor.

Tellis was breathing like he had run a marathon. A bruise darkened his left cheek. The armor over his left forearm had lost integrity, turning dull.

Arland dropped his buckler and attacked. His mace whistled through the air. Tellis blocked, letting the blow glance from his right sword, and stabbed with his left. The blade sliced a hair above Arland's right shoulder. Arland lunged forward and punched Tellis. It was a devastating left cross. Tellis stumbled and Arland swung his mace into Tellis' left arm. The groom shied back. Arland swung again and Tellis danced away.

They circled the battlefield, Tellis fast and agile, Arland unstoppable like a tank on a rampage.

They made a full circle.

Tellis kept backing up. Arland stalked him, but the other knight never let him get within reach.

Arland stopped and waited. Tellis stopped too.

The lawn was silent.

Arland took a step forward. Tellis took a step back.

Otubar called out, "It's not a dance. Fight or get off the field."

Tellis looked at the eight bodies lying on the grass. Some moaned, others simply lay still. His eyes were wide and glassy. Maud had seen that look before. It was the look of someone who had seen his own death. Tellis had forgotten this wasn't a real battlefield. The urge to survive had taken over. He had nowhere to go. Back was dishonor; forward was Arland, pain, and death. So, like the bodies on the grass, Tellis held still.

Arland shrugged his massive shoulders, powered down his mace, turned his back to Tellis, and walked off the field. Maud let out a breath she didn't know she was holding.

He stopped by the table, beat up and splattered with blood, and looked at her. You could hear a pin drop.

"We didn't finish our discussion, my lady."

Oh, she was more than ready to have a discussion. It would feature topics like *Why the hell would you let nine knights pummel you?* and *What were you thinking?* If he was bleeding internally, this was the only way for him to make a graceful exit. She had to get him out of here and out of that armor.

Maud rose, aware of every stare. "In that case, my lord, I

suggest we retire to your quarters so we may carry out our debate in private."

"I'd be delighted." Arland extended his hand toward the path.

Maud bowed her head to Ilemina and Otubar. "My apologies."

Ilemina waved at her. "Think nothing of it, my dear."

Maud started down the path, aware of Arland only a step behind her.

"Ahh, young love," Ilemina's voice floated to her. "Where is our medic?"

———

As soon as they got to the tower and the door slid shut behind them, Arland swayed and sagged against the wall.

"You're such an idiot," she whispered through clenched teeth.

Arland smiled. "Maybe. But I won."

Ugh. She had no idea how badly he was hurt. He probably didn't know how badly he was hurt. They had to get him out of the armor. She could just pull it off him here. Every House crest contained the basic supplies necessary for emergency medical intervention. But if she took the crest off him now and applied it, he would have to remain stationary in this tower. They had to climb the stairs, cross the bridge, and get to either his room or hers and they had to do it with Kozor and Serak watching. Any show of weakness would dilute Arland's victory.

The value of the beating he delivered wasn't in the humiliation of Kozor and Serak. It was in fear and uncertainty. Both House Kozor and Serak came to the fight reasonably sure of what to expect. They had done their research, they had watched the fight in the Lodge, and they expected Arland to be a superior fighter. They didn't expect him to be invincible. If he had been carried off the field by medics or had limped away obviously hurt, they could quantify it. "We almost beat him with nine knights; we can kill him with ten!" But he had crushed them and walked away like it was nothing. Now they didn't know how many knights it would take, and they didn't know how many Arlands House Krahr could field. They feared what they couldn't see and didn't know. Arland had to appear invulnerable.

She slid her shoulder under his arm. He leaned on her. His weight settled on her and her knees almost buckled. It was bad. He wouldn't have put that much weight on her if he could have helped it. He had to be on his last legs.

Arland bared his fangs, his face grim. "Stairs."

"One at a time, my lord."

They staggered up the stairs.

"'The Road Lodge offered me seven,'" she growled in her best Arland voice.

"It's true."

"That was different. The fight in the Lodge was a brawl against bandits and scumbags in outdated armor. You could kill them. You went up against nine knights in prime condition, in good armor, and you couldn't kill any of them without ruining the wedding. Who does that?"

"Well, sure, it sounds unwise when you put it like that. But I won."

They paused on the landing. His breath was coming out in ragged gasps.

"Do you feel cold or drowsy?" she asked.

"I'm not bleeding out."

"Well, we don't know that, do we?"

"I would know."

"Shut up."

He grinned at her.

"What?"

217

"We're like we were before. At the inn."

She glanced at his face. "Beat to hell and bleeding out on the stairs?"

"No. You are talking to me again. Really talking to me. You've been so...distant since you arrived. I like when we're like this."

They started up the second flight of steps.

"If I had to fight nine knights every week..."

"Don't say it," she warned him.

"...to keep you talking to me..."

"I will throw you down the stairs, Arland. I mean it."

"No, you won't. You like me. You are impressed."

She rolled her eyes. "That you can't walk, unassisted, up a flight of stairs? Yes, my lord, very impressive."

He grunted and swayed. For a moment they tottered on the last step, careening back and forth, and she thought they would lose their balance, but they pitched forward and conquered the final stair.

"As I was saying," Arland said, a sheen of sweat covering his face, "if I had to fight nine knights every week for the pleasure of you berating me, I would do it gladly."

"You are an idiot. I abandoned my sister and a perfectly good inn and traveled halfway across the galaxy for an idiot."

The door slid open in front of them. The breezeway stretched in front of them, suffused with sunshine and impossibly long. They would be watched by the vampires on the lawn for every step of it.

Arland grunted again, gently pushed away from her, and stood on his own.

"You can do it," she told him and slid her arm in the crook of his elbow.

They walked into the sunlight side by side, as if out for a leisurely stroll.

"If I fall, don't try to catch me," he warned.

"You are not that heavy."

"Yes, I am."

They kept strolling. One step at a time.

One step.

Another.

Another.

"Did it have to be nine? Couldn't it have been five?" She knew the answer but talking would distract him.

"It had to be more than there were at the Lodge. Beating seven again wouldn't be as exciting. I already did that."

"You make me despair, my lord. Is there no common sense in your head? None at all?"

He gave her a dazzling smile. "No, not right now."

Maud sighed. "Figures."

"You should stay with me. Here. You and Helen. Don't leave me. I don't want you to go."

Her heart sped up.

"Marry me, or not, I will take what you're willing to give me. Don't leave."

There it was. He just came out and said it. He went for it. She had to give him an answer and this time it couldn't be a maybe. "Lord Arland?"

He sighed quietly, his voice resigned. "Yes, my lady?"

"I'm not going anywhere, you fool. You are mine. But if you decide to fight nine random knights again because you want to make a statement, I swear, I will leave you bleeding right there and walk away."

"No, you won't. Next time you can help."

She swore, and he laughed.

TwENTY FEET FROM THE FORK IN THE HALLWAY THAT LED TO BOTH their rooms, Arland's harbinger chimed. He glanced at it and continued. She was almost carrying him now. The unit chimed again and again.

"Soren," Arland told her.

They reached the spot where the hallway split. They had a choice, his room or hers. Soren likely had a direct channel to Arland's quarters with priority access. If they went to Arland's room, they would get no peace.

"Does Lord Soren have an override code to my quarters?" she asked.

"No."

She turned right, to her room, and he went with her. The last fifty feet of the hallway were pure torture. Her knees shook and her back burned from the strain.

The door whispered open. They stumbled through and it slid shut behind them. His full weight hit her. His face had gone blank and almost soft. He was done.

"Bathroom," she squeezed out. "We have to get you into the bathroom."

His face jerked, and he staggered to the bathroom, fueled by pure will.

"Medbed!" she ordered as they crossed the threshold.

A shelf shot out of the wall and she half-lowered, half-dumped Arland on to it. He landed on his back, his mane of blond hair fanning over the bed. His right leg hung off the edge. Maud heaved it on to the shelf.

Arland tapped his chest. The syn-armor cracked along its seams, pieces of it falling off. Maud pulled parts of the breastplate off him, dropping them on the floor.

"First aid kit!"

A tray slid out of the wall, offering the usual vampire assortment of stimulants, antibiotics, wound sealants, and anesthetics. She got the last piece off of him. Arland was built like a vampire hero of legend. Saying that he had wide shoulders, a chiseled chest, and a washboard stomach didn't do him justice. He was big. There was really no better word for it. Hard, powerful muscle sheathed his massive frame. When you looked at him, you saw pure force in physical form. A large, athletic human male would look like a fragile teenager next to him.

All of that muscle came with a price. He had endurance and could deliver bursts of devastating power, but he couldn't run for hours the way Sean, her sister's boyfriend, did. Sean, being an alpha strain werewolf, had almost unlimited speed and stamina. Arland was designed to stand his ground. And that's exactly what he had done. His entire left side was an oblong bruise. His right bicep bled in two places, where something had punctured the armor. His right hip had turned dark red, the result of blunt force trauma. He'd gotten hit in the back too, but she would deal with it later.

Maud took a smooth nutrient cartridge from the tray, slid it into the injector with practiced ease, found a vein on his left arm, and shot it. Vampires healed faster than humans, but they required a lot of fuel to do it.

"Scanner."

A mechanical appendage slid from the wall with two prongs about eight inches apart. She pulled it forward, positioning the prongs horizontally over the bruise on Arland's left side. A screen shimmered into existence between the prongs, showing her a black and silver view of Arland's bones. Two hair-line fractures. Not great, but not awful. She had half expected to find broken ribs puncturing vital organs. If he had been human, she would have.

Maud moved the scanner to his right arm. Whatever punctured it had missed the major blood vessels. The bleeding had already slowed.

His right hip was next.

"A little to the left and down," he said, his voice quiet.

"Do keep in mind that I have a whole tray of tranquilizers."

"That would be nice, too."

The pain killers would have to wait until she finished evaluating the extent of his injuries.

The hip offered her a muscle contusion, bruised bone, and hematoma. A lump had formed as a pool of blood saturated the injured tissue. It hurt like hell, which had contributed to him limping, but wasn't fatal.

She grasped his shoulders. "I need you to sit up."

He sat upright. She moved the scanner over his back. He'd taken the blow on his left shoulder blade. Fractured scapula. Crap.

"Lift your left arm."

Arland raised his arm a couple of inches out to his side and stopped. "No."

"Does it hurt to breathe?"

"I've had worse."

"You need a medic."

"I'm fine."

Human, vampire, werewolf, didn't matter. If they were male and severely injured, they all thought they could just "walk it off."

"Take a deep breath, my lord."

"We're back to 'my lord,'" Arland said dryly.

Right. Misdirection was a wonderful strategy, when it worked. Maud smiled and clapped her hand on his back. Arland jerked forward, sucking in a sharp breath.

She plucked a heavy-duty pain reliever cartridge from the tray.

"No," he said. "I don't want to be sedated. It will make me slow and sleepy. I don't have time for a nap."

"You have a fractured scapula and two cracked ribs. You've lost the full use of your arm and every breath is torture. You need some quality time with a bone knitter."

"Maud," he said.

"No. You aren't a teenager. We both know you require sedation and a visit to a medward. Why are we even having this con—"

He reached out with his left arm and caught her wrist in his fingers, drawing her close. Suddenly they were face to face and he was looking at her. His eyes were very blue.

It would have been easy to pull away. A part of her, the part that panicked and kept her alive on Karhari, warned her to be cautious. But she was so damn tired of being careful and prudent. Something wild swept through her like a scorching sariv.

She kissed him.

His lips were warm on hers and she opened her mouth and let him in. He tasted just as she'd imagined, hot and male, and he kissed her like she was the only thing that mattered. It started tender, then turned hungry, as if they both couldn't get enough. Her whole body strummed with need. He kissed her until she could think of nothing except stripping off her clothes and climbing on top of him to feel him against her skin.

They broke apart. His eyes had turned dark. She saw raw naked lust in his face and it thrilled her.

"Looks like I still have some use of my left arm," he said.

"It does," she said and emptied the cartridge of sedative into his back.

———

MAUD STARED AT THE DISPLAY PROJECTING FROM HER HARBINGER. The medic didn't answer, which wasn't unusual. Medics often ignored direct calls because they were occupied, and Arland's handiwork on the lawn guaranteed the medical staff would be busy. But after calling him directly, Maud had tried the medward and hadn't received an answer either. That didn't happen. There was always someone in the medward.

She had to find some way to get Arland down there. Leaving him alone wasn't an option. He was sedated and had to be under observation. Besides, his injuries needed to be treated. They weren't life threating, but they were urgent.

She tried the medward again.

No answer. What the hell?

She could try Soren. Arland was ducking his uncle, but given that he was peacefully sleeping, Soren couldn't exactly bug him with whatever duties Arland had been avoiding. She tried Lord Soren.

No answer.

A cold heavy weight landed in her stomach and rolled around. Something was wrong. Something bad had happened or was happening.

Helen.

Maud snapped a brisk order. "Helen, priority override." The parental override would pierce through whatever Helen was doing. It would interrupt a video, or another call, and it would supersede a silence setting.

No answer.

Panic hit her in an icy rush. She used logic to surf the wave of fear, keeping on top of it. Either nobody was answering her calls, or her harbinger had been jammed. If someone was jamming her calls, it meant only one thing. An attack was coming.

A door chime, normally soothing, lashed her senses. Maud unsheathed her sword, priming it. The blood blade screeched.

Another chime.

"Show me," she ordered.

A screen ignited above the door, showing the hallway and Karat, alone. Karat's face was paler than usual, her expression tight, her eyes focused. Only House Krahr had enough power and resources to jam her unit. She was on their communication grid. The other vampire Houses didn't have access to this part of the castle, and they didn't have the capabilities to penetrate the House communication network and isolate her, specifically.

She and Karat were friendly. If House Krahr had turned on her, that's exactly who they would send.

"Audio," Maud said. The audio icon flashed in the corner of the screen. "Yes?"

"Open the door," Karat said.

"I'm indisposed at the moment. Can it wait?"

"It's an emergency."

Sure it is. "What sort of emergency?"

"Maud, we don't have time for this." Karat put her hand against the door. "Command override."

The door slid open. Maud backed away, putting herself between Karat and Arland, giving herself room to work.

"Put that away!" Karat waved her hand. "You have to come with me. Helen was poisoned."

[14]

Maud ran.

She had heard two words: poisoned and medward.
She didn't wait for anything else. She just sprinted. Hallways flew
by, the doors flashing one after another. The air in her lungs
turned to fire, but she barely noticed. Karat chased her but had
fallen far behind.

The medward loomed ahead. There were people in the
antechamber, Ilemina, Otubar, Soren, but they might as well have
been ghosts. Getting to the door was all that mattered. She tore
past them and burst into the triage chamber.

Maud saw it all in an instant, the image was seared into her
mind in a fraction of a second: Helen lying on a medbed, tiny and
pale; a dozen metal arms hovering over her; the spiderweb of an
advanced iv drip; and the medic sitting next to her, his face grim.

She charged to the bed, and then Karat was on top of her,
pulling her back with all of her strength, and the medic was in
front of her, holding his arms out, saying something. She fought
her way forward, dragging Karat, and the medic rammed into her,
pushing her back, his voice insistent.

Finally, the words penetrated. "...do not touch..."

She had to stop. It took a few more seconds for her body to catch up with her mind. Maud stopped struggling.

"...stable for now," the medic said.

Her mouth finally worked. "What happened?"

Karat gently but firmly pushed her back to the antechamber. "Not here."

"I need to see her."

"Stop," the medic said. "Look at yourself."

Maud forced her gaze away from Helen and looked at her armor. She was smudged with Arland's blood. She'd washed his arm and sealed the wounds, but some of it must've gotten on her when he kissed her.

"I've got her stabilized," the medic said. "You're carrying a horde of germs and you're covered in blood. You can't help her by going in there. You can only hurt her."

Maud had to walk away. Everything in her screamed to get back into the room, as if just walking up to the bed would magically fix everything, and Helen would sit up and say, "Hi, Mommy." But it wouldn't.

It didn't seem real. It felt like a dream, like some nightmare, and she wished desperately to wake up. She wanted to undo this. If only there was some button she could press to rewind it all back to normal.

"Come with me," Karat said.

There was nothing she could do. Maud turned and walked into the antechamber. The medic and Karat followed.

"What happened?" Maud asked again. Her voice sounded strange, like it was coming from someone else.

"Helen was at the lake with other children," Soren said. "The bugs were there as well, swimming in their designated area. After a while, the chaperones made the children get out of the water to take a break, warm up, and snack. The children ate and decided to play hunt and run."

Hunt and run was the vampire version of tag. Helen would've loved it.

"Helen ran close to the tachi," Soren continued.

"Then one of them bit her!" Ilemina snarled.

"Helen collapsed," Soren said. "She was rushed here, to the medward. The tachi was apprehended, and the rest of them are confined to their quarters. We tried to question him, but he refuses to talk. None of them are talking to us and harming him is out of the question until we know if Helen will survive."

That "if" hit Maud like a sledgehammer. She wanted to sink to the floor, ball up her fists, and scream. But she had no time.

"He bit a child." Ilemina's face was terrible. She bared her fangs, eyes blazing. A primal snarl shook her lips. It was like looking at rage personified. "I will slaughter every single one of them. I will decimate their planet. Their grandchildren will tremble when they see a vampire coming."

From anybody else, it would seem like grandstanding. But Ilemina meant every word. Otubar snarled in response. Karat gripped her blood sword. The entire room was a hair away from violence. This was how wars started.

"It's more complicated than that," the medic said. "We have data on tachi venom, but there is a synthetic compound in her system that is inconsistent with what we know of the tachi."

The sharp, jagged pieces snapped together in Maud's head. Vampires cherished children. There was no greater treasure. They cherished Helen, too. They considered her one of their own. And then a bug bit her, like she was prey. It had awakened a primal response, the collective racial memory of Mukama, of invaders who devoured vampire children.

"Where is the tachi now?" she asked.

"Across the hall," Soren told her. "You can't hurt him, Lady Maud. He may hold the key to your daughter's recovery."

"I need to speak with him." She sank steel into those words.

"Come with me." Soren marched out of the room and into the hallway, to the door opposite the medward.

Maud followed him, aware of Ilemina, Otubar, Karat, and the medic directly behind her. The door slid open, exposing a small cell. Inside it, a male tachi sat on the floor, bound in a captivity suit. Made from tough polymer and weighted, it wrapped around him like a straitjacket. His exoskeleton had faded to barely visible gray.

Maud marched into the room, dropped to her knees in front of him, and released the lock on the captivity suit. It fell away, and he sprang up to his full height above her.

She jumped to her feet and bowed her head. "Thank you for saving my child."

The tachi turned brilliant indigo blue. "You're welcome, daughter of the innkeepers."

———

"Somebody better explain this to me," Ilemina growled.

"Tachi venom isn't lethal to most species." Maud stepped aside, giving the tachi room to stretch his wings. "It's meant to put the prey into a suspended state, slowing down its life functions to preserve the freshness."

Karat winced.

"If he wanted to kill Helen, he would've just sliced her head off," Maud continued. "As soon as you said he'd bitten her, I knew it wasn't an attack."

Ilemina turned her glare onto the tachi. "Why didn't you say something?"

The tachi spread his indigo appendages. The gesture looked so much like a human spreading his arms in a Gallic shrug, as if to say "None of this is my fault; I didn't mess it up, you did. Deal with it."

Ilemina turned to Maud. "What does that mean?"

"It means he thinks you are a xenophobic species prone to rash and violent reactions, so he saw no point in explaining himself. You wouldn't have believed him anyway."

Ilemina's eyes narrowed. She pierced the tachi with her stare.

"I can't make it simple for you," he said.

Ilemina flashed her fangs. "Try me."

The tachi turned to Maud, switching to the Akit dialect. *"They think I killed the child; the royal is angry. Now they know I saved the child; she is angry. I do not comprehend this species. How have they ever managed to achieve interstellar civilization without self-destructing?"*

"Could you please tell me what happened to my daughter?" Maud didn't even try to keep the desperation from her voice.

The tachi's color lightened for a moment. "Yes, of course." He folded his arms in an apologetic gesture. "I will use short thoughts. We were bathing. The children were running and making excited noises. Your child ran close to us. She was not afraid like the other children. They could not catch her. She ran too close and almost ran into me. Then she apologized for disturbing my *tegah*."

Maud had given Helen a primer on tachi manners. Until now she had no idea any of it had stuck.

"She is such a polite child," the tachi said. "We spoke. Something hit her in the neck, on her left side. She fell. I caught her. I saw a wet spot on her skin. It smelled wrong. Her eyes rolled back in her head. I knew I had to act. I bit her to keep the poison from spreading."

"Which way was she facing when it hit her?" Soren asked.

"She was turning away from me to rejoin the game. She was facing the rest of the children. The lake was on her right and the castle was on her left."

"A sniper shot from the bluff," Otubar said.

Karat bared her teeth in a grimace. "There is a clear line of sight from the western edge of the game grounds to the lake. They distracted us with the krim match, then goaded Arland into a fight, and while we were watching, they shot Helen."

"Pull the video feed," Ilemina ordered. Karat took off at a run.

There were implications and conclusions to be drawn from all of this, but right now, none of them mattered. "Did you recognize the poison?" Maud asked.

"No," the tachi said. "I would know it again. It smelled strong."

The vampire medic failed to identify it and the tachi didn't know it. The tachi coma wouldn't last forever. It could fail at any moment. She had to do something now, or Helen would die. There was only one place she could turn to.

"I don't have anything to trade."

Everyone stopped and looked at her. She realized she had spoken out loud.

Before she could explain, a half-dressed Arland rounded the corner, somehow managing to look angry and confused at the same time. "What the hell is going on?"

Soren blinked. "Why are you out of armor?"

"Maud?" Arland closed in on her.

She looked up at him, feverishly rummaging through the list of her meager possessions in her head.

"What is it?" he asked.

"Helen has been poisoned, and I don't have anything to trade."

"Will someone explain this to me?" Ilemina demanded.

Understanding sparked in Arland's eyes. "But I have things to trade. They will trade with me or I'll twist their heads off."

"Who?" Ilemina snarled.

"Explain things to your mother," Otubar boomed.

"No time." Arland grabbed Maud's hand and pulled her down the hallway. Behind them the sound of a pissed off Preceptor shook the air. Arland sped up.

"How are you still walking?" Maud squeezed out.

"Booster. Activated it before you took my armor off. I had plans. None of which involved a sedative."

"Arland Roburtar Gabrian of Krahr!" Ilemina roared. "Stop this instant!"

Arland ignored her. They were almost to the bend in the hallway.

Suddenly Arland braked, and then the lees flooded all available space, their veils swirling, their jewelry shining, tails and ears twitching. Maud saw Nuan Cee in the center of the lees mob and reached out to him. "Helen..."

Nuan Cee took her hands into his furry paw-hands. "I know."

The rest of the lees rushed past them, washing over them like a wave, and rolled down the hallway, parting around Ilemina, Otubar, and Soren.

"I have nothing to trade," she said.

Nuan Cee's turquoise eyes shone. He grinned, displaying sharp, even teeth. "I am sure we can come to an arrangement."

"Get out of my medward, vermin!" the medic screamed.

"Do not worry yourself." Nuan Cee patted Maud's hands as a mob of lees carried the medic out of his medward. "All will be well now."

[15]

M aud slumped in an oversized chair in Lord Soren's study. She felt wrung out like a piece of wet laundry about to go in the dryer. The lees had treated Helen for the better part of an hour, and when Nuan Cee finally emerged from the medward, Maud felt ready to tear her hair out. He had announced that the danger had passed, Helen would be up in a few hours, and there was no need to worry.

Maud had been allowed to see her daughter and to kiss Helen's warm forehead, and then the enraged vampire medic kicked everyone out. She wanted to be back in the medward, sitting by the bed, watching for minute signs of improvement, but it would accomplish nothing and Ilemina had requested her presence in her brother's study.

The Preceptor of House Krahr sat in a chair by Lord Soren's desk, looking grim. Otubar sat on his wife's right, Arland sat on Maud's left. He had put on his armor and his booster kept him awake, but she could tell by the slightly feverish look in his eyes that a crash was coming. Karat took a spot at the opposite end of the room. Soren presided over it all, sitting behind his huge desk as if it were a castle wall and he was watching a horde of invaders gather for a siege. Except this time the invaders looked back at them not from a field before the castle but from a massive screen, where the recording of the events on the mesa played out.

Maud had picked the farthest chair from the screen, maybe twenty feet away. It felt like miles. The room contained the Krahr, not the huge House, but the small nuclear family who ran it. She didn't really belong here.

"So we have no useable footage," Arland said.

Karat frowned. Her fingers danced across the tablet in her hand. The recording zoomed in past the game of krim, showing distant figures at the edge of the mesa. The image sped up and the figures jerked around in a slightly comical dance as knights mulled about.

"We know members of both Kozor and Serak were at the edge of the game grounds and had opportunity to fire the shot at Helen," Karat said. "We know none of them had a gun on them, so they had to have assembled it on location. See how they keep crowding each other? They could've assembled a small space craft and we would've been none the wiser."

"We should upgrade the surveillance," Otubar said.

Soren grimaced. "Do you want to assign each of them a personal drone?"

"If that's what it takes," Otubar said.

"We would be breaking every rule of hospitality," Soren said. "They would accuse us of cowardice and paranoia and claim we made the wedding impossible. We already failed to protect a child in our care and we were almost too late to prevent a confrontation between our other guests and these...*ushivim*."

Karat jerked. "Father!"

Maud blinked. Of all the words she had expected the Knight

Sergeant to use, the expletive meaning the bloody diarrhea of diseased vermin was the last on the list.

The corners of Otubar's mouth rose a couple of millimeters. It was the closest she had ever seen the Lord Consort come to a smile.

"It was planned and premeditated," Karat said. "As I pointed out, they had to have brought the weapon in pieces, assembled it on the spot, shot her, and disassembled it after. We scoured that entire area, on top of the mesa and down by the beach. If they had dropped any part of it, our scans would have picked it up. Each of them must have carried a small piece of it. It's smart."

"They switched targets," Arland said. "They must have planned to take me out after the krim match in a final effort to uncover the Under Marshal, but they allowed for the possibility of failure. So, when I won the bout and walked away, they shot Helen."

Maud turned to him. "Why her? She's just a child."

"Not her," Ilemina said. "They used Helen to target you. If the tachi had truly injured the child, would you still negotiate with them on our behalf?"

"If she survived, yes," Maud said. "But if she died, everything would be over for me."

"And what would the tachi and lees do if Helen had been injured by one of them?" Ilemina asked.

"They would evacuate," Maud said. "Neither delegation has the numbers to oppose a large attack and neither party wants to antagonize you. They want the trade station and access to your space. If their presence became an issue or caused any inconvenience, they would remove themselves from the situation rather than risk aggravating you. They would wait the wedding out and resume negotiations after the other guests left."

"You see now?" Ilemina leaned forward, resting her hands on Soren's desk. "You are the key to the tachi and lees. Without your intervention, the tachi might have left already and Nuan Cee, who loves money above all things, dotes on you as if you were his own child. Congratulations. You've made enough of a difference to become a high-value target."

"Yes," Soren agreed. "The Kozor and Serak stooped to attacking a child just to remove you. They are willing to weather the shame if it means running off the lees and the tachi."

Otubar leaned forward. "The ends justify the means."

"But we're back to why," Karat said. "What possible detriment could the lees and the tachi be to their plan?" She turned to Maud.

Great. "I don't know."

"That reminds me," Ilemina said. "Could a lees have poisoned Helen? They are devious enough to injure her and then magnanimously provide the cure. It would put Maud in their debt."

Maud shook her head.

"It needed to be said," Otubar said.

"No," Arland said. "That was the first thing I checked. None of the lees were anywhere near the game grounds or the lake. Their equipment is sophisticated and can render them practically invisible, but I have seen their disruptor in action and Nuan Cee knows it. The disruptor relies on a maa emitter, and once you know what to screen for, it's not hard to find. They've been using plain stealth to get around the castle and record candid videos of us, but they had nothing to do with poisoning the child. It would be too heavy-handed for them anyway."

"Why?" Karat asked.

"The lees seek balance," Arland said. "A good bargain is the highest honor they could strive for. Saving a child and collecting a favor from the parent satisfies the need for balance. Hurting a child to save it and then collecting the favor is not a balanced transaction."

Maud almost did a double take. He flashed her a grin.

"Is he right?" Ilemina asked.

"Yes. The lees pride themselves on being clever. To set us up by hurting Helen would go against Nuan Cee's clan's code." Maud took a deep breath. "However, I do owe him a favor. He will collect, which means he will ask me for something and I won't be able to refuse. I am now a security risk."

Ilemina waved her hand. "Eh."

"You are a security risk if we don't know about it," Soren said.

Arland leaned back in his chair. "What do the lees and tachi have in common? Why do Kozor and Serak want them gone?"

Maud sighed. "The two species couldn't be more different. The lees live in clans, the tachi are a monarchy. The lees prize wealth, the tachi seek knowledge. The lees are secretive ambush predators, the tachi swarm their target. The lees encourage personal achievement and strive to earn individual recognition, the tachi win or lose as a whole. They don't have much in common. They're both omnivorous species. They are both interested in a trade station and an alliance with Krahr. They both arrived in spaceships…"

"Battle station," Karat said.

Everyone looked at her.

She hit her fist on her father's desk. "The scum. They want the battle station."

Arland sat up straight. "The battle station has limited personnel and a central control point. Two hundred wedding guests, the elite of their Houses, would pose a real threat."

Karat nodded. "Once they have control of the battle station, they can pound the planet to dust. Even the full power of our fleet might not be enough."

"They don't have to face the fleet," Otubar growled.

"He's right," Arland said. "If they gain control of the station, they can hold the planet hostage while they clear the system."

Maud blinked. "Did you actually put a warp drive on that thing?"

"Of course we did," Ilemina snapped. "What good is a weapon if you can't move it where your enemy is?"

"It's a bold plan," Soren said. "If they pull this off, they would be untouchable. The bragging rights alone would guarantee them a seat at the big table."

"They would still have to take it from us," Karat reminded him. "The only way for them to get on to the station is through the wedding boon."

According to tradition, the couple about to wed could request a small favor from their hosts. To deny the boon was the height of rudeness.

"They will request that the wedding be held on the station," Karat continued. "We deny the request. Problem solved."

"On what grounds?" Ilemina asked.

"On the grounds that we know they're up to something."

Soren heaved a sigh. "So, you want to accuse our honored guests of plotting behind our backs. With what evidence? Do you have any proof to support your baseless claims?"

Karat opened her mouth and shut it.

Her father nodded. "Silence that speaks volumes. We have no proof, only guesses, deductions, and suspicions. Furthermore, we already permitted them to tour the battle station when they arrived. We can't claim that it's forbidden, unfinished, or secret now, because we invited them for wine and pastries on the observation deck."

Of course they would invite the rival Houses to tour the battle station. *Look at our big new super-awesome weapon. Behold the might of Krahr. We are the greatest and you could never compare.* Ugh.

"If we refuse to grant the boon," Soren continued, "we would have to do so without any explanation. At best, we would be viewed as discourteous and uncouth. At worst, timid and cowardly. How could we, with all our might and our planet only a shuttle flight away, be so wary of two hundred wedding guests? Even if we do refuse to step into the trap, they score a wounding blow."

He was right. Reputation was everything. It wasn't enough to stop the scheme. House Krahr had to do it in a way that brought them credit.

"There has to be more to their plan," Arland said. "Some scheme, some ploy to minimize the risk. There's something we don't know that makes them think they could win. And they view the aliens as a wildcard."

"Both the lees and tachi have battle ships in orbit," Maud said. "Between the two of them, they pack a lot of fire power. The tachi have the technological superiority, and the lees fight dirty and hold grudges for generations."

Ilemina bared her teeth. "The pirates are afraid the aliens will come to our aid. What kind of world is it that a vampire from another House is my enemy and bugs and Merchants are my allies?"

Soren turned to Maud. "Would they help us?"

"Hard to say," Maud said. "I'm leaning to yes. If you promise them the trade station, then definitely."

"The plan you're contemplating requires a military alliance," Ilemina told Soren. "Do you truly want this? An alliance of one House and another species against other Houses has never been done. How would this be received by the rest of the Anocracy?"

"How would the end of our House be received, my lady?" Soren asked.

Maud took a deep breath. "The rest of the Anocracy doesn't have to know whether this alliance was forged before the other houses broke the rules of hospitality or after."

Ilemina pivoted toward her.

Maud met her gaze. "The Kozor and Serak will request to hold the wedding on the battle station. By virtue of their presence, the lees and the tachi, honored guests of House Krahr, would be invited to said wedding. If during the ceremony, the other Houses commit an act of treachery and attack their hosts, it would be only natural for the lees and the tachi to defend themselves against a common threat. If, in the course of such a battle, they are so impressed by the might of House Krahr that they seek an alliance, who could blame them? And wouldn't House Krahr, moved by their bravery, then be honor-bound to accept such an alliance, if for no other reason than to compensate for the danger the guests had experienced? After all, who would stand with the Houses who drowned so deeply in dishonor that even the aliens have judged them unworthy?"

Silence claimed the room.

"Draft it," Ilemina said to Soren. "Maud, once it's drafted, take it to the aliens. Tell them that if they agree, I will personally open negotiations for the trade station."

Otubar's eyebrows rose a hair.

Ilemina bared her teeth. "Kozor and Serak are wary of them, so I will use them. 'He who is feared by my enemy is my shield.'"

[16]

Maud rushed down the hallway. The meeting with the lees and the tachi was in less than ten minutes, but her harbinger had pinged, letting her know Helen was awake. Maud tore through the castle at a near sprint. Logic told her that everything would be fine, but emotion trumped logic, and her emotions were screaming at her that something would go terribly wrong in the time it would take her to get to the medward. By the time she reached the door, she was in a near panic.

The door whispered open.

In a flash, Maud saw the room in excruciating detail: the bed, the white instruments, the blue readouts projected on the wall, the medic standing to the side, and Helen, upright on the bed.

"Mommy!" Helen cleared ten feet in a single jump.

Maud caught her and hugged her, hoping with everything she had that this was real, and her daughter wouldn't disappear out of her arms, fading back into the hospital bed.

"Full recovery," the medic said. "I uploaded a monitoring routine to her harbinger and synced it to you. If she takes a turn for the worse, which I do not anticipate, her unit will flash with yellow and you will get a warning. Should this occur, I want to see her immediately."

"Understood." Maud kissed Helen's forehead, inhaling the familiar scent of her daughter's hair. *It will be okay, she's okay, everything is fine, she's alive, she's not dying...* "Thank you for everything."

"You're welcome," the medic said. "I did very little. All I could do was keep her alive for a little longer. Eventually she would have slipped away. Are you going to speak with the lees?"

"Yes." She was still clutching Helen tightly to herself, unwilling to let go.

"I want the recipe for that antidote."

"I will try, but the lees hoard their secrets like treasure. They will only trade, for something of equal or greater value."

The medic pondered the wall for a moment and tapped his unit. A round ceramic tower slid out of the floor and opened, revealing a core lit from within by a peach-colored glow and rows of tubes, vials, and ampoules arranged in rings around it. The contents of the tower glittered like jewels, some filled with amber liquid, others containing glowing mists or small dazzling gems in a rainbow of colors. It was oddly elegant and beautiful, the way vampire technology often was. The medic plucked a twisted vial filled with green mist and held it out to her.

"A gesture of good faith."

"What is it?"

"It's a biological weapon we developed during the Nexus conflict. It renders the lees infertile."

He just pulled a species-ending toxin out of the shelf like it was nothing. And he had dozens more in there, of all different shapes and sizes. How many other species could they neuter with one of those shiny bottles? She'd just watched him reach into a Pandora's box like he was grabbing a sandwich out of a picnic basket.

242

Her reaction must have shown on her face, because the medic shrugged. "It was never used. It was judged to be against the code of war. Also, it's a poor weapon. It doesn't kill the enemy. It's something one might use in retaliation for being beaten, and we do not lose."

"I need a carrying case for this," she said.

"Why? The vial is unbreakable by normal means and is hermetically sealed."

Maud smiled. "You don't just hand someone a terrible evil without impressive packaging. We need a chest filled with velvet or a high-tech vault container with an elaborate code lock. Something that makes it seem important and forbidden."

The medic's eyes lit up. "I have just the thing."

———

THE MEETING WITH THE LEES AND THE TACHI WAS SET IN THE Maven's Gardens, located at the top of a small mesa that jutted next to the Marshal Tower. Consisting of a small stone plaza ringed by lush greenery, the gardens were at once a very private and completely exposed space, accessible only by a long, covered breezeway that curved around the tower from one of the bridges connecting it to the rest of the castle. The trees and shrubs hid the plaza from outside observers, and its location, on the very edge of a sheer drop, made outside surveillance impossible. However, the cameras and turrets, mounted on the walls of the tower directly above, had a perfect view of everything that transpired.

From inside the plaza, the gardens looked calm and inviting. Blue, turquoise, and pink blossoms rose from the flower patches beneath old trees. Here and there, plush furniture, some made for vampires, some made with other bodies in mind, offered comfortable places to sit and reflect.

In the center of the plaza rose a ten-foot-tall replica of the neighboring mesa. Water cascaded from the top of the mountain into a basin made to resemble a lake, complete with a narrow sandy beach and foot-tall trees. The soothing sound of the waterfall added another sound screen to the dampeners placed along the perimeter of the gardens.

Helen splashed through the shallow edge of the lake, waving her arms like a giant about to take on a mountain. If there was an inch of water available, her daughter would be in it, Maud reflected. None of this seemed real. Only a few hours ago, Helen was dying, and now she looked like she'd never even been poisoned. Things were moving too fast and she kept trying to get a grip.

Maud fought the urge to shift in her seat, aware of Otubar looming to her left. She still had no legal status, and for negotiations to succeed, she needed to borrow some authority. She would've preferred Arland as a backup for this meeting, but he was sleeping off his booster, and she had to admit Otubar had authority in spades. The Lord Consort projected quiet menace. Emphasis on the quiet. He didn't speak, he made no small talk, he asked no questions. He just towered like some legendary bastion of vampire might ready to pummel any offenders into bloody mush.

She couldn't screw this up.

The lees and the tachi arrived at the same time, each delegation led by a vampire knight through the side tunnel. Nuan Cee wore his usual silk apron, the kind Maud saw him wear at his shop, and a necklace of white and blue shells that matched his silver-blue fur. It wasn't the bejeweled ensemble he donned for important meetings. The two lees behind him bounced up and down as they walked, looking like two fluffy, excited kits.

The tachi queen strode next to the Merchant, elegant and

seemingly weightless despite her size. Her exoskeleton was a cheery, beautiful azure, like the waters of the Mediterranean Sea. Maud had expected a neutral gray. A pleasant surprise. The two tachi following the queen exhibited color as well, one deep lavender, the other a familiar green. Ke'Lek.

Good. The tachi are in a receptive mood.

Maud rose and bowed. "Lady of sun and air. Great Merchant. Welcome."

Nuan Cee waved his paw-hands magnanimously. "No need, no need. We are all friends here."

Dil'ki bobbed her head. "I am relieved to see you well, Maud of the Innkeepers. And your child."

"Please," Maud murmured and pointed to a table with four chairs. Two were the typical vampire seats, large, solid, with simple but functional lines. The third chair, to Maud's right, was a divan, piled high with soft pillows. The fourth chair, on Maud's left, looked like a mushroom with a plush, padded cap and round protrusions to the back and sides. It had taken Maud a good half hour of drawing and explaining to convince House Krahr's fabricator supervisor to manufacture one. She still wasn't sure if the proportion of the stem to cap was off by an inch or two, but it looked right and it was the best she could do.

The queen saw the chair. Maud held her breath.

A flash of deeper color rolled over the royal and she perched on the chair, locking her vestigial appendages on the protrusions. Nuan Cee sprawled on the divan like a Roman patrician.

The tachi bodyguards split up. Ke'Lek remained behind the queen, while the other tachi headed to the fountain. The Nuan Cee's relatives followed the tachi to where Helen was splashing. The significance wasn't lost on Maud. If anything happened to either Nuan Cee or the tachi queen, Helen would be a primary target. The thought should have disturbed her, but she took it with easy calm. *Either too much has happened, and I am now inoculated, or I've gotten used to high-stakes negotiations.*

A vampire retainer delivered pitchers of green wine and red spiced juice along with platters of baked snacks and artfully arranged fruit and vegetable slices, and withdrew. It felt like an odd tea party. Here she was serving cosmic cookies and wine to a queen of enlightened predators and the head of a clan of ruthless assassins. Nothing much at stake except an interstellar alliance. Whee!

Maud sipped some juice. This would have to be done very carefully. If she offered either of them a finger, they would bite her entire arm off. No time like the present.

"Have you rested from the interstellar travel?" she asked. "I always find being planetside to be a relief." Not the best opening, considering they had both been on the planet for the last two weeks, but it would do.

The tachi queen glanced at her. "This planet is rather beautiful."

"I do so enjoy being planetside," Nuan Cee said. "However, as regrettable as it is, one must commit to the unpleasantness of space travel to pursue one's goals."

So far, so good. "I do wonder how space merchant marines do it. Long voyages, expensive cargo, and I hear there are pirates in certain quadrants."

Nuan Cee's eyes narrowed slightly. "Yes. One does have to make sacrifices in the name of profit."

"Or scientific achievement." The tachi queen speared a cookie with a long talon. "The quest for knowledge cannot proceed without the fuel of labor."

"It always rankles when opportunistic beings attempt to cash in on the labor of others." Maud studied the contents of her glass.

"Some of them go so far as to plan to invade their hosts' stronghold and claim them for their own."

"It is both unfair and predatory," Dil'ki said. "Should we witness such an act, of course, we would be obliged to intervene."

"Indeed," Nuan Cee said. "But then there are personal costs to consider. Such assistance often results in tragedy for those who offer it."

They didn't even bat an eye. Both the lees and the tachi either knew what the Kozor and Serak were planning or strongly suspected. And Nuan Cee had gone straight for the jugular. *We could all die if we help you.* Yeah, right. She would have to choose her words carefully.

Maud smiled. "If one were to provide a safe harbor, a protected haven, for courageous seekers of wealth and knowledge, perhaps new routes could be plotted to take full advantage of it and the great gains for all would dull the pang of tragedy."

Nuan Cee sat up straighter. "If such a harbor were to appear, one would be a fool to not take advantage of it."

Maud pretended to toy with her glass. Ilemina was very clear on what could be promised.

"A safe harbor in space has three major applications. First, it is a base of scientific inquiry, a natural gathering place where multiple species could come together in comfort and security to share their findings. Second, it is a hub of shipping and supply, a port where cargo can be bought, sold, and moved, and weary sailors can rest before resuming their journey. Third, it is a military installation, equipped to repel attacks and shelter those within. The military might of the Holy Anocracy, and House Krahr in particular, is unmatched. If only suitable partners could be found to fulfil these other roles." Maud sighed. "Of course, such cooperation could only be possible if iron-clad alliances could be agreed upon, and financial and other obligations were determined and evenly assumed by all involved, and only after an instance of spontaneous mutual cooperation had occurred."

The queen's color darkened. "An even contribution from each species would only be fair. Such a place would require advanced technology and modern construction to be truly effective."

"And of course, it would require a sufficient infusion of capital coming from a partner intimately familiar with the peculiarities of space trade." Nuan Cee bared his teeth in a quick smile.

"If such plans were to be put in writing, in secret, of course, progress could be made on the path of mutual benefit." There, she laid it out. Help us retain the battle station and we'll get the ball rolling on the trade station, provided you agree to military alliances.

Nuan Cee turned to Otubar. "Does the Under Marshal agree?"

Oh crap.

Otubar stared back at the Merchant. "I'm standing here with her, am I not?"

Maud had to seal the deal. She nodded at the retainer waiting at the other end of the plaza. The woman disappeared behind the tree and returned with a huge metal chest. Square and reinforced, it looked impregnable enough to contain a grenade blast. The retainer carried it over with obvious strain, set it on the ground next to Nuan Cee, and withdrew.

"A gesture of good faith from House Krahr," Maud announced. "We are grateful for Helen's rescue and hope Clan Nuan will share the antidote with us for future use."

Her harbinger, which she had programed prior to the meeting, sent a signal to the box. It split with a clang, and a metal spire shot out, like the pistil of a flower. The top of the pistil unfolded. A bottle of green mist slid upward on a pedestal.

"A weapon of Nexus," Maud said, "meant to render the lees infertile."

Nuan Cee jerked back.

"House Krahr has no need of such things now that it has found a willing and reliable trade partner in Clan Nuan," Maud said. "We do not commit lightly and once we do, we stand fully behind it."

"The depth of your commitment is stunning," Nuan Cee said. "It is a proper bargain. We shall share the antidote."

"It brings me and the Lord Consort great joy," Maud said.

Lord Consort projected all of the joy of a boiling thundercloud.

Everyone sipped their drinks.

The royal tachi rose. "This has been a most enlightening meeting, Maud of House Krahr. We have many plans to make."

[17]

Maud strode down the length of the bridge, measuring it with her footsteps. It was early morning, and the sky was lightly overcast, the sun playing tag with ragged clouds. Next to her, Helen yawned and rubbed her eyes.

Last night Maud had reported the conversation with the lees and the tachi to Soren and Karat. She had no doubt the Lord Consort would give a complete account of it to Ilemina. Soren agreed with her assessment—Serak and Kozor were targeting the battle station and wanted both alien species out of the way, but how exactly they were planning to pull it off was anyone's guess.

Afterward she returned to her quarters to check on Arland. His door was locked, and he didn't respond to her harbinger message. It drove her nuts. She kept imagining wild scenarios, each of which involved him dying in his sleep, defenseless. Eventually she surrendered and used the private passageway to check on him. He was asleep in his bed, his chest rising and falling in a smooth steady rhythm. She'd considered climbing into bed next to him to hold him but decided it would be creepy and made herself walk back to her suite. Nothing was going to happen to

Arland; he would sleep off the booster while a cocktail of drugs the medic had administered repaired his injuries. There were a lot of injuries. It was perfectly reasonable for him to remain asleep for another day or more.

Maud kept moving. A refreshing wind pulled at her hair, throwing the short strands in her face. The exile to Karhari had shocked her. By then she was used to Melizard's schemes. He was always creating problems, but he was the younger son, beloved and spoiled. His sins, however grievous, were always forgiven. Except that time.

From the moment she'd seen her former mother-in-law's face, Maud had learned to expect the worst and her imagination obliged. If Melizard was delayed, it was because he was dead. If Helen ate a piece of unfamiliar fruit, it was surely poisonous, and she would likely die. If Maud met strangers on the road, they were assassins sent to kill her. And Karhari had proven her right again and again, feeding her paranoia.

Now Arland had joined the short list of People Whose Death She Imagined. There were only four names on the list: Helen, Dina, Maud, and now, Arland. Last night she kept waking up, checking on Helen, and when she drifted off, Arland died in her dreams, and she would jerk awake. A couple of times she got up and prowled on her balcony, like a caged cat.

If only she could have seen him this morning; if she had touched him and felt the warmth of his body, it would have reassured her that he was alive. She had rolled out of her bed planning to do exactly that. Instead, Karat had barged into her quarters as soon as the sun was up, announced that Ilemina required her presence, and took off.

Maud and Helen passed through the arched entrance to the Preceptor's tower.

"What are we doing today, Mama?"

"Today we're going on a hunt," Maud said.

She'd reviewed the day's agenda late last night, after giving up on getting any sleep. At their core, vampires were mostly carnivorous predators, and hunting was in their blood. They liked to kill, cook their catch, and eat it.

Humans had retained some of those primitive memories, too. No matter how civilized they became or how evolved the art of cooking became, nothing beat a piece of meat roasted over a fire.

The Holy Anocracy was not that civilized. They didn't bother to make any excuses or to distance themselves from their predatory past. As soon as a vampire House claimed territory, they did two things. They planted a vala tree and they designated hunting grounds.

House Krahr maintained a huge hunting preserve. Today, at noon, they would be riding through it. Missing the hunt was unthinkable. She could get away with missing games, skipping a formal dinner, even being late to the wedding ceremony, although that last one would require reparations for the offense to the newlyweds. If she missed the hunt, however, the insult to the hosts would be monumental. Even children were brought to the hunt as soon as they were old enough not to fall off the mounts.

"What kind of hunt?" Helen asked.

"Do you remember when Daddy and I took you to House Kirtin and we rode out to hunt bazophs?"

It had been one of the rare bright moments in their exile. Melizard had landed a position with a stable House and for two months they had a brief taste of normal Anocracy life. And then he had punched the Kirtin Marshal and it all ended.

Helen's eyes lit up. "Can I come on the hunt?"

"Yes."

Maud realized that if she had told an average Earth woman that she would be taking her five-year-old daughter onto a temperamental alien mount and allowing her to ride in a large pack of homicidal vampires to hunt an unknown but surely dangerous beast, the woman would have tried to take Helen away from her on the spot. Some people had PTA meetings, she had hunts.

Helen would enjoy it and Maud wanted her to be happy. Plus, after the poisoning, letting her daughter out of her sight without an army of bodyguards ready to tear any attacker to pieces was out of the question.

Whatever Ilemina wanted would likely take place before the hunt.

They reached the Preceptor's study. The door was retracted, the doorway framing Ilemina bent over her desk. The older vampire woman seemed deep in thought, her expression focused and harsh.

A feeling of dread mugged Maud. *Now what?*

She halted in the doorway. "My lady?"

Ilemina raised her head. "Come inside."

Maud walked into the room, bringing Helen with her. The door slid shut behind them. *Trapped.*

Ilemina fixed her with a heavy gaze. "Lady Onda and Lady Seveline have invited you to the bride's wassail."

The wassail was a long-standing vampire tradition. Despite the grand name, it was basically a brunch, light on food, but heavy on drinks, which, for vampires, meant caffeine. An average vampire could drain a bottle of whiskey and remain perfectly sober, but Maud had seen them down an expresso and dissolve into a soggy mess of slurred words and draping arms, declaring their undying love and devotion to a stranger they met ten minutes ago.

The wassail involved a large punch bowl filled with a caffeinated beverage and each guest would be served from it, toasting the host. It was common before a wedding; in fact, the tradition prescribed having several wassails for both the bride and groom. Maud had attended a few of these before and every time proved to be a hilarious experience. Inevitably someone challenged her to a drink off, which ended with them under the table and her, completely sober, urgently looking for a bathroom.

Ilemina's face held very little humor. It promised doom. Definitely doom.

"Is the invitation cause for alarm?" Maud asked.

"No female members of House Krahr received an invitation. It is a family wassail. You are the only outsider."

She would be isolated and surrounded by knights of House Kozor. House Krahr was honor bound to respect their guests' privacy. If something happened, there was no guarantee back-up would arrive in time or at all. To decline the invitation would be both rude and cowardly, and Onda and Seveline were counting on that.

"It's a trap." The words came out flat.

Ilemina nodded. "They'll provoke you. They'll try to test you to see what you know. Failing that, they'll seek to humiliate you."

"They're counting on Arland. If they insult me enough, and I run to him crying, he'll be honor bound to do something about it. They're getting bolder."

Ilemina's gaze was direct and cold. Maud had seen this exact expression on Arland's face, right before he threw himself at a world-destroying flower. Ilemina had made up her mind. Neither Kozor nor Serak would get off this planet unscathed. It chilled Maud to the bone.

"Do you want the post of Maven?" Ilemina asked.

She didn't even have to think. "Yes."

Ilemina turned to the screen glowing on the wall. A recording began playing. Onscreen, Seveline dashed at a group of otrokar.

Each of the five Horde warriors was bigger than Seveline. Maud had fought the Hope-Crushing Horde before; they had earned their name and then some. Seveline danced through them, slicing limbs, cutting bodies, graceful, lethal, unstoppable...A radiant smile played on the vampire knight's lips. Blood stained her blond hair. She looked like a berserker, lost to the slaughter, but she moved like a fighter completely in control of her body. Fluid. Precise. Aware. Underneath a caption glowed.

Seveline Kozor
57 confirmed kills

Shit.

Onscreen, Seveline beheaded a warrior with a single swing and laughed. She seemed to know where every one of her opponents was at all times, anticipating their movements before they made them.

Ilemina sank steel into her voice. "You will go to this wassail and you will endure every assault on your honor and dignity. Under no circumstances are you to draw your sword. Do you understand me, Maven?"

"Yes, Preceptor."

———

"So, is it customary for humans to be kept as pets?" Seveline asked.

Maud sipped her coffee. It was genuine Earth coffee, given as a gift to the bride by House Krahr, and sweetened with some local syrup until it was less drink and more dessert. The bridal party about lost their minds when they watched her pour cream into it.

She was painfully aware of both Onda and Seveline starring at her. The questions started the moment she sat down and became progressively more outrageous. The last one was an insult. If she were a vampire, by now there would be blood.

It wasn't a bad plan. Isolate her. Get her drunk. Insult her until she threw the first punch, then kill her. They were likely recording this to absolve themselves of blame. Maud had done a mental sweep of the room when she entered. The situation hadn't changed. They were in a tower, in a round chamber. Eight tables, four vampires each. She could hold her own, but nobody was that good. Ilemina was right. *If I draw my sword, I won't make it out of here alive.*

Her best defense was to pretend to be dense. "I don't know what you mean," she said.

Seveline heaved a sigh. Onda leaned forward, brushing her chestnut hair out of the way. "It's a logical question. You are not a member of our society. You have no rights, no purpose, and offer no benefit to House Krahr."

"Aside from sexual amusement for the Marshal," Seveline added.

"In other words, you're being kept around as a source of comfort, much like a dog."

"That's not true," Seveline said. "Dogs serve a purpose. They warn you of intruders and add to your safety."

"Very well, not a dog then." Onda waved her arm. "A bird. A pretty, ornamental bird."

Maud raised her eyebrows. "So, what you are saying is, I'm here for the Marshal's sexual amusement like a pretty bird? Are members of House Kozor in the habit of copulating with their pet birds? I had no idea you had such exotic tastes."

The two women blinked, momentarily derailed.

Seveline switched to Ancestor Vampiric. *"I'm going to wring her neck."*

The bride chose that moment to float by, all smiles. She smoothly turned, rested one hand on Seveline's shoulder, and still smiling, said, *"Do it and I will personally jab a knife in your eye. You have a simple job—provoke this bitch. How hard could this be? The hunt is about to start. Get on with it."*

Interesting.

Kavaline offered Maud a bright smile. "Are you enjoying yourself? These two aren't bothering you, are they?"

The temptation to answer in Ancestor Vampiric was almost too much. "Not at all. They've been the soul of courtesy."

Onda looked like she was about to have an aneurism.

The bride's smile sharpened. "So glad to hear it."

She floated away.

"So, you're content with being a bedwarmer?" Onda asked. "How will this reflect on your daughter? Or do you expect her to learn by example?"

"What a good question," Seveline said. "Perhaps you have already selected a client for her?"

Amateurs.

"What a disturbing thought," Maud said. "Sexual contact with a child is forbidden. It's incredibly damaging to the child. I'm surprised this is tolerated within House Kozor. This is turning out to be a very educational conversation. Birds, children...Is anything off limits to your people?"

Onda turned gray, shaking with rage.

Seveline glared. "We do not have sex with children!"

Vampires at other tables turned to look at them.

"So, just birds, then?" Maud asked.

Seveline picked up the pitcher of coffee, jumped to her feet, and hurled the contents at Maud. There was no time to dodge. The coffee was barely warm, but it drenched her completely.

Onda's eyes were as big as saucers. The room went silent.

Seveline stared straight at her, anticipation in her eyes.

Maud looked back. *It's still your move, bitch.*

Seveline unhinged her jaws. "Coward."

Under the table, Maud sank her fingernails into her palm. In her mind, she flipped the table, gripped her sword, and drove her blade into Seveline's gut.

A moment passed.

Another.

The sticky coffee slid down her neck, dripping from her hair.

Another.

Seveline bared her fangs in a vicious grimace, spun on her heel, and stomped off. The door hissed shut behind her.

Maud sat very still. This could still go bad. If they came at her now, her best bet would be to jump out the window. It was a thirty-foot fall to the ledge below, but she could survive it.

Kavaline opened her mouth. Every pair of eyes watched her.

"My lady, we are dreadfully sorry. I do not know what came over her."

"Clearly," Maud said, her tone dry, "some people just can't handle their coffee."

A light ripple of laughter spread through the gathering.

"You are most gracious," the bride said.

Oh, you have no idea. "I implore you, think nothing of it. Please excuse me, I must now change."

"We wouldn't dream of keeping you."

Try and you'll regret it.

———

MAUD GRITTED HER TEETH AS THE LONG ELEVATOR SPED downward, through a shaft carved in the heart of the mountain. Getting the sticky coffee mess out of her hair had taken forever.

Getting it off her armor had taken even longer. She'd had no time to apply any cosmetics or make herself in any way presentable.

She was never fond of caking makeup on her face, but she'd always loved eye shadow and mascara. In exile, mascara became an unattainable luxury and often a hinderance. Having mascara bleed into your eyes while you sweated buckets trying to kill an opponent twice your size before she did you in wasn't exactly a winning strategy. But as soon as Maud had gotten to the inn, Dina invited her to raid her makeup stash. Maud had worn eye shadow, mascara, and a light lipstick every day since landing on this planet. Now, her face was bare, her hair was wet, because she didn't dare to waste three minutes drying it, and she still, somehow, smelled of that damn coffee.

Maud tapped her foot. The elevator refused to descend faster.

This was not the way she intended to appear at the hunt. If the hunts she'd attended were anything to go by, this would be an almost ceremonial occasion. Everyone would look their best as they rode in a procession. Armor polished, weapons ready, hair styled. When they finally tracked down whatever they were hunting, the strikers would move forward and close in for the kill. The strikers were determined in advance. To be chosen was an honor, and she was sure the strikers for this hunt would be the groom, the bride, possibly Arland, Otubar, Ilemina or Karat. Whoever was chosen from House Krahr would be there solely to make sure the bride and groom got the kill. Everyone would cheer and record the event so later it could be shown to family and friends. Then, the whole party would turn around and go home.

All she had to do was get to the stables on time, ride in the middle of the procession, exchanging pleasantries and looking well put together, then express admiration at the strategic moment, and ride back. She couldn't even manage that. She was at least ten minutes late. More like fifteen. And that's if they'd left on time.

Maud tapped her foot again. The elevator kept going with a soft whisper. She'd checked the message from Helen again. Her daughter's excited face flashed before her, projected from her harbinger. "Hurry up, Mommy. We're going on a hunt."

A message from Ilemina had followed. "I have your child with me." Which didn't sound ominous at all. Maud heaved a sigh. Damn vampires.

The elevator finally stopped. The doors parted, opening to a tunnel leading to wide open doors. Daylight flooded the doorway. Maud broke into a jog and emerged into the sunshine.

A wide pathway, completely straight and paved with flat stones, rolled out before her, leading to a gate. On both sides of her, large corrals lined the path, secured by massive fences. Behind each row of corrals lay a large stable.

The corrals were empty.

The vihr, the big-boned massive mounts vampires preferred, were gone.

She spun around and saw the Stablemaster off to the side. Middle-aged, huge, grizzled, with a mane of reddish hair going to gray, he scowled, checking something on his harbinger. A younger male vampire with grayish skin and jet-black hair stood next to him with a long-suffering expression. Maud strode to them.

"Salutations," Maud said. "Where is the hunting party?"

The Stablemaster didn't look up. "Gone."

"Gone where?"

He stopped and gave her a flat look. "Hunting."

"In which direction?"

"North."

"I need a mount."

The Chatty Cathy of the vampire world favored her with

another look. "I don't have any."

"You were supposed to hold a vihr for me."

"Someone took it. Hunting. North."

Maud summoned the last reserves of her willpower and kept her voice calm. "Do you have any other mounts that I could ride?"

"No."

Okay. "Do you have any mounts at all here? Anything that can run fast?"

The young stable hand glanced at her. "We have savoks. But you can't ride the damn things." He looked at the Stablemaster. "Why do we even have them?"

"Gift from the Horde, after Nexus," the Stablemaster said.

Maud's heart sped up. The otrokar of the Hope-Crushing Horde lived in the saddle. They prized mounts like treasure. They wouldn't offer a gift of anything less than spectacular.

"I'll take a savok," she said.

"The hell you will," the Stablemaster growled. "They will throw you, trample you, gut you with those claws, and bite your head off. And then I'll never hear the end of it from the Marshal."

That did it. She didn't have time to argue this. "You had orders to provide me with a mount. Bring the savoks or I'll get them myself."

"Fine."

The Stablemaster flicked his fingers at his harbinger. The closest gate in the stable on their left opened. Metal clanged and three savoks galloped into the corral. Two were the typical rust red and one was white, an albino. Incredibly rare. The sun caught the velvety short hair of their pelts, and they almost shone as they ran. If they were horses, they would be at least eighteen hands at the withers. Muscular, with four sturdy but lean legs, they moved with agility and speed. Their hind legs ended in hoofs, their front had three fused fingers and a raptor-like dewclaw. Their thick, short necks supported long heads armed with powerful jaws that hadn't been seen on Earth since the extinction of bear dogs and hell pigs.

They thundered past her, the white male flashing her a vicious look from its emerald-green eyes, and kept running along the fence, testing the boundaries of the enclosure, their narrow long tails whipping behind them.

They took her breath away. Growing up in her parents' inn, Maud had seen hundreds of otrokar mounts, but none quite like these three.

The savoks came around again, snapping their fangs at them as they passed. The big male drove his shoulder into the fence and bounced off. They galloped on.

"Told you," the Stablemaster said. "Un-rideable."

They had no idea of these animals' value. By otrokar standards, these were priceless.

The vampires, with their crushing physical power, evolved on a planet rich in woods. They were ambush predators. They hid and sprang at their prey, overpowering it. They were not great runners or great riders, and their mounts, huge, sturdy vihr, who had more in common with bulls and rhinos than racing horses, served their purpose perfectly. They could be loaded with staggering weight, carry it for hours, and they were guaranteed to deliver you from point A to B. They wouldn't do it quickly or gracefully, but they would get you where you needed to go.

The otrokar home world was a place of endless plains. The otrokar were lean and hard, and they could run for miles to exhaust their prey. Their mounts were like them; fast, agile, and tireless. They would eat anything: grass, leftovers, prey they could run to ground, and they were as smart as they were savage.

The savoks kicked the fence. They seemed stir-crazy. "When was the last time they were even out?"

"We let them out once a week," the stable hand said.

Maud resisted the urge to scream. She had to resist very hard.

"Did they provide you with saddles?"

"Yes," the stable hand said.

"Bring me one. The one that came with the white one."

"How will I know which one it is?"

She closed her eyes for a few painful seconds. "The one that has white embroidery."

The stable hand looked at the Stablemaster. The older vampire shrugged. "Go get it."

She didn't wait for the saddle. The savoks had halted at the far end of the corral. Maud climbed the heavy metal fence.

"Hey!" The Stablemaster roared.

The white savok saw her and pawed the ground, preparing for a charge.

Maud inhaled and stuck two fingers into her mouth. A shrill whistle cut through the air.

The savoks froze.

The Stablemaster had lumbered over to the fence and was obviously trying to decide if he should grab Maud and pull her back.

When Dina told Maud about brokering peace on Nexus, she'd mentioned the Khanum, the wife of the Khan, and her children. They were northerners; they would train their savoks in the northern way. Maud whistled again, changing the pitch.

The savoks dashed to her. The Stablemaster made a lunge for her, but she jumped off the fence, down into the corral.

The white savok reached her and reared, pawing the air with his forelegs. Behind her, the Stablemaster swore.

"So beautiful," Maud told the savok. "Such sharp claws. Such a pretty boy." He wouldn't know what she was saying but he would recognize and respond to the tone of voice.

She whistled again, a soft ululating sound, and the savoks pranced around her, nudging her with their muzzles and showing off impressive sharp teeth. The white male hopped in place like a wolf dancing in the snow to scare the mice out of hiding.

"So good. So imposing."

She whistled again. The white savok bent his knees, laid his head down, and waited. She vaulted onto his back and hugged his neck. He leaped up and took off in a dizzying gallop, circling the corral. It took all of her strength to stay on his back. Finally, she whistled him to a slow trot.

The Stablemaster and his helper, a traditional otrokar saddle in his hands, stared at her, openmouthed. She rode the savok a bit more and dismounted. "The saddle."

The stable hand passed it to her through the fence.

"Does the white one have a name?"

"Attura."

Ghost.

Perfect. Let's hope he can fly like one.

She was so late.

————

THE GREEN PLAIN FLEW BY AS ATTURA DASHED THROUGH THE GRASS. The savok hadn't run for a while, and the moment she gave him free rein, he burst into a gallop. For a few happy breaths, after they started off from the stables, Maud let all of her anxiety go and lost herself to the exhilaration of the wind, speed, and power of the beast below her. Attura ran, fueled by the pure joy of it. She felt that joy and, swept up in his need to run free, she let him do it and shared in it.

Eventually though, reality came back like a heavy blanket wrapping around her. She checked her harbinger. They had swung too far to the west, nearing the mesas rising on her left. The hunting party rode through the center of the plain, to the east and just about four miles ahead. Reluctantly, she shifted in the saddle, whistling softly. Attura whined, slowing.

"I know, I know." She promised herself that the next time she had a few hours free, she would bring Attura back out here and let him run himself out. But now they had a hunting party to catch.

The savok settled into a fast canter, which wasn't really the best term. The canter of Earth horses was a three-beat gait, while the savok launched himself forward with his powerful hind legs and pawed at the ground with his forelimbs. It was a stride more reminiscent of a wolf or a greyhound. But it was one rung slower than his sprint, so she called it a canter. Maud steered her mount on an interception course and soon they found a comfortable rhythm.

She checked her harbinger again. It obediently projected the target of the hunt, a large vaguely feline beast the size of a rhinoceros with dark-green fur marked by splotches of deep rust red. The House Krahr Huntmaster was tracking it, but the main hunting party, and Maud, had no idea where it would come from. The vampires didn't like hunts with training wheels.

Daesyn really was a beautiful planet, Maud decided. Soft green grass with flashes of turquoise and gold lined the floor of the plain. Mesas rose on both sides, the gray stone of their walls weathered by rain and sun to almost white. The sky was tinted with emerald green, the golden sun shone bright, and the wind smelled of wildflowers. It was so easy to lose herself in it all and just breathe.

The mesa on her left curved, protruding. Maud rounded it. Far ahead, a long procession trotted across the plain, the massive vihr stomping forward like they were trying to crush the ground with every step, like oversized tan Clydesdales. She was too far off to hear the hoofbeats, but her mind supplied the sound all the same. *Boom. Boom. Boom.* They were moving kind of fast. They must have sighted the prey.

Her harbinger chimed, synchronizing, and projected a stylized map, tagging the individual vampires in the party. Eight people in the lead represented by red triangles, followed by a larger group of white triangles, followed by a smattering of green circles. Red signified the killing team, white indicated adults, and green was reserved for children.

"Tag Helen."

Among the green circles, one turned yellow. She was in the center of the group of children. Likely protected by several sentinels and perfectly safe. Still, the fights were unpredictable.

I really am getting too paranoid.

As if on cue, the hunting party split. The red group at the front peeled off, the slow vihr speeding up. The white group remained steady, holding to their original course.

If she didn't hurry, she would miss the kill. She couldn't offer congratulations to the soon-to-be-married couple unless she actually witnessed them bringing the beast down.

Maud gave a short harsh whistle, and Attura surged forward.

A distant roar shook the air. A huge creature burst from between the mesas, running for the killing team, his green fur blurring with the grass. Damn it.

The killing team fanned out, seeking to flank the beast. It would be over in a matter of minutes.

Her harbinger screamed, the shriek of alarm piercing her. Something was happening in the main procession. The formation broke, too chaotic to see. On her display, a big red dot appeared in the mass of green circles.

Panic punched her. Maud threw her weight forward, almost lying on Attura's neck. The beast galloped with all his might.

266

Individual riders shot out of the procession in all directions. She chanced a quick glance at the projection. There were three red dots now. The children were fleeing, while the adults bunched at the center, trying to contain the threat. The yellow circle indicating Helen angled southwest, another green circle in her wake.

Maud shifted her weight to her left, and the savok angled west.

The group of vampires broke, bodies flying, and through the gap Maud glimpsed a creature. Enormous, mottled gray and stained with dirt and reddish clay, the hulking beast bellowed, swinging its huge scaled head side to side. It caught a knight and the force of the blow hurled him off his mount. The orphaned vihr screamed. The beast's great jaws unhinged and clamped the vihr. The creature swung away and a bloody half of the vihr toppled to the ground.

What the hell was that? It looked like a dragon. A huge scaled dragon.

She had to get to Helen. She had to get to Helen now.

Another dragon, this one pale yellow like an old bone, tore out of the clump of the vampires, and charged southwest. The two riders on juvenile vihr kept fleeing, oblivious to the danger.

It's going after the children.

Maud screamed. Helen's head whipped around. She looked over her shoulder and shrieked.

Maud fused with Attura as if they were one creature, willing him to go faster.

The vihr were running for their lives, the kids bouncing in their saddles, but they weren't fast enough. The dragon came after them, paw over paw, like a sprinting crocodile, jaws gaping, a forest of fangs wet with its drool.

It was gaining.

Faster. Faster!

They were almost there. Almost. A few dozen yards.

The dragon lunged, roaring. *The teeth. Huge teeth.*

This wasn't a dream. The monster from her nightmares had come to life and was trying to devour her daughter.

The little boy's vihr shied, screaming in panic, and stumbled. The boy and the beast went tumbling into the grass. The dragon loomed over them. Maud saw it all as if in slow motion, in painful clarity: Helen's terrified face, her eyes opened wide, her hands on the vihr's reins; the vihr turning, obeying her jerk; and then she was on the ground, between the boy and the dragon.

Twenty yards to her daughter.

A sound ripped the air around Maud, so loud it was almost deafening. A small clinical part of her told her she was howling like an animal, trying to make herself into a threat.

Helen drew her blades.

The dragon opened its mouth. Its head plunged down and Helen disappeared.

Something broke inside Maud. Something almost forgotten that lived deep in the very center of her being, in the place where innkeepers drew their power when they connected to their inn. She had no inn. She had nothing, except Helen, and Helen was inside the dragon's mouth. Everything Maud was, every drop of her will, every ounce of her strength, all of it became magic directed through the narrow lens of her desperation. It tore out of her like a laser beam and she saw it, black and red and ice cold, committed to one simple purpose: *Stop!*

Time froze. The dragon halted, locked and immobile, and the bulge about to travel up its neck stopped in its tracks. The vihr, one fallen, the other about to bolt, stood in place, petrified. The vampire boy sprawled in the grass, unmoving.

This is the magic of an ad-hal, that same clinical voice informed her. *You shouldn't be able to do this.*

But she was moving through the stillness, her sword in her

hand, and as Attura tore into the dragon's hide, Maud slit a gash in its cheek. Blood gushed, red and hot. Maud thrust her arm into the cut. Her fingers caught hair and she grabbed a fistful of it and pulled. She couldn't move it, so she planted her feet, dropped her sword, and thrust both arms into the wound. Her hands found fabric. She grasped it and pulled.

The weight shifted under her hands.

The edges of the gaping cut tore wider.

Her daughter fell into the grass, soaked in spit.

Is she dead? Please, please, please, please...

Helen took a deep, shuddering breath and screamed.

The magic shattered.

The dragon roared in pain and swiped at Attura, who was clinging to its neck. The savok went flying, flipped in midair, landed on all fours like a cat, and charged back in.

The dream haunting her since she arrived on Daesyn burst inside her, popping like a soap bubble, and in a flash, she remembered everything: her parents' inn, the monstrous dragon, the deep inhuman voice that reverberated through her bones, "**Give me the child.**"

There were two children behind her, and she was the only thing between them and the dragon.

Maud attacked.

She tore at it with all the savagery of a mother forced into a corner. She stabbed it, she cut it, she pierced it, her blood blade the embodiment of her rage. There was no fear left. She'd burned it all in the terrifying instant she saw Helen being swallowed. Only fury and icy determination remained.

The dragon struck at her and she dodged. When it caught her with a swipe, she rolled back to her feet and came back in, her teeth bared in a feral snarl. She stabbed it in the throat. When it tried to pin her with its claws, she cut off the talons. She wasn't a whirlwind, she wasn't a wildfire; she was precise, calculating, and cold, and she cut pieces off of it one by one, while Attura ripped into the monster's flesh.

The dragon reared, a bleeding wreck, one eye a bloody hole, paws disfigured, and roared. She must have lost her mind, because she roared back. It came down on her, trying to trap her with its colossal weight. She had the crazy notion of holding her blood blade and letting it impale itself, then something hit her from the side, carrying her out of the way. The dragon smashed into the ground, and in a lightning flash of sanity, Maud realized she would have been crushed.

Arland dropped her to her feet. His mace whined, and he charged the dragon, his face a mask of rage. She laughed and dove back into the slaughter.

They cut and slashed and crushed together. At some point she caught a glimpse of the children stabbing at the crippled dragon's legs. Finally, it swayed like a colossus on sand feet. They drew back and it crashed to the ground. Its remaining eye closed. It lay unmoving.

Maud gripped her sword, unsure if it was over. She had to make sure. She started forward, aiming for its face.

Arland rose out of the gore, jumped up onto the dragon's head, and raised his mace, gripping it with both hands. They hit it at the same time. She sank her blade as deep as it would go in its remaining eye, while he crushed its skull with repeated blows.

They stared at each other, both bloody.

Helen hugged Maud's leg, her lip trembling. Arland slid off the dragon's ruined head and clamped them to him.

His voice came out strained. "I thought I lost you both."

Maud raised her head and kissed him, blood and all, not caring who was watching or what they thought.

[18]

Maud knocked on the door separating Arland's quarters from the passageway leading to her rooms. Yesterday she would have hesitated. Today she didn't even pause.

The door swung open. Arland stood on the other side, barefoot and out of armor, wearing a black shirt over loose black pants. His hair was damp, and he'd pulled it back into a loose ponytail. He must've just stepped out of the shower. The afternoon had turned into evening, and the light of the sunset tinted the room behind him with purple, red, and deep turquoise.

His gaze snagged on her. She was wearing a white robe of fonari spider silk, its fabric so thin and light, she barely felt it. The wide sleeves fell over her arms like a cloud. She'd cinched the robe at the waist with the belt, but it was cut so wide that the voluminous skirt swept the ground behind her, the gossamer silk swirling at the slightest breeze. When the light caught it just right, it shimmered, nearly translucent.

The robe was a Christmas gift from Dina. Her sister had handed her the gift, smiled, and walked away, giving Maud her privacy. Maud had opened the gilded box and stared. At the time it seemed like an unbelievable luxury. On Karhari it would have paid for a year of water for her and Helen.

She'd touched the robe, feeling the delicate fabric, and it stirred something inside her, something gentle and fragile she had hidden deep within her soul to survive, the part of her that loved beautiful clothes, and flowers, and long soaks in the bath. Something she'd thought she lost forever that first night on Karhari, when she cut off her hair and sat alone on the floor among the dark locks and cried. Now, that part came awake and it hurt, and she'd cried again from pain and relief.

She wished so much she'd had her hair now.

Arland opened his mouth.

Nothing came out. He just looked at her. An exhilarating flash of female satisfaction surged through her.

Silence stretched.

"Arland?"

He closed his mouth and opened it again. "How is Helen?"

"Very tired. We washed all of the blood off and she fell asleep."

"Understandable. She was fighting for her life." His voice trailed off.

"Arland?"

"Yes?"

"Can I come in?"

He blinked and stepped aside. "Apparently, I lost my manners somewhere on the hunt. My deepest apologies."

She swept past him into the room.

He shut the door and turned to her. "Have you sustained any inju—"

She put her arms around his neck and stood on her toes. Her lips met his, and he held very still.

Does he not want me?

Arland's arms closed around her. He spun her, and her back

pressed into the door. His rough fingers slid along her cheek, caressing her skin. She looked into his blue eyes and caught her breath. His eyes were hot with lust, need, and hunger, all swirled together and sharpened with a hint of predatory anticipation.

His lips trembled in the beginning of a growl. He smiled wide, showing his fangs, and lowered his mouth to hers. Her instincts screamed in panic, not sure if she was mate or prey, but she had waited so long for this and she met him halfway.

They came together like two clashing blades. His mouth sealed on hers and she opened for him, desperate to connect, to feel him, to taste...His tongue glided over hers. He tasted of mint and warm spice. His fangs rasped against her lip.

Her head swam. She felt light, and strong, and wanted...

He kissed her deeper, his big body bracing hers. She nipped his lip. A snarl rumbled deep in his throat, the sound a predatory warning, or maybe a purr, she wasn't sure. He kissed the corner of her mouth, her lips, her chin, her neck, painting a line of heat and desire on her skin. She was shaking with need now.

"I've wanted this for so long," he groaned.

"So have I."

"Why now?"

He was kissing her neck again, each touch of his lips a burst of pleasure. She could barely think, but she answered anyway. "We almost died today. I can't wait any longer. I don't want to be careful, I don't want to think about the consequences or things going wrong. I just want you. I want you more than anything."

"You have me."

"Always?"

"Always," he promised.

———

Maud stretched, sliding her foot along the heated length of Arland's leg. He pulled her tighter to his body. Her head rested on his chest.

"What were they? The creatures."

"The closest thing to Mukama in my generation. On the vampire home world, there were predatory apes, like us, but not quite us. A distant relative, less intelligent, more feral, more vicious."

"Primitive?"

"Yes. The Mukona, the creatures that attacked us, are the Mukama's primeval cousins. They are to the Mukama what feral apes are to us. An earlier evolutionary branch that didn't grow. Daesyn is the birth place of the Mukama, after all. The Mukona possess rudimentary intelligence, more of a predatory cunning, really, and inhabit caves deep below the planet's surface. When we took over the planet, we had hunted them to extinction, or so we thought. Apparently we were mistaken."

"There were three of them," Maud said. "A mated pair and an offspring?"

"I don't know. Possibly. I'd never seen one before today. I'd heard stories." He made a low growl. "Once this damn wedding is over, we'll have to send survey drones into the caverns. Find out how many of them there are, and if any are left, we'll have to take measures to preserve them."

She raised her head and looked at him.

He smiled at her. "Today we are legends. We killed a Mukona, the next thing to the Mukama, the ancient enemy, the devourers of children, the cosmic butchers who almost exterminated us. Once the word gets out, every House will be beating on our door for a chance to hunt one. They really are magnificent beasts. We have to protect their future and manage their numbers. I have no idea what brought them to the surface for this hunt, but whatever it was ensured its place in history. Oh well, at least something good will come out of this wedding."

"It was Helen," Maud said.

He frowned.

"When I was a little girl, a Mukama came to stay at our inn."

Arland jerked upright in the bed. "A living Mukama?"

"Well yes, it wasn't a dead one that somebody brought with them. No, he was very much alive and wanted a room. They are out there somewhere, Arland. Think about it. They were an interstellar civilization with an armada of ships. You didn't really think you got them all, did you?"

"Yes, I kind of did. What happened?"

Maud sighed. "I was very young, so I only remember bits and pieces. My brother told me most of it. He is older than me by three years and he saw the whole thing. He had nightmares for years after. The inn had lain dormant for a long time and my parents had just recently become its innkeepers. They were not in a position to turn down guests, and when the Mukama came, he was brimming with magic. The inn desperately needed sustenance and giving him a room would go a long way to restore the inn's strength."

"I understand," he said. "That's why your sister agreed to host our peace summit after everyone else turned us down."

Maud nodded. "My parents offered him quarters with a separate exit, completely away from all the other guests, on the condition that he refrain from harming anyone. Supposedly, I had walked into the garden at this point. I was maybe five. I should remember it, but I don't. All I recall is a monster chasing me through the garden. And then there were teeth. Really scary teeth."

She slid deeper under the blanket. Arland lowered himself back down next to her and wrapped his arm around her waist.

"I was running for my life and then my father stepped onto the path in front of me. His robe was black, and his eyes and his broom were glowing with blue light. I ran behind him and kept running, and then there was this awful roar. My parents had restrained the Mukama. It had taken all of their combined power and everything the inn had. When my father demanded to know why he shouldn't just kill the Mukama now, the creature told him that it couldn't help itself. That I was full of magic and he would do anything to devour me. He offered them a fortune. He told them they could always make more children, but it was vital that he be allowed to eat me."

Arland swore.

"He raved about it. My father was worried that they wouldn't be able to contain him, and he appealed to the Innkeeper Assembly. They sent the ad-hal and the ad-hal took him away. That's why the Mukama are barred from inns."

"Why didn't you ever tell me? Why didn't anyone tell us?"

Maud sighed. "I didn't tell you because I had forgotten it. I've had nightmares about it every night on this planet, but I must have repressed it. It was just too scary. All of my energy was spent either tending to your wounds or trying to not throw myself at you."

His eyebrows crept up.

"As to why nobody told the Holy Anocracy, the vampires are just one of the thousands of species who come through Earth's inns. We maintain our neutrality and we keep the secrets of our guests."

Maud frowned. "What is it about the children? The Mukama and their relatives seem uncontrollably drawn to them. Three creatures who had survived on a vampire world all this time burst out of hiding just to eat my daughter. Why now?"

"I don't know," Arland said. "But we will find out."

They lay together in a comfortable silence. Maud basked in it. Warm and safe and...

"Tell me something. When I was running to you, I could have sworn the Mukona froze in mid-move. Was it you?"

She groaned and pulled the covers over her head.

Arland peeled the blankets back. "That's not an answer."

"It was me."

"How?"

"I don't know."

He pinned her with his stare. "It reminded me of Tony. The ad-hal Tony. When he walked into the battle at your sister's inn and froze the attacking Draziri."

She narrowed her eyes at him. "Why do you have to be so observant?"

"A lifetime of training and a few moments of fear," Arland said. "When you see the woman you love and your daughter about to be eaten alive, it sharpens your senses a bit. Why do you have the magic of an ad-hal?"

"I wish I could tell you. I've never done that before. Nobody knows how the ad-hal are made or trained. When a child is chosen to become an ad-hal, and the family consents, they are taken away for a while. Sometimes a few months, sometimes a year. The older you are, the longer the training takes. They don't talk about it, even with their families. Sometimes they come back, like Tony, sometimes they choose not to."

"Are the ad-hal highly prized? Are they rare?"

"Yes," she said.

His expression hardened.

"Are you formulating a battle plan in case the ad-hal show up here and try to take me or Helen away?" she asked.

"They will not take you away. You are the Maven of House Krahr. Nobody comes to take you away. They would have to kill the entirety of our House. You said it yourself, their numbers are few. Should they try, there would be a lot fewer of them."

She gave a mock shudder. "So bloodthirsty."

He flashed his fangs at her.

"It doesn't work like that," she explained. "Becoming an ad-hal is strictly voluntary. If I go back to Earth and demonstrate my new time freezing ability, assuming I can do it, because I don't know how I did it and I've been trying to do it again with no success, the Innkeeper Assembly may want to ask me some questions. But I am not an innkeeper. They have no authority over me unless I break the treaty. But I like the way you think, my lord."

Arland kissed her shoulder. "That's excellent news."

The kissing made it difficult to carry on a conversation. "Mhm. So when did you know your mother made me the Maven?"

"She informed me after the fact." He nuzzled her neck. "Do you like being the Maven?"

"I'm thinking about it. What are you doing?"

"Since my wounds don't need tending, I am seeing if I can get you to throw yourself at me."

"Already?"

"A knight always rises to the occasion, my lady."

———

THE THREE OF THEM WERE EATING BREAKFAST ON HER BARREN balcony. She and Arland sat at the table, enjoying mint tea and a platter of meats, cheeses and fruit, while Helen had taken her plate and sat cross-legged on the stone wall, contemplating the dizzying drop below. Every time she shifted her weight, Maud had to fight the urge to leap into action and pull her back from the edge.

"The child is completely fearless," Arland said quietly.

"Karhari was flat," Maud said. "I'm not sure if she understands the danger or is just ignoring it."

Arland raised his voice. "Helen, do not fall."

"I won't."

Arland glanced back at Maud.

Well, of course, that fixes everything. She hid a smile and drank her mint tea.

"I have a gift for you." Arland pushed a small tablet across the table.

On the tablet, a slightly worse for wear but still impressive vessel appeared on the screen. It was patched, repaired and obviously scarred but the battle-damaged nature of the ship seemed to make it even more imposing. It was like an aging fighter, battered but unbowed.

"The *Star Arrow*? Renouard's ship?"

Arland nodded. "The pirate."

"What about it?"

"Would you like him killed?"

She blinked.

"He insulted you. You seem to dislike him, so I sent a frigate to track him down. We've been watching him for the past half-cycle, and we have more than enough firepower to reduce him and his ship to cosmic dust."

"Let me see if I understand correctly. You didn't like the way a pirate and slave trader spoke to me, so you sent a frigate to track him down and murder him and his crew at my convenience?"

"You seemed to really dislike him."

She stared at him for a long moment and then began counting on her fingers. "Fuel cost, hazard pay, an entire crew sent into deep space..."

"The man is a menace, and the galaxy would be better off without him."

She squinted at him. "Are you jealous of Renouard?"

"Not anymore. You are here with me and he is somewhere in the Malpin Quadrant, about to impersonate a supernova." Arland sipped his tea.

She laughed. "Would you like me to tell you about him?"

"If you wish."

"We met at a Road Lodge, a year and a half ago. He is a smuggler, occasional slave trader, and pirate of opportunity. I don't know which House he was in, but I do know that he was born out of wedlock and it caused an issue. Depending on who you asked, he was either cast out or he left of his own free will, but he has been a pirate for the last two decades. I ran into him again after Melizard died. I was desperate to get off the planet, and he offered me passage."

"At what price?"

Maud shook her head. "Human, vampire, doesn't matter. You want to know if I slept with him." It was rather adorable that it was bugging him that much.

"I would never presume to ask." Arland's face was very carefully neutral. If he appeared any more disinterested, he would fade into the stone wall.

"I never had sex with Renouard. He hinted at first, then he offered me passage for it, but even if I had found him attractive, which I didn't, I never trusted him. He is the type to screw you until he's bored, and then sell you to the highest bidder to make a quick credit. Even if I had been by myself, I wouldn't have taken him up on it. I was responsible for Helen. I wasn't about to take any chances. Shooting him now serves no purpose."

"It might be entertaining to watch him explode." Arland smiled wide, showing her his splendid fangs.

Maud rolled her eyes. "Keep him. He's not stupid. He's been a pirate for twenty years; he's a survivor. He knows a lot of creatures. He's also vain and he hates the Holy Anocracy, which makes him predictable. He may prove a valuable resource. Alternatively, you can storm his ship, put him in chains, have him dragged here and hidden in some dark hole, and when you're suffering from an attack of melancholy, you could go and poke him with a stick. It would cheer you right up."

"I don't do melancholy." Arland sat up straighter. "I am the Lord Marshal of House Krahr. I have no time to mope."

Maud shrugged. "There is your answer then."

Arland took the tablet back and typed something in a very deliberate fashion.

"I recalled the frigate. The man is a scumbag but blowing him to pieces after this conversation would be unseemly. I have to avoid the appearance of pettiness."

"What happens the next time somebody is mean to me? Will you scramble the fleet again?"

"I'll handle it. I just won't tell you about it until it's done."

She laughed. "Do you feel I need assistance defending my honor?"

Arland leaned back and glanced into her quarters.

"What are you doing?" Maud asked.

"Checking to see where your sword is before I answer."

She leaned back in her chair and laughed again. She couldn't remember the last time she had so much fun at breakfast. *You could have this every day*, a small voice told her. Just like this, the three of them, together, making jokes about pirate hunting and watching to see if they needed to rescue Helen.

"Do you think I could get some plants for this balcony?"

Arland stopped chewing halfway through his smoked meat.

"Do you want plants? Make a list. I'll have them delivered before sunset."

"Thank you. It needs some flowers," she said.

"You don't need to even ask. Anything you want is yours, if it is within my power to grant. Besides, as Maven, you have a discretionary spending account and the authority to use it as you wish."

Maud toyed with her spoon. "I don't even know what to get…"

"Can I have a kitty?" Helen asked.

The two of them turned to her.

"If Mommy gets flowers, can I have a kitty?"

Arland looked abashed. "We don't really have kitties. Would you settle for a *rassa* puppy or a *goren* puppy?"

Helen checked her harbinger. "Yes!"

"Then we'll go to the kennels when we finish breakfast. If your mother approves."

Smart man. "I approve," Maud said.

Their harbingers chimed at the same time. Maud read the short, one-sentence message, and her stomach tried to crawl sideways.

The happy couple want to wed on the battle station.

– Karat.

[19]

Maud followed Arland into the HQ of House Krahr. The large room churned with activity. Desks and displays sprouted from the floor, each station a focal point for the House Krahr elite, and between them a dozen knights and retainers hurried to and fro. Screens shone on the walls, flashing with data and images. A clump of retainers surrounded Ilemina on the left and an equally large group crowded Lord Soren.

"Lord Marshal!" Knight Ruin emerged from the rush, a look of determination on his face. As far as she could tell, Knight Ruin's mission in life was to ensure that Arland was where he was supposed to be when he was supposed to be there so he could be taking care of pressing matters, of which Knight Ruin always had a long and detailed list. She had a feeling the russet-haired knight considered her to be a permanent threat to his success.

Arland veered left to what had to be his desk, with Ruin following and speaking in urgent low tones. Several knights peeled off from the crowd and closed in on Arland like starved sharks.

Maud halted, taking in the controlled chaos around her. The

entire wedding venue had to be relocated to the battle station, where things would finally come to an end. The logistics of moving the celebration alone were enough to give one kittens but selecting who would be in attendance to the wedding added an entirely new dimension. Planetside, House Krahr had an over-whelming numbers advantage. In space, with a limited capacity, half of which was taken up by the wedding "guests," every attendee counted.

The gauntlet was thrown, the war banner unfurled, and the fangs bared. House Krahr had risen to the challenge.

In his wildest dreams, that's what Melizard had envisioned. A thriving House, bustling with activity and preparing for war. The hum of voices, the chimes of communication alerts, the rapid rhythm of running footsteps...Spacecraft taking off on the moni-tors. Knights in battle armor. An electric excitement saturating the hall, sizzling along his skin. Her former husband would have drunk it in like it was the nectar of the gods. Melizard would've killed, in a very literal sense of the word, for a chance to be a part of this. He had once told her he felt like he was born into the wrong House. She never understood it until now. House Ervan could have never delivered *this*, not on this scale. This was what he must've seen in his head.

He must've felt suffocated.

She imagined his ghost standing next to her, a thin translucent shadow, and waited for the familiar pinch of bitterness. It didn't come.

I've moved on.

She was free. Finally. All her memories and bitter lessons were still there but they lost their bite. The present mattered so much more now.

Everyone around her was busy. She should make herself

useful. At least she could contribute in some small way. Someone somewhere could use her assistance…

A young vampire knight slid to a halt in front of her. If Melizard's ghost had any substance, she would have torn right through him. She was tall, with a deep-gray skin and a wealth of blue-black hair braided from her face. She held a tablet in her hands, a communicator curved to her lips, and a secondary display projected over her left eye.

"Lady Maven."

Maud moved to step aside and froze in mid-step. She was the Maven.

"Yes?"

"I'm Lady Lisoun. I'm your adjutant. What should we do about the chairs?"

"What about the chairs?" What chairs? Adjutant?

Lady Lisoun took a deep breath. The words came out of her in a rapid sprint. "The battle station banquet hall chairs."

Maud waited.

"They are sojourn style chairs."

Sojourn style chairs had a solid back. There was no way the tachi would be able to sit in the sojourn chairs. Their vestigial appendages would be in the way.

"Your desk is this way." Lisoun began weaving her way through the crowd.

Maud marched next to her. "Can we substitute different chairs?"

"No, my lady. They are part of a unit, one table and eight chairs."

"Are they attached to the table?"

"Yes, my lady."

"Whose bright idea was that?"

"I don't know, my lady. They stow away for the ease of storage."

"Are they at least height adjustable?" The lees couldn't sit in vampire-sized chairs either.

"I don't know." Lisoun braked to a stop before a desk surrounded by people. "I'll find out."

The retainers crowding the desk saw Maud and swarmed them. Everyone spoke at once.

"One at a time!" Maud barked.

A familiar looking retainer—where had she seen him? Ah, feast hall—thrust a tablet under her nose. On it glowed an elaborately arranged platter of fruit and vegetables. "Menu for approval!"

Maud stared at the arrangement. "Take out all of the kavla—the tachi are allergic. Make sure the honey doesn't contain any kavla either." She waved her fingers at the tablet, scrolling through the pictures. "No. None of these make any sense. The tikk igi dishes need to have a pattern. You can't just put a bunch of pretty fruit randomly on a platter. There must be a progression of taste or color, ideally both. A circular arrangement would start with sour fruit on the edge and then progressively get sweeter toward the center. Or, you start with purple berries and work your way through a spectrum to yellow. This is a haphazard mess. Take this back, bring me an updated menu."

He took the tablet and broke into a sprint.

"The chairs are not adjustable!" Lisoun reported.

"Get me a station engineer." Maud looked at the crowd. "Next!"

Konstana thrust herself into Maud's view. They hadn't seen each other since the Communal. The red-haired knight's arm didn't show any signs of ever being broken.

"I'm your security chief," she said.

She had a security chief. Huh. "How many people do we have?"

"Three squads, sixty knights total, but they are only letting me take six. They expect me to secure thirty-eight aliens with six vampires."

Maud raised her eyebrows. "Is that a problem?"

Konstana scoffed. "Of course not. But I do need to know how they are getting to the battle station. Are we transporting them or are they transporting themselves? And if they are transporting themselves, are we going to let them dock or are they shuttling over via their shuttles or via ours?"

"What does the Knight-Sergeant say?"

"He said to ask you."

Thank you, Lord Soren. "Get battle station security chief on the line and figure out if a non-regulation shuttle can even dock there. Let me know what you find out."

Lisoun pushed her way back into the circle. She grasped Maud's arm and half-guided, half-propelled her behind a podium next to her desk where a large screen presented her with a tough looking female vampire standing in a large hall. The smooth black floor split, a glossy onyx contraption spiraled out of it and unfolded into a round table ringed by eight sojourn style chairs. The chairs were big, rectangular, and blocky. The worst-case scenario.

"How wide are those chair backs at the seat?" Maud asked.

"Twenty lots," the engineer reported, which Maud's implant helpfully converted into twenty-eight inches. Right.

"I need you to cut a hole in the back of the chair at the seat level, twenty-four inches wide and eight inches tall."

The engineer stared at her, incredulous. "You want me to deface the an-alloy chairs?"

"Yes." She glanced at Lisoun. "I need the seating chart."

A diagram popped out on a side screen. Oh universe, what in

the world..."This is wrong," she told Lisoun. "We cannot put the royal in the back of the hall."

"Lord Soren said..."

"Go back to Lord Soren and ask him if he would like to have a war with the Tachi Protectorate. Lady Dil'ki is not just a scientist, she is a member of the royal house. She and Nuan Cee have to be seated in the front. This needs to be reworked."

Lisoun took off.

"These chairs are a marvel of function and durability," the engineer growled. "The an-alloy is nearly indestructible."

"I have..." Maud checked her harbinger. "Thirty-eight aliens, of which twenty-two are too small to sit in these chairs and the others have vestigial appendages which prevent them from sitting at all."

"These chairs were never designed for aliens!"

"Well, now they have to accommodate some, so find a way to destruct the indestructible chairs. I will send over an updated seating chart. Every chair marked 'tachi' must have a hole. Every chair marked 'lees' must be adjusted for a being of three to four feet in height."

The engineer bared her fangs. "On whose authority?"

"On my authority. I'm the Maven. Look at it as a challenge."

The engineer opened her mouth.

Maud loaded steel into her voice. "When these aliens go off into the galaxy, they will praise House Krahr's hospitality instead of telling the universe that the elite of vampire engineering couldn't solve the trivial problem of appropriate seating. We won't embarrass ourselves. Have I made myself clear?"

"Yes, my lady."

"I see you're settling into your role," a familiar voice said.

Maud raised her head from the screen. "Lord Erast?"

The Scribe nodded at her and passed her a tablet. "The

Preceptor would like you to make the necessary edits. She wishes to deliver the document to the parties in question as soon as possible."

Maud raised the tablet. The green spark of a scanner flashed at her. The contents were locked to her. The screen flared into life.

Mutual Cooperation Pact.

The following Articles are to outline the involvement and voluntary participation of Clan Nuan and the tachi Protectorate...

Oh no. "This won't work."

"What's wrong with it?" the Scribe asked.

"It says involvement."

"Involvement is a perfectly good word."

"We're dealing with the lees. It's like making a deal with..." the devil. She grappled with her knowledge of ancient sagas, looking for a reference. "Yarlas the Cunning."

Lord Erast raised his eyebrows.

"If we leave any gap, any hint at an alternative interpretation, they will drive a space cruiser through it. We have to make this super simple. Short, clear sentences. No ambiguity at all or we will end up explaining to Lady Ilemina why the lees now own the station and half of the planet. This will require an extensive edit."

She stared at the gathering. Six vampires. If she could cull this to a reasonable number, she could devote all of her attention to editing the articles.

"Everyone with an immediate need step forward. Everyone whose issues can wait, see me this evening."

The six vampires in front of her took a step forward in unison.

It was going to be a long day.

———

MAUD STOOD IN THE MIDDLE OF THE OFFICER HALL AND WATCHED

the entrance ceremony unfold on a large screen. The banquet room, a large space meant to accommodate five hundred diners, spread out before her, an expanse of smooth onyx-black floor punctuated by rosettes of tables and chairs made of the same glossy black. The crimson banners of House Krahr stretched along the walls, the gold catlike predator on them snarling to remind the gathering in whose house they were about to dine.

The blast shields of the massive battle station were down, and the far side of the hall was all window, the universe glittering beyond, with the turquoise and blue orb of the planet rising slowly to the right. A spray of radiant stars winked from beyond, the Krahr Home World Fleet displayed for the guests in a show of power and strength.

A dais had been raised in the center, with the windows as the backdrop, and in the middle of it a small vala tree spread its gnarled black branches, its red leaves glowing against the cosmos, at once fragile and indomitable, a testament to the power of life that flourished given the slightest chance.

Both the Kozor and Serak were already seated, taking up the center swath of tables. The lees and the tachi, in the newly butchered chairs, were also in their places, the tachi on the left, and the lees on the right, with the heads of both delegations nearest the dais. The one hundred and twenty knights of House Krahr would take the back rows of the tables. The addition of the thirty-eight aliens brought their numbers to one hundred and fifty-eight. If either Kozor or Serak recognized that they were being boxed in, they could do nothing about it.

She had spoken to both factions only a couple of hours ago about what to expect in greater detail.

"We will do our part. But why won't the Krahr simply bring additional numbers to overwhelm the other Houses?" Dil'ki had asked her as they strolled through the Maven's Gardens. "It would avoid the loss of life."

"It's about face," Nuan Cee had said, drawing his paw-hand over his muzzle. "One must never lose it."

"It's a challenge," Maud had explained. "The Kozor and the Serak hope to accomplish an incredible feat, worthy of the old sagas. The response from the Krahr must be equally heroic. They will reject any numbers advantage. This isn't just about winning. This is about winning against the odds. Every moment of this wedding will be recorded."

"Do the vampires of Krahr truly believe themselves to be that good?" Dil'ki had asked.

"Yes," Maud had told her.

The royal sat quietly now, clad in the diaphanous veils and glowing jewelry of her kind. Her warriors waited around her, all a saturated, even color. Despite what was coming, the tachi were at ease.

At the other side of the hall, Clan Nuan, in their best gold and jewels, all wearing soft silky aprons, chattered and giggled without a care in the world.

The Herald announced Ilemina and Otubar. The hosts entered the hall last, according to tradition, and Ilemina and Otubar walked to their table, Ilemina elegant in her ornate armor and Otubar stalking next to her like a hulking krahr in a bad mood, while the Herald barked out their titles: Supreme Predator, Killer, Destroyer, Marauder, Slayer...

Maud wished with all her heart that she could hug Helen again. She left her on the planet. The battle station was no place for a child, especially if things proceeded as expected. She had to do what she did best: survive. Eliminate the threat and go back, to her daughter, her future husband, and her new home.

Easier said than done.

Arland approached. She felt his presence, rather than saw him, and turned. He towered above her in full syn-armor with a crimson cloak that made him seem even more enormous. His blood mace rested on his hip. He'd pulled his long blond hair from his face and secured it at the nape of his neck, and his features looked carved from granite, his blue eyes hard and cold. A Marshal in every sense of the word, meant to inspire fear.

He held out his arm to her. "Ready, my love?"

"Yes." She put her hand on his wrist, her fingers light as a feather.

They entered the long narrow hallway leading to the banquet hall, moving in step.

Ahead the microphone-enhanced voice of the Herald recited their titles, booming through the room.

"Arland Rotburtar Gabrian, son of Kord, son of Ilemina, 28th Heir of Krahr, Lord Marshal of his House. Bloodmace, Bone Crusher, Ravager of Nexus, Destroyer of the World Killer. Kill count of two hundred and twenty-four."

Maud caught their reflection in the polished walls. In it a strange woman glided next to Arland, wearing black armor and carrying a blood sword, a narrow crimson sash of the Maven wrapped around her left shoulder, crossing over her collarbone and draping over her right shoulder to trail behind her to the floor. She was graceful and strong, and walked next to a vampire prince like she belonged there.

A giddy, electric anticipation surged through her. They were walking to a fight. Finally, an end to all the pressure. One way or the other, it would be decided. Her lips threatened to curve into a smile, and she forced an arrogant cold mask over her face. Today she was Cinderella and her sword would be her glass slipper.

"Matilda Rose, daughter of Gerard, daughter of Helen, Lady and Heir of Demille, Maven of House Krahr."

The hallway ended, and they strode into the banquet hall. The entirety of the room was watching them.

"Maud the Red, the Sariv, the Learned One."

They were approaching the table where Onda and Seveline sat. Both women were staring daggers at her.

"Kill count of sixty and eight."

A muscle in Seveline's face jerked. *That's right, precious. I'm coming for you.*

Arland led her to their table, directly behind the one occupied by the parents of the bride and groom. The two couples had arrived just this morning for the happy occasion.

She took her seat, keeping her face flat. Behind them, the Herald was announcing the next guest.

"Alvina, daughter of Soren, daughter of Alamide, Lady Renadra, Karat, Commander of Krahr..."

Maud sipped the light mint drink and watched the hall fill. Finally, everyone was seated.

Twelve vampire women entered the hall, moving in a column two abreast. Each wore a long white robe with a hood and carried a vala tree branch decorated with bells and golden thread. A low chant rose from their lips, a melodious song that floated through the chamber. Beautiful and timeless, it reached deep into one's soul and found that vulnerable place hidden within. It wrapped around Maud and suddenly she missed her parents, Dina, Klaus, and Helen. She wanted to gather them all to her and hold on, because life was short and fleeting.

The procession split just short of entering the dais, the women moving along the main floor to encircle the raised platform, holding their branches straight up, as if guarding.

Twelve vampire knights entered the chamber, out of armor and dressed in plain black tunics, matching black pants, and wearing tall black boots. Each carried a simple black blade. A second chant rose from the men, joining the song of the women, deepening the melody, like a twin vine growing around the first. The song was everywhere now, echoing from the walls, reverberating back on itself, and Maud breathed it in.

The second column split in two and the men took position between the women, each with their blade straight down, its point resting on the floor.

The song changed, gaining strength and speed.

A Battle Chaplain entered the chamber. He was tall, his skin gray with a slight blue tint. A mane of black hair shot through with gray fell on his shoulders in dozens of long braids. His vestments, the color of fresh blood, were split into ribbons, each about eight inches wide, and as he strode forward, they moved and shifted like the robes of some mystic mage. He carried an ornate spear draped with a red cord and decorated with golden bells. Two glowing yellow orbs about the size of a large orange dangled from it.

The song erupted, suddenly full of joy and triumph.

Behind the Chaplain, the bride and groom strode into the chamber in unison, both out of armor. The bride's gown swept the floor, long, diaphanous, and white. The groom wore an ornate silver doublet over darker pants and soft boots. They had removed all jewelry. Their hair hung loose, brushed back from their faces.

It was one of the rare few moments that vampires permitted themselves to be vulnerable in public. Maud hadn't fully grasped the significance of it during her own wedding but now she understood. You came to the altar as you were, hiding nothing from your future spouse.

Arland reached over and squeezed her hand. She smiled at him.

The Chaplain ascended the dais. The couple followed and the

three of them took their places in front of the vala tree. The Chaplain raised the spear and touched its end to the floor.

The chant died.

The Chaplain opened his mouth.

An alarm blared through the chamber.

A screen opened in the middle of a wall, showing a male vampire knight on the bridge of the battle station.

Arland rose to his feet. "Report."

"We are showing multiple unidentified craft entering the system," the knight said, his voice calm. "We are under attack."

THE BANQUET HALL HAD GONE COMPLETELY SILENT. WHEN THE huge screen projected on the wall, it showed three merchant barges racing from the gate, deeper into the system, squeezing every drop of speed out of their protesting engines. Behind them, a pirate flotilla swelled like a swarm of angry hornets. A single barge could've fit all of its attackers in its bloated hull, but the pirate ships made up for their lack of tonnage in maneuverability and armaments. No two vessels were alike, but, limited only by the imagination of their crew and the laws of physics, all of them bristled with every possible weapon they could rig onto their hulls, from kinetic cannons to missile batteries. They chased after the lumbering merchants like barracudas ready to tear into an injured whale.

Arland watched the chase, his face impassive, as if unaware that every person in the hall was waiting for him to make his move.

"We're receiving a distress call from the barges," the officer from the bridge reported. "They are begging for our assistance, my lord."

"Put it through," Arland said.

A scratchy, static-filled distress call played from hidden speakers, screams of beings in pain, spearheaded by an urgent, desperate female voice, "...rear thrusters lost...hull integrity compromised...requesting immediate aid. We're at your mercy..."

The call cut out.

"Will House Krahr stand idly by and permit this piracy?" the father of the groom demanded. His voice boomed through the hall.

Maud glanced at Ilemina. Arland's mother sipped her wine, appearing fully unconcerned.

"Lord Marshal!" the bride called. Tears stained her cheeks. "Please. Don't let this travesty stain my wedding."

Arland turned to the bride, concern obvious on his face. "Do not worry, my lady. You have my word that I will allow nothing to ruin this day."

Arland turned to the screen. "Give me the feed from the *Eradicator*."

The screen flashed with white, and a new image snapped into view, a swarm of sparks silhouetted against the dark cosmos, and then, as if by magic, huge elegant vessels appeared on both sides and above, framing the screen—the House Krahr armada, waiting in formation between the battle station and the incoming invaders. If the barges could reach the firing envelope of the leading Krahr vessel, they would be safe.

"Lord Harrendar," Arland said.

The image of a middle-aged vampire with a blue-black mane appeared in the lower left corner. "Lord Marshal." Lord Harrendar sounded like a lion who somehow became a vampire.

"How close are the leading pirate vessels to the barges?"

"We expect them to reach firing range in forty seconds."

Arland waited.

The division in the banquet hall was obvious now. The members of House Krahr waited in tense silence, while the wedding guests appeared almost frantic, as if they were barely able to contain themselves. From her spot, Maud had a clear view of the groom's mother and the woman looked ready to explode. Next to her the bride's mother tapped her fingers on the table, looking as if her armor was on too tight.

Seconds ticked by.

"Do something," the bride's father growled.

Arland ignored him. Maud's heart hammered. She forced herself to reach for her drink and take slow measured sips. The tension in the hall was so thick, you could cut it and serve it in slabs on a plate.

"They've launched the opening volley," Lord Harrendar reported.

"Missiles?"

"No, my lord. Long-range kinetic bombardment."

Maud had little experience with space battles, but her harbinger assured her that kinetic bombardment amounted to lobbing chunks of matter, such as stone or metal, in the direction of the target. Kinetic bombardment was deployed primarily against stationary targets, because they couldn't dodge.

"Damage?" Arland asked.

"Slight," Harrendar reported, his tone sharp.

"Well, of course they're not using missiles," the mother of the groom snapped. "They clearly want the cargo, desperately enough to chase it into your territory. If you do not do something, we will."

"Is this what House Krahr stands for?" the father of the bride asked.

"Do not trouble yourself, my lord and lady," Arland said. "We have the situation well in hand."

"You're going to let those merchants get slaughtered by pirates," the groom growled.

"Second volley," Harrendar reported. "Damage minor. The barges have passed the outer beacon. Still mostly intact."

"Show me the relative position," Arland said.

A projection appeared on the screen. The pirates were clustered around the barges now, forming a loose cloud about to engulf the three larger ships.

"Velocity?"

".4 lightspeed," Harrendar reported.

"Initiate firing solution Revelation."

"Finally," the groom muttered.

"Yes, my lord." Harrendar bared his fangs in a joyous grin that would give some people nightmares.

The screen flashed back to the view from the *Eradicator*. For a torturous moment, nothing happened. Then, the entire armada simultaneously belched a missile salvo. The missiles sparked with bright green and vanished.

"Impact in three," Harrendar started. "Two. One."

The screen exploded with white. Maud shut her eyes against the blinding flash. When she opened them, the explosion had faded, and the long-range projection glowed on the left half of the screen.

The barges were no more. The leading third of the pirate fleet had vanished. Chunks of debris hurtled through space in their stead, turning it into a localized asteroid field. The vessels in the center of the swarm reeled, initiating evasive maneuvers.

Stunned silence claimed the hall.

"Direct hit," Harrendar crowed into the quiet.

"Excellent work, admiral," Arland said. "The field is yours."

Harrendar grinned. The House Krahr armada accelerated toward the remaining pirates.

Arland turned. His gaze swept the hall and settled on the table where the elite of Kozor and Serak waited. "When I became aware of your asinine plot to take over the battle station, one thing kept nagging at me. Our fleet is in-system, and you are, like most pirates, cowardly. You shy from an honorable fight. You had to have a way to neutralize our fleet."

You could hear a pin drop.

"A few days ago, I happened to come across a pirate. He is a knave and a brigand, exiled by his own House and burning with rage. I planned on killing him, but my betrothed reminded me that even a knave could be useful. I asked myself, who would find this pirate, once a Knight Captain and now an enemy of Holy Anocracy, useful? So, I bribed his communication officer and then I listened, and for a paltry sum, he told me your entire battle plan. The three barges loaded with explosives, set to go off as soon as they reached our fleet, and the pirates meant to mop up what was left while you used the chaos to take over the battle station. My lords and ladies, please take these few precious seconds remaining of your lives to contemplate where it all went wrong and prepare to cross death's threshold. You will not be granted another chance to reflect."

That was her cue. Maud stood up, turned to Seveline and Onda, and said in Ancestor Vampiric, *"Did you get all that or do you need me to translate it for you into your backwater gibberish?"*

For a moment nothing moved. Then Seveline leaped onto the table and charged her, her blood sword screaming.

THE BANQUET HALL ERUPTED AS EVERY ARMORED VAMPIRE JUMPED to their feet. Maud caught a glimpse of Seveline swinging her sword at someone in the distance. Maud's instincts screamed, and she jerked out of the way, turning, and saw the father of the bride, huge and raging, lunging at her from his seat. She'd dodged but not fast enough. His steel fingers clamped her right shoulder. He jerked her to him and roared, baring his fangs.

She grabbed a fork from the table with her left hand, jammed it deep into the roof of his mouth, and twisted. The fork snapped in half. Blood poured from his mouth.

The vampire yanked her off her feet and slammed her onto the table, pinning her shoulders with his hands. The impact reverberated through her, shaking her bones. If she didn't break free now, he would crush her, armor or no. Maud dropped her sword, locked her left hand on his right wrist, and drove her right palm into his elbow. The power of the blow and the sudden pressure on his left elbow forced him to her left, and she hammered her armored knee into his exposed face with a sickening crunch.

He reared above her, breaking her hold, face bloody, nose broken, eyes insane, and ripped his blood mace off his thigh.

Maud rolled left.

The mace slammed into the table with a telltale whine and bounced off.

The engineer was right. These are really good tables.

Maud swiped her sword off the ground, priming it, and lunged right, putting the table between them. The father of the bride gurgled something, letting out a sound of pure rage saturated with blood.

"Use your words."

His face twisted with fury. He jumped onto the table. She dove underneath, caught herself on the table's smooth narrow base, and used her momentum to swing around it on the glass-slick floor, landing a crouch.

The father of the bride leapt down off the table. He'd tried to put some distance into his jump, but he was huge and heavy, and he hit the floor with a thud. For a moment, all of his weight rested on the backs of his feet.

Maud lunged. Her blood blade kissed the back of his right ankle, its edge slicing through the segmented armor like it wasn't even there. She didn't stop. Instead she rammed her shoulder into the back of his thigh.

The big vampire went down like a felled tree. She scrambled up his back and rammed her blade into the back of his neck, just above the collar of his armor. He jerked once and went still.

Maud straightened.

All around her the battle raged. Vampires clashed, blood weapons shrieked, and bloody mist filled the air. Roaring and screaming and the sounds of weapons clashing filled the hall, and the din nearly deafened her.

To her left, Arland tore into two attackers. To the far right, Ilemina and Otubar raged, back to back, as attackers came at them over the bodies of the wounded and dying. On the left, the tachi, their exoskeletons so saturated with color they looked almost black, formed a protective ring around their royal and sliced at anyone who came near. On the dais, the Battle Chaplain skewered the bridal attendants as they piled onto him. Most of them were unarmored, but his odds were one to twenty. Karat was methodically cutting her way to the dais to assist the outnumbered cleric.

I should help.

"Mommy!"

Oh my God.

Maud whipped around. Helen scrambled toward her, weaving between combatants, her blond hair flying.

How? How did she get here? What is she doing here? She was supposed to be planetside.

Her legs were already moving. Maud dashed forward. Nothing else mattered.

Helen dove under a table, slid on her knees and crawled forward, disappearing from Maud's view.

"Stay! Don't move!"

A vampire got in her way, her armor marked with Kozor colors. Maud stabbed her in the gut, driving the sword through the armor with detached precision. The vampire groaned, Maud pulled her sword free and kept moving. Nothing mattered except getting to the table.

Another knight lunged at her. Maud leaned back a hair out of the way. The blade whistled through the air, fanning her face. She gripped the wrist attached to the hand that held the sword, jerked it up, thrust her blade into the exposed armpit, freed it, shoved the body out of the way, and kept moving. She was almost there.

Two knights, snarling and locked in combat, blocked her view. She halted. They tore into each other and moved to the right.

Onda stood by the table, holding Helen by her throat with one armored hand.

The world screeched to a halt. Maud went ice cold.

Helen dangled from the Kozor woman's grip like a helpless kitten. Her face was turning blue.

Onda smiled wide and turned to Maud.

Helen jerked her hands up and drove both of her daggers into Onda's face. The vampire woman screamed. A shimmer appeared on the table next to them and snapped into Nuan Cee. The merchant tossed a handful of pale powder into Onda's ruined face, caught Helen as Onda collapsed, and dashed across the table tops, leaping nimbly over the larger armored fighters like he could walk on air. A blink and he landed among the lees.

"Let me go!" Helen snarled and kicked, but the lees swarmed her, petting her hair and making cooing noises.

Maud let out a shuddering breath, exhaling so much pressure, it felt like pain, then something burned her side. She spun out of the way of the pain, turning around.

Seveline grinned at her. "I've been waiting for this."

Maud's side was on fire. The armor kept most of the blood in and it drenched her, so hot it felt scalding. She forced a yawn. "Bring it, bitch."

Seveline lunged, opening with a classic overhead stroke. The bitch was fast. Maud dodged left. Seveline reversed the swing, turning into an upward slash. The blood blade grazed Maud's breastplate. The armor held. Maud danced back.

"Running?" Seveline sneered.

"I want you to feel like you're doing well."

"Is that so?"

"You're so scared, you stabbed me from behind, so I'm trying to boost your confidence."

Seveline bared her fangs.

Maud struck, lunging fast. Seveline parried. Maud let her blade slide off the other woman's sword and thrust, aiming at Seveline's throat. The vampire woman shied back and launched a furious counterattack. They clashed in a flurry of blows and blocks, neither fully committing, their swords meeting and parting too fast to follow.

Seveline ducked, and Maud's sword whistled over her head. The vampire woman thrust from a near crouch. Maud knocked the blade aside and kicked but missed. They broke apart.

Sweat soaked Seveline's hairline. Maud held completely still, trying to catch her breath. Her whole side was drenched in pain now. Every movement, even deep breaths, hurt. Fighting Seveline required everything she had, and she had attacked and parried on pure instinct. The more she bled, the slower she would be. Time was not on her side.

Seveline charged. Maud parried the slash. The power of the

blow traveled up her arm into her shoulder, stabbing the joint. Seveline had switched tactics, banking on her greater strength. The blows rained down on Maud, big, wide, fast. She danced away, dodging and ducking. Her back touched a table. Seveline had backed her into a corner. An electric pulse of alarm burst through Maud.

I will survive this.

The vampire gripped her sword with both hands and brought it down with all the subtlety of a sledgehammer. Maud angled her blade down, catching Seveline's sword at just the right place, and guided it down, out of the way. The momentum pitched Seveline forward and off-balance. Her face was wide open, and Maud hammered a punch into it.

Seveline stumbled back.

The world acquired a slight fuzziness. She was losing too much blood. She needed to end this now, or there would be no time with Helen, no evenings with Arland, and no holidays with Dina.

"You can't beat me," Maud said. "You're not good enough."

Seveline snarled and marched forward. Maud saw her eyes. Murder burned there, hot and blinding. They clashed again, cold and vicious this time. Maud thrust her blade past Seveline's guard. It bit just above the vampire's hip, piercing armor and flesh. Seveline backhanded her. The blow rang through Maud's skull. The world turned black for a terrifying second.

Somehow, she knew even through the darkness that Seveline was coming. Maud slashed blindly. Her sword met resistance, and she charged forward, throwing all of her weight into the swing. Her vision cleared. She caught a glimpse of Seveline's kick right before it landed.

Agony blossomed in her right side, the impact throwing her to the side and knocking the wind out of her. Suddenly there wasn't enough air. Panic tore through her. Maud scrambled back to her feet, holding her blade out in front of her.

Across from her Seveline gripped her sword with her left hand, her right arm hanging uselessly at her side. The floor around them was slick with blood.

Seveline bared bloody teeth at Maud. "Die."

"You first."

Seveline screamed and charged. The world slowed to a crawl. Maud watched her come, one powerful step after another, face skewed with rage, mouth gaping, fangs on display, her blond mane streaming behind her. Her own heart was beating like the toll of a massive bell, steady and somehow too slow. Heartbeat...another...

Maud thrust. Seveline lashed at her, but she was too slow. Maud's blade pierced her chest.

Too low. Missed the heart. Missed my chance.

Seveline dropped her sword, still impaled, and locked her hands on Maud's throat. The air in Maud's lungs turned to fire. Spots exploded in her vision. There was no way to break the hold. Seveline was too strong. Maud clamped both hands on her sword's grip and dragged the blade, still buried in Seveline's chest, upward, through the muscle and bone.

She will not kill me. I will not die here, with her hands around my throat.

Seveline was screaming, loud, so loud, spitting blood into Maud's face. Maud's lungs turned to molten lead. She forced the blade up farther, sawing through living flesh.

The light dimmed, Seveline's face swimming out of focus.

With a last desperate jerk, Maud twisted the blade. The hands crushing her neck fell away. Seveline stumbled back and collapsed, her blond hair fanning out as she fell. Maud dropped to her knees. Her stomach spasmed and she retched.

Red liquid burst from her mouth and she didn't know if it was wine or blood.

Get up. Get up, get up, get up.

She crawled to Seveline on her hands and knees and locked her hand on her sword. Seveline's dead face glared at her with empty eyes. Maud forced herself up, into a crouch, then to her feet. She gripped her sword, put her foot on Seveline's chest and pulled the weapon free.

The fighting around them was drawing to an end. She saw Arland walking toward her, armor stained with blood. Their gazes met and suddenly Maud knew that everything would be alright now.

———

THE CEILING OF THE MEDWARD WAS PRISTINE AND WHITE. EVERY cell in her ached, as if her whole body had been through such a long and grueling punishment that it simply gave up and now wallowed in self-pity and pain.

Maud blinked at the whiteness above her. She remembered many different medward ceilings from the last two years: the grimy mud-brown stone of the Karhari's East Plateau, the thick metal plates of the Kurabi Fort, the multitude of chains hanging from the darkness at the Broken Well...She had woken up a few times like this, in pain and unsure, surprised to be alive. This ceiling was, by far, the cleanest.

I survived again.

She didn't remember losing consciousness. There was Arland coming toward her, covered in blood, and after that, soft darkness.

To the side, quiet voices murmured. Maud focused on them and the formless noise congealed into words.

"...what if she doesn't wake up?"

Helen.

"She will wake up." Arland. "Her injuries are serious but not life-threatening."

"But what if she doesn't?"

Maud turned her head. Arland lay in an identical medcot. Helen sat by his feet, her blond hair drooping over her face. A smile played on Maud's lips. *There you two are.*

"Am I in the habit of lying?" A touch of steel crept into his voice.

"No, Lord Arland."

"Your mother will wake up. Have you thought of what you will tell her?"

"Nothing she can tell me will make me less mad," Maud said. "There will be repercussions. Huge repercussions."

Helen flew off the medcot and jumped the five feet separating them. Maud barely had a chance to move her legs out of the way. Helen threw herself at Maud, small arms wrapping around her neck. "Mommy!"

Maud hugged her daughter to her. "You're in so much trouble."

Helen stuck her face into Maud's shoulder, like a kitten waiting for a stroke.

Arland was looking at them. His eyes were so blue.

Maud reached over to him, but her arm fell short.

"Hold on." He fiddled with the controls on the side of his medcot. It slid toward hers. The two beds touched. Arland moved toward her and held out his arm. She slipped under it, ignoring the muscles screaming in protest, and settled on his chest. He kissed her. A hot electric thrill dashed through her, from her neck all the way down into her feet. Maud laughed softly. They stretched against each other, their bodies touching. Maud pulled

Helen closer to her. Arland sighed next to her, sounding completely content.

"How did you get on the battle station?" Maud asked.

Helen didn't say anything.

"Go ahead," Arland said. "Tell her."

Helen pulled the blanket over her head and burrowed under it. Maud looked at Arland.

"She walked onto the transport and presented herself to the guards," he said. "When they asked her what she was doing there, she told them, 'My mommy is the Maven and she is waiting for me.'"

Maud drew in a theatrically shocked breath. "Helen! You lied!"

Helen curled into a ball, trying to make herself smaller.

"And nobody thought to confirm this?" Maud asked quietly.

"No. When I asked them why they let a child onto the transport going to the battle station, I was told she was very convincing and had an air of confidence. She didn't try to sneak in or ask permission, she walked up to them and looked them in the eyes, as if reporting for duty, which apparently persuaded the battle-hardened knights that she was following orders and was exactly where she was required to be. All of our iron-clad security measures have been defeated by a five-year-old," Arland said, his tone dry. "I'm less than pleased."

That was pure Melizard. He could talk anyone into anything with a wink and a smile.

"What were you thinking?" Maud squeezed her daughter to her.

"I was helping," Helen said in a small voice. "Am I punished?"

"Yes," Maud told her. "As soon as I can think of a floor large enough for you to scrub with your brush."

"I don't care," Helen said. "I helped. You didn't die."

Maud sighed and kissed her daughter's forehead. "What are we going to do with you?"

"Command training," Arland said. "As soon as she is old enough, in about two years, maybe sooner. She needs to learn responsibility for the people she will lead, or we will all be in a lot of trouble when she reaches adolescence."

"I can't think about that right now." Maud shivered.

Arland wrapped his arm tighter around her. The heat of his body warmed her. She could've stayed like this forever.

"I love you, Arland," she whispered. "You know that, right?"

"I know," he told her. "I love you, too, with all my heart. Will you have me?"

"I will." She brushed his lips with hers.

"Even though I am an arrogant idiot who took on nine knights at once?"

"Even though. You're mine. All mine."

He grinned at her.

The medward's doors opened and Ilemina and Otubar marched in.

"You're awake," Ilemina announced. "Good."

Maud had a powerful urge to bury her head under the blanket. Arland let out a low growl.

"Have you told her?" Ilemina demanded.

"No. I was about to, Mother."

"Well, I'll tell her." Ilemina smiled at Maud. "We won. We destroyed over half of the pirate fleet. The rest of the cowards fled. We captured seven vessels and picked up a few dozen escape pods, all of them crewed with members of Kozor and Serak. Of the two hundred wedding guests, only sixty-eight survived. It was a resounding victory." She turned to her husband. "Well? Say something to the boy."

Otubar fixed Arland with a heavy stare. "You did well."

Arland looked like hiding under the blanket had occurred to him as well and he was seriously pondering the merits of that idea.

"We are breaking the survivors up into small batches and shipping them off to Karhari," Ilemina said. "We have several drop points around the planet, so there will be little chance of them reuniting."

"What about the Kozor and Serak Houses?" Maud asked. "Who will be in charge now?"

Ilemina sneered. "House Krahr doesn't concern itself with the petty political squabbles of minor Houses. I can tell you who won't be in charge: the idiots who thought to test the might of Krahr. If they want to travel to Karhari and retrieve what's left of their former leaders, that is their burden. I have a feeling they will be in no hurry to do so. No matter; on to more important things. I understand my son has asked you to marry him?"

"Mother," Arland snarled.

"Yes," Maud said.

"Did you accept?"

"Yes."

Ilemina smiled, baring her fangs. "Excellent. We have some impressive recordings of the both of you from the battle on the station, lots of blood, many severed limbs. They are working on it now. We will splice it in with the wedding announcement. Shall we say a month from now? The valas will be in full bloom. You don't want to get married on the battle station, do you?"

Arland put his left hand over his face.

Both Ilemina and Otubar stared at her.

"Ummm, no?" Maud said, not sure if she should brace herself. "I would prefer a traditional wedding..."

"That's my girl," Ilemina said. "Recuperate now. I will give the two of you the rest of today. Tomorrow the Marshal will need to assess our losses and the assets we've seized, and the Maven will have to go back to the negotiating table, because the aliens want edits to the pact and trade station plans and I cannot be trusted to not kill them while they bargain with us."

Otubar reached over and plucked Helen from the bed. "Come with me, child. It's time we tested you with other weapons."

"If you do well, I will give you cake," Ilemina said.

Helen's eyes lit up. "What kind of cake?"

"The delicious kind," Otubar told her. He set her on his massive shoulder like she was a parrot and carried her out of the room. Ilemina watched them go with a smile, followed them, and paused in the doorway.

"By the way," she said, "I was going to tell you once you both had properly recovered, but since you're awake, I might as well. A human is here to see you. I was going to turn him away, but he is an Arbitrator, which presents some difficulties. His name is Klaus. He says he is your brother."

THE END

ALSO BY ILONA ANDREWS

Kate Daniels Series

MAGIC BITES

MAGIC BLEEDS

MAGIC BURNS

MAGIC STRIKES

MAGIC MOURNS

MAGIC BLEEDS

MAGIC DREAMS

MAGIC SLAYS

GUNMETAL MAGIC

MAGIC GIFTS

MAGIC RISES

MAGIC BREAKS

MAGIC STEALS

MAGIC SHIFTS

MAGIC STARS

MAGIC BINDS

MAGIC TRIUMPHS

The Iron Covenant

IRON AND MAGIC

UNTITLED IRON AND MAGIC #2

***

Ilona Andrews is the pseudonym for a husband-and-wife writing team, Gordon and Ilona. They currently reside in Texas with their two children and numerous dogs and cats. The couple are the #1 *New York Times* and *USA Today* bestselling authors of the Kate Daniels and Kate Daniels World novels as well as The Edge and Hidden Legacy series. They also write the Innkeeper Chronicles series, which they post as a free weekly serial. For a complete list of their books, fun extras, and Innkeeper installments, please visit their website at http://www.ilona-andrews.com/.

Lightning Source UK Ltd.
Milton Keynes UK
UKHW021116041019

351006UK00007B/125/P